THE PERFECT GENTLEMAN

Mr. William Mainwaring was everything that Elizabeth could want in a suitor. He was ruggedly attractive, immensely wealthy, thoroughly charming, impeccably well born and bred. What was more, he was undeniably smitten with her, and made no bones about declaring his honest affection and honorable intentions.

Unfortunately, his best friend in the world was Robert Denning, the Marquess of Hetherington, and he had brought Robert with him on this visit to William's country estate.

With this marquess from Elizabeth's hidden past so close at hand, and with the insidious effect he still had on her so powerfully plain, how could she pledge true love to William when her heart proved her so false . . . ?

A Chance Encounter

More Delightful Regency Romances from SIGNET

Mary Balogh

A Chance Encounter

A SIGNET BOOK

NEW AMERICAN LIBRARY

NAL BOOKS ARE AVAILABLE AT QUANTITY DISCOUNTS WHEN USED TO
PROMOTE PRODUCTS OR SERVICES. FOR INFORMATION PLEASE WRITE TO
PREMIUM MARKETING DIVISION, NEW AMERICAN LIBRARY, 1633 BROADWAY,
NEW YORK, NEW YORK 10019.

 SIGNET TRADEMARK REG. U.S. PAT. OFF. AND FOREIGN COUNTRIES
REGISTERED TRADEMARK—MARCA REGISTRADA
HECHO EN CHICAGO, U.S.A.

SIGNET, SIGNET CLASSIC, MENTOR, PLUME, MERIDIAN and
NAL BOOKS
are published by New American Library,
1633 Broadway, New York, New York 10019

First Printing, December, 1985

1 2 3 4 5 6 7 8 9

PRINTED IN THE UNITED STATES OF AMERICA

1

Mr. Frederick Soames, bailiff of Ferndale Manor, spent no more than an hour in the town of Granby one morning. He spent half of that time at the blacksmith's forge having his horse shod and the other half in the road outside the rectory exchanging civilities with the Reverend Claridge. Yet that short visit furnished the townspeople and the families of the surrounding countryside with enough food for gossip to keep them all happy for a week.

Mr. Mainwaring was finally coming to take up residence in the manor that had been willed to him on the death of his uncle more than a year previously. The blacksmith told the innkeeper and the innkeeper told the butcher, who told everyone who came to his shop to purchase their meat supplies, that the master was coming for a lengthy stay, the Season in London being over for another year. He was to be expected within the next week or ten days.

The vicar told his wife, who told all her lady acquaintances, that the housekeeper at Ferndale had been given the most intriguing instructions. She was to open up and prepare not only the master bedroom, but several guest chambers as well. It appeared that Mr. Mainwaring was not coming alone.

During the week of excited anticipation, Ferdie Worthing, only son of the squire, Sir Harold Worthing, basked in sudden and unexpected fame. Ferdie was young and good-natured, but not particularly handsome or intelligent or talented. On this occasion, though, he had a distinct advantage over all his social peers: he knew Mr. Mainwaring.

Of course, Ferdie did not really *know* the man. He had seen him twice from a distance the previous winter when a former university crony had invited him to London for a two-week visit. William Mainwaring had been pointed out to him one afternoon at a race meet, and Ferdie had taken a good look because he had recognized the name as that of the new owner of Ferndale. He had also glimpsed the man at church one Sunday morning from a distance of eight or nine pews back.

His acquaintance with his new neighbor was, therefore, very slight. But it was enough to catapult him into the limelight when no one else near Granby knew whether to expect an infant or an octogenarian, a gargoyle or an Adonis.

"The fellow's regular top-of-the-trees," Ferdie told Mrs. Claridge and Miss Anne Claridge when his sister, Lucy, had persuaded him to escort her on a visit to the rectory one afternoon. "His tailor must be Weston, without a doubt. Looks as if he must have been poured into his coats." Ferdie sounded wistful.

"Is he a young gentleman?" Mrs. Claridge asked.

Ferdie considered. "Thirtyish, ma'am, at a guess," he replied.

Anne sighed. "And is he handsome, Ferdie?" she asked, getting to the important point.

"Great tall, dark fellow," Ferdie said. "He's well enough, Anne."

She gazed at him worshipfully.

The following afternoon saw Mrs. Claridge and Anne at the home of Mr. Thomas Rowe, gentleman farmer, two miles outside town. Anne and Cecily Rowe were bosom friends and spent a great deal of time together exchanging confidences. Mrs. Claridge and Mrs. Rowe visited only when there was significant gossip to be exchanged. The occasion did not arise nearly as often as either of them could have wished.

"Well, I declare, it will be most gratifying to have Mr. Mainwaring in residence at last," Mrs. Rowe told the room at large. "I have always said it is a sad shame to have a large estate like Ferndale standing empty for so long, have I not, Cecily?"

"Yes, indeed, Mama," her daughter agreed obediently.

"Ferdie Worthing says that Mr. Mainwaring is young and handsome and quite top-of-the-trees," Anne Claridge said to Cecily.

"Yes, Ferdie would say that," Cecily said unkindly. "He has been quite insufferable ever since he spent those weeks in London last year. It is amazing he did not claim to have been quite intimate with Mr. Mainwaring."

"You are being unkind, love," said Elizabeth Rossiter, Cecily's governess-turned-companion, looking up from her embroidery. "It sounds to me as if Mr. Worthing has merely provided information that we have all been longing to hear."

Cecily shot her a cross glance. "As usual, you are probably right, Beth," she sighed.

"It is high time Mr. Mainwaring came to the manor," Mrs. Rowe said, nodding sagely. "I always tell Mr. Rowe that we are so dull here in the country that we might as well not bother to dress and set an elegant table. When there is any entertainment, we see the same faces and the same gowns over and over again."

"Do you really think there will be balls and parties at Ferndale, Mama?" Cecily asked eagerly. "Oh, I do hope Mr. Mainwaring brings a whole pile of young men with him."

Elizabeth Rossiter gave her charge a speaking glance, but that young lady was so enraptured with the mental image she had of herself glittering in the midst of an admiring group of eligible young men, that she did not notice.

"Papa is going to call on Mr. Mainwaring the moment he arrives," she said finally to Anne. "I was dreadfully afraid he would not, that he would say it was not his business to pay social calls on newcomers, but he told us he would at dinner last evening, did he not, Beth?"

Elizabeth inclined her head.

"He says that Mama and I should not go because Mr. Mainwaring seems to be a single gentleman, but if he brings house guests and some of them are ladies, then perhaps we may call, Papa says."

"Yes, my papa means to call, too," Anne said, not to be outdone. "The front pew is kept for the master of Ferndale, you know. Papa wonders if Mr. Mainwaring will want new cushions for the seat."

The topic of conversation in the Rowes' drawing room did not change even after the Claridge ladies had left. In fact, little else had been talked about for two days past. Mrs. Rowe already had Cecily all but betrothed to the unsuspecting Mr. Mainwaring.

"It stands to reason, my dear," she said to Elizabeth, "that if he is still not married after living in London and Brighton, he just does not like the ladies of the *ton*. They are too starchy and artificial for him, you may be bound. He will find a country girl refreshing. And Cecily is excessively pretty, you must admit."

"Oh, indeed I do," Elizabeth replied gravely, trying to hide the amusement she was feeling, "but I should not get my hopes up too high, ma'am. We do not know that he is an agreeable man or, indeed, for sure that he is not married."

"I do not think he can be, my dear," Mrs. Rowe said. "Soames would surely have told the vicar if there were a Mrs. Mainwaring."

Elizabeth bowed her head in acquiescence.

"Cecily," her mother said briskly, "tomorrow we shall go to Miss Phillips and have her make you some new gowns. We cannot have the London visitors thinking us country bumpkins. It is most provoking, indeed, that your papa will not take us to Bath to a more fashionable modiste, but he always says that forty miles is too great a distance to travel merely for trifles."

"Mama, shall I have a new ball gown?" Cecily cried. "And a fashionable one, too?"

"Yes, yes, my love," her mother agreed. "You are eighteen years old this year, and I cannot see that Mr. Rowe will ever agree to a Season for you. We will have to make the best of our opportunities."

Mrs. Rowe, who had risen from her chair to pace excitedly about the room, suddenly stopped and turned to her employee.

"Indeed, my dear Miss Rossiter," she said kindly, "you must accompany us and order some new gowns as well. It would also do you a great deal of good to meet Mr. Mainwaring and his friends. You are a gentlewoman, for all that you have been in our employ for six years. Now that Cecily is growing up, you should be thinking of returning to your own proper station. I am sure you could still make a quite respectable marriage if you applied yourself."

"It is very kind of you to say so, ma'am," Elizabeth said, rising decisively to her feet and folding her embroidery into her work bag, "but I am in the sort of position in which I belong. And I have no wish to marry. Come, Cecily, love, it is time to go to your room to get ready for dinner. You know your papa does not like it when you are late."

Elizabeth escorted Cecily to her room, rang for her maid, and retired to her own room to get ready for dinner. She too was to dine with the family, as she had done for the past year, since Cecily was declared too old for the schoolroom and the governess's title was changed to that of companion. Even before that, Elizabeth had frequently been asked to dine. Mrs. Rowe was very conscious of the fact that the governess had been born a lady and that only straitened circumstances had forced her to seek employment. She had tried for all of the six years to treat Elizabeth as a friend rather than as an employee. The governess had gently but firmly resisted. She had been quite determined, in fact, to leave the house and seek a

position elsewhere once Cecily no longer needed her, but
Mrs. Rowe had pleaded so convincingly that her daughter
needed a companion to restrain her wilder impulses that
Elizabeth had agreed to stay for another few years.

Elizabeth Rossiter was six and twenty years old. She
looked the part of a governess as she dressed for dinner
without the help of a maid. The gray cotton dress, with its
high, unadorned neckline and long, fitting sleeves, was
changed for an evening dress that was almost identical
except that the fabric was silk. She loosened her long
chestnut hair, which was tied in a severe knot at the back
of her neck, brushed it until it shone and crackled against
the hard bristles of the brush, and arranged it in the same
style. The face that looked back at her from the mirror
was calm. There was no self-pity in the look.

Elizabeth had been considered an exceptionally beautiful girl when she made her come-out in London at the age
of twenty. Not pretty, but beautiful. The fact that she had
spent five years running her father's home after the death
of her mother had given her a maturity that many other
debutantes lacked. She had acquired a dignity in face of
the difficulties of her situation. Her father had been
frequently in his cups; he held gambling parties in his
country home and was often beset by creditors. Through
it all, Elizabeth had tried to run the house as if it were a
home for the sake of John, her younger brother. But when
John, under the sponsorship of his godfather, had gone to
Oxford, Elizabeth had finally given in to the frequent
pleadings of Lady Crawford, her maternal aunt, and had
gone to London to be introduced to the *ton*.

Things might have gone well for her there. She had
made friends, she had had admirers, her engagement
calendar had constantly been filled. Aunt Matilda had
been hopeful of her making a good match despite her lack
of fortune. Elizabeth often wondered what might have
happened had she not met Robert, but, of course, such
thoughts were useless conjecture. She *had* met Robert
and fallen in love with him and. . . . But she had trained

herself over the long years not to think of that episode in her life.

The fact was that even before the end of the Season she had been back in the country with her father and that within a year he had been dead. No one had been more surprised than she to discover that her father had left no debts. Even so, the estate was impoverished, and bringing it back to prosperity would be a long and tedious business for her brother, who was still only eighteen years old. A good bailiff had been hired to reverse the neglect of years, while John finished his studies at university. Elizabeth had reached the decision to seek employment and had found a position with the Rowes in the West Country. John had been upset and, in fact, had constantly tried to persuade her to resign her position and to move back home. But Elizabeth had been adamant. She would never marry— her experience in London had assured that. And she would not burden her brother with her presence. She had been glad of her decision when John married at the age of two and twenty and a child arrived the following year. She was delighted, too, to know that the estate, though still not prosperous, was beginning to pay its way.

Elizabeth descended to the dining room when the bell sounded, and spent the next hour listening, in some amusement, to Mrs. Rowe rhapsodizing about the expected pleasures of the coming weeks.

"So you think our new neighbor will soon be riveted to Cecily, do you, my love?" Mr. Rowe asked, chuckling at the blush that immediately brightened his daughter's cheeks.

"Papa!" Cecily cried. "I do not even know if I shall like him. I do not even know that he is handsome, though Ferdie says he is."

"What does that signify if he has the handsome fortune that I have heard he has?" her father replied with a twinkle.

"Well," Cecily said doubtfully, "but I should hate it, Papa, if he were positively ugly."

"Depend upon it, my love, if he is wealthy, he is probably handsome too," Mrs. Rowe comforted.

Mr. Rowe chuckled. "Is it not a blessing, Miss Rossiter," he commented, "that our country is not ruled by a woman's logic?"

She smiled. "Ah, but it is a woman's romantic view of life that keeps it from becoming dull," she replied.

"Then we must look for a duke, at least, to be part of the Ferndale party," Mr. Rowe said, directing his attention back to his plate again, "for you, of course, Miss Rossiter. Who could be more romantic than a Cinderella figure?"

"That would be very fine," she agreed gravely, "but we should have to prevail upon Mrs. Rowe and Cecily to conspire to keep me busy in my rags so that I could not attend the ball."

"But it is your idea not to have anything to do with elegant company, my dear," Mrs. Rowe interjected. "I would like nothing better than for you to meet a duke. The idea of my trying to prevent such a match! *Is* there to be a duke as a member of the party, Mr. Rowe?"

Her husband smiled fleetingly at his plate, but directed at his wife a secretive look that raised her curiosity and anticipation of the proposed arrivals to near-fever pitch.

The topic of Mr. Mainwaring and his anticipated arrival had hardly begun to flag one week later when it was given a reviving boost. The ostler of the Granby inn told the butcher, who as usual told all comers for the rest of the day, that two grand traveling carriages had stopped at the inn to ask directions to Ferndale. The first carriage had apparently been carrying passengers, though they had not been obliging enough to step down and be counted. The second was loaded down with trunks and bandboxes. Two gentlemen riders had accompanied the carriages, both dressed in the height of fashion. Indeed, it was one of these gentlemen who had asked directions of the innkeeper.

Mrs. Rowe had to live with her impatience for two whole days before her husband made the promised call on the new arrivals. Her only consolation was that the other gentlemen of the neighborhood would be feeling similar scruples about descending too early on the new owner of Ferndale. Mrs. Claridge would surely have found an excuse to call if she had had any information, and Lady Worthing would have found a more subtle way of informing her supposed inferiors if she knew anything of the identities of the visitors.

No soldier marching into battle has been more lovingly sent on his way by his womenfolk than was Mr. Rowe when he departed for Mr. Mainwaring's house. He was sent back upstairs once to change his coat because the first one was too loose for current fashion. He complied with his wife's demands with an amused indulgence and pinched his daughter's chin as he made his escape to his waiting horse.

Mrs. Rowe and Cecily jumped to their feet in unrestrained excitement when he strolled into the drawing room a little less than two hours later, and Elizabeth smiled up at him from her embroidery.

"Well, Cecily," he began, "it seems that your mama is right again. Mr. Mainwaring is, in fact, both young and handsome."

"Oh, Papa," Cecily squealed.

"I am so gratified that you went today to pay your respects," his wife added ecstatically. "I vow that you must have stolen a march on Squire Worthing, which is only as it should be, my second cousin Harriet being sister-in-law to an earl."

"No one in his right mind would argue that that connection gives us a position of undisputed superiority in the county, my love," her husband replied indulgently, "but Worthing was there before me, with Ferdie in tow."

"How provoking!" said Mrs. Rowe. "But do tell all, my dear Mr. Rowe. What manner of man is Mr. Mainwaring, and who are his guests? Will they feel it a condescension to associate with us? Or are they prepared to join in the social activities of the neighborhood? Oh, depend upon it, Lady Worthing will have them all to dine before we can make plans. She will be pushing that pasty little Lucy at him, mark my words, though the chit is only seventeen and much too young to be setting her cap at a gentleman from town. But then, Lady Worthing always did lack something of breeding. Father a cit, you know, Miss Rossiter."

"Am I to answer your questions now, my love?" Mr. Rowe asked meekly. "The gentleman of the house is tall, dark, and handsome, Cecily—definitely the answer to a maiden's dreams, I believe. He might be difficult to bring to the point, though, love," he added as Cecily clasped her hands to her bosom and gazed adoringly at him. "His manners are quite correct, but there is a certain stiffness about the man. He is not perfectly amiable, I would guess."

Cecily seemed quite unperturbed. If a man were tall, dark, handsome, wealthy, *and* single, what more could a girl ask for?

"It seems that there are two more gentlemen and two ladies at the house," her father continued, "though I met only a Mr. and Mrs. Prosser, a youngish and perfectly amiable couple. Mrs. Prosser's sister is also of the party, we were told, and another mysterious gentleman, whom I heard referred to only as 'his lordship.' There, my dear, have I not made you happy today? Your family has been put upon visiting terms with our new neighbor, I have discovered the answers to many of your questions, and I have left you with an intriguing mystery."

"'His lordship,'" Mrs. Rowe repeated. "We have a member of the aristocracy in our midst. Now I wonder if he is a handsome man."

"He is probably a hunchback with a squint and not a groat to his name," her husband suggested with a straight face.

Mrs. Rowe chose to ignore this witticism. "When may

one decently invite them to dine?" she asked of no one in particular. "Next week for an informal dinner of, say, twenty people? Could we have dancing too? Or would cards only be more appropriate for a first visit?"

"I think none of those plans would be suitable, Dorothy," her husband said quite firmly, "until Mr. Mainwaring returns my call and shows that he wishes for our acquaintance."

"Oh, but, Papa," Cecily wailed, "we might wait forever."

"Precisely, my love," her father replied unsympathetically. "But, Miss Rossiter, I see a very promising future for you. 'His lordship' cannot be a prince or a duke, but it is very possible that he is an earl. He surely could not be so unromantic as to neglect to fall in love with a gentlewoman turned governess and raise her to the exalted rank of countess—now, could he?"

"He would not be so rag-mannered," Elizabeth agreed. "I shall lose all my faith in romance, sir, if I do not have him groveling at my feet within a sennight. Provided he is also handsome and wealthy, of course."

"Depend upon it, my dear," Mrs. Rowe said soothingly. "If he is a member of the aristocracy, he will be handsome."

Mr. Rowe smiled with amused affection at his mate.

2

It was Elizabeth Rossiter who saw the visitors arriving the following afternoon, all on horseback. One was a lady, she could see. Elizabeth had returned just half an hour before from a visit to the rectory. She had taken flowers from the garden to decorate the church while Cecily paid a call on Anne to divulge all the information she had learned at the dinner table the evening before. Now Elizabeth was sitting in the window seat of the drawing room, her embroidery in her lap. Mrs. Rowe and Cecily were looking through patterns, though the directions for the new dresses had been given to Miss Phillips days before.

"I should warn you, ma'am, that I believe we are about to have visitors," Elizabeth said calmly. She did not look through the window again for fear that the riders would look up and laugh at her curiosity.

Mrs. Rowe shrieked. "Mr. Mainwaring?" she asked. "And I would put on this old lace cap after luncheon when something told me that I should wear the new."

"Beth," Cecily cried, "is my gown creased? Have my ringlets lost their curl? That new bonnet will flatten my hair so."

"You look your usual pretty self," Elizabeth assured her. "And I am sorry now that I alarmed you both. The visitors must call upon Mr. Rowe first. It is just possible that they will not call upon you ladies at all today."

"Oh, yes," Mrs. Rowe agreed, "and it would be just

like him to keep them all to himself in the library and never think of bringing them to the drawing room."

But five minutes later Mr. Rowe had ushered the three gentlemen and a lady into the drawing room and was performing the introductions. Mrs. Rowe and Cecily were on their feet. Everyone seemed to be moving and talking at once, as Mr. Mainwaring, Mr. and Mrs. Prosser, and the Marquess of Hetherington were introduced to the ladies of the house.

Only Elizabeth was still seated, frozen into the shadows of the window seat where she had shrunk when the visitors first entered the room. Her eyes were fixed on the marquess; for the moment no one else existed in the room. My God, but he had not changed! She saw a man only a little above average height, but graceful and athletic in build. His fair hair was as shiny and as thick as it had been then, his face just as open and full of vitality. It was not exactly a handsome face, but the dancing blue eyes and the perfect white teeth made the beholder unaware of the fact.

He was bowing now over Cecily's hand, gazing into her face with frank admiration. Robert. Elizabeth had frequently wondered what it would be like to see him again. Well, now she knew, some dispassionate part of her brain told her. Numb. Totally and completely numb. But not for long.

Mrs. Rowe turned with a magnanimous gesture to the employee that she insisted on treating like a lady. "I wish you to meet Cecily's lady companion, Miss Elizabeth Rossiter," she said, directing all eyes to the window seat.

But Elizabeth was aware only of the slightly jerky movement made by Hetherington as he heard the name and turned in her direction. For a timeless, frozen moment their eyes met. Blank disbelief, sudden recognition, and shock flashed across his face all within seconds. It was unlikely that anyone except Elizabeth even noticed.

Then, his expression wiped clean of all expression except polite reserve, he inclined his head with a muttered "ma'am," while the others were presumably doing the same, and Elizabeth, snapping back to reality, rose to her feet and curtsied.

He seated himself with his back to her and engaged Cecily in conversation while Mr. Mainwaring and Mrs. Prosser talked to Mrs. Rowe. Mr. Prosser, a man in his early forties, Elizabeth estimated, balding and slightly paunchy, strolled over and conversed with her for a few minutes, though she could not recall afterward what had been the topic. After twenty minutes, the company departed with promises of future visits and invitations.

Another half-hour passed before Elizabeth could escape from the raptures of her employer and her charge. Mrs. Rowe was vastly impressed with the good looks and the presence of the owner of Ferndale. Cecily seemed more pleased with the rank and the charm of the marquess. But on one thing they were agreed: Cecily would surely be able to engage the interests of one of the two men, or possibly of both. Had not the marquess had eyes for no one else? Had not Mr. Mainwaring positively glowered when his friend sat next to Cecily before he had a chance to do so himself?

At the earliest opportunity Elizabeth retired to her own room on the pretext of having to wash her hair before dinner. She was very badly shaken by the unexpected encounter and felt that she needed a few hours in which to assess what had happened and what its implications for her immediate future would be.

She had never really expected to meet Robert again. She had known, of course, that he was now Marquess of Hetherington. The vast difference in their ranks should have ensured that their paths would never cross. Elizabeth had tried to make doubly sure by taking a position with a less-than-prominent family in a place quite remote from London, where she assumed he spent most of his time, and from Hetherington Manor in Sussex, where he had his country seat.

But it had happened by some bizarre twist of fate. And

she thought again of how achingly familiar he had looked
in the drawing room earlier before he had become aware
of her presence. She supposed there must have been some
changes had she had the chance to look more closely to
show that he was now a man of eight and twenty rather
than two and twenty, but the experience of six years
before seemed to have left no mark on him. He had
appeared as friendly and as charming as he ever had.
Elizabeth wondered if there were any visible sign of
change in her. But she knew that there must be. Even
though her name had brought his eyes in her direction
earlier, it had taken him a moment to recognize that she
was the same Elizabeth Rossiter he had known.

Of course she had changed! Elizabeth thought back to
the young, eager girl that she had been when she arrived
in London at the age of twenty. She had worn her chestnut
hair long, in thick curls and ringlets. Her aunt's hairdress-
er had advised her not to imitate the current fashion for
cropped hairstyles; her hair was too rich and too healthy,
he declared. Her aunt's dresser had decided that Elizabeth's complexion needed no artificial aids. Her cheeks
always had a natural bloom. Her gray eyes were large and
always looked directly into a companion's. Her figure was
slender but unmistakably feminine. She was of average
height.

Elizabeth remembered that she had had many admirers, who had shamelessly flattered her beauty. But although she had laughed, she had had to believe in their
sincerity. She had no wealth or dowry that could have
attracted mere fortune-hunters. After the hard years
spent keeping her father's home, she had thrown herself
with unabashed zest into the activities of the Season. The
fashion was to appear bored, but Elizabeth had refused to
conform. She had ridden, driven with a variety of escorts,
and attended balls, routs, Venetian breakfasts, soirees,
and a dizzying array of other events.

Yes, Robert must have noted a huge difference in her.
Elizabeth's eyes strayed to the mirror over her dressing

table. Her hair was as rich and as healthy as it had been, but was worn now in a severe knot. Her face was pale; it appeared to have lost its youthful bloom. And her prim gray governess's gown hardly compared to the white and pastel-colored muslins and silks and laces that she had worn the year she met Robert.

Elizabeth was staring unseeingly now at her own image. She was reliving that first meeting at a particularly crowded and stuffy ball. She could not even remember who the hosts had been. Her aunt had introduced them. He was Robert Denning, younger son of the Marquess of Hetherington. At first he had been just another dance partner. But it had not taken many minutes for Elizabeth to respond to his charm and his obvious enthusiasm for life. He, too, ignored the trend toward affected boredom. He was very different from the languid, dandified young men with whom the ballrooms were usually filled.

When the supper dance had begun later in the evening, Elizabeth was delighted to be claimed yet again by Robert Denning. He had led her to a table apart in the supper room instead of joining a group of acquaintances, and they had talked animatedly for a full hour, sharing stories of their childhood. She had learned that he had been a lonely boy, eleven years younger than his only brother. His mother had died at his birth; his father was almost constantly in London, very involved in the business of the House of Lords; and his brother had been away at school or university during his boyhood. Robert had spent those years at Hetherington Manor with a secretary, a tutor, and a housekeeper for companions. His father, a man very conscious of his own superiority, had discouraged him from making friends of his own age in the neighborhood.

But for all that, he did not speak with bitterness about his family or his childhood. Somehow a natural sunniness of nature had carried him through unscathed. But he was restless. Life did not have much in the way of challenge to offer a younger son. He wanted to enlist, but his father had steadfastly refused to buy him a commission.

Elizabeth had parted from him at the end of supper to dance with other partners. She would not, she reflected now, have been heartbroken if she had never seen him again. It had certainly not been a case of love at first encounter. But she remembered feeling a pleasant hope of meeting the charming, fair-haired man again. She had thought they could become friends.

Elizabeth became conscious of her own reflection again. How she wished now that they had not met again! Or did she? Someone somewhere had said that it was better to have loved and lost than never to have loved at all. Did she agree? She was not quite sure. But she did know that if she arrived at the dinner table with unwashed hair, someone might think to comment on the fact.

She rang the bell and instructed the maid to bring several jugs of hot water.

Elizabeth finally calmed herself that night by deciding that she need not see Hetherington again. It was true that he was a house guest at Ferndale for an undetermined length of time, true too that there was almost certain to be some social interchange between the Rowes and the Ferndale party. But she need not be a part of any of the meetings. She was a mere servant. And even though she was Cecily's companion, she guessed that Mrs. Rowe would herself be anxious to accompany her daughter to any social functions that might arise from the new arrivals. Elizabeth's presence, then, would be superfluous. She went to sleep comforted by her thoughts.

Two days later she did not feel so hopeful. She and Cecily were outdoors sketching in the warm summer air when a servant came from the house to say that Mrs. Rowe wanted them immediately. Elizabeth did not recognize the phaeton drawn up before the door, but that very fact alerted her to the identity of the visitors who were obviously inside. She went straight to the schoolroom with the easels and sketching pads while Cecily, fluffing the muslin of her light summer dress around her and checking her curls with eager hands, disappeared in the direction of the drawing room.

Ten minutes later Cecily herself appeared in the schoolroom, her cheeks flushed, her eyes shining.

"Mr. and Mrs. Prosser and the Marquess of Hetherington have invited me to walk with them," she said breathlessly, "and Mama says I may go, provided you come too. We may even go as far as Granby, Beth, as Mrs. Prosser wants to purchase some ribbons."

Elizabeth arranged the charcoal pieces more neatly on their shelf, her back to Cecily. "It is a delightful day for a walk," she said calmly. "You must go, Cecily, but I cannot think my presence necessary. I am sure your mama will consider Mrs. Prosser chaperone enough."

Cecily pulled a face. "But I particularly wish you to come, Beth," she coaxed. "You see, I feel shy. I shall not know what to talk about."

Elizabeth smiled. "What?" she teased. "I have never known you to be at a loss for words before, Cecily."

The girl looked rather shamefaced. "Say you will come, please, Beth. You are always so sure of yourself. I know you will not feel a qualm at being in such company."

Elizabeth felt completely trapped. "Oh, very well," she said finally, and went to her room to fetch a straw bonnet.

Mr. and Mrs. Prosser smiled cordially when the two ladies returned to the drawing room. Hetherington bowed stiffly in Elizabeth's direction and smiled dazzlingly at Cecily.

"You look most charming, Miss Rowe," he said, eyeing appreciatively the blue bonnet and parasol that complemented the white muslin of her dress. "Shall we leave?" He extended his arm to the girl, and she laid her hand within it.

On the stroll to Granby, two miles distant, Elizabeth was left to walk behind with the Prossers. She found them good company. Mrs. Prosser, a plain but sensible woman in her middle thirties by Elizabeth's estimation, did not say much, but her husband conversed easily, not suggesting any condescension to the inferior status of his companion. He made her feel a social equal, in fact, as he talked about the welcome they had received from several families in the neighborhood. He talked about his life in the diplomatic service, about a year he had spent on government business in Lisbon.

All the while Elizabeth watched the couple walking ahead of them, arm in arm, talking and laughing together. Hetherington was obviously turning the full force of his charm on this new victim, she decided bitterly. She had once considered that charm to be natural and unforced. Elizabeth felt an actual pain in the region of her throat as she saw the fair head bend closer to Cecily's to listen to something she was saying. As he had once done with her.

When the group reached Granby, Cecily immediately led the way to a haberdasher's and turned eagerly to Mrs. Prosser, so that the five people came together.

"Mrs. Leigh has a fine selection of ribbons," Cecily said. "Shall we see if she has what you need?"

"Yes, indeed," Mrs. Prosser answered. "And do come with me, Henry. You always say I do not have a fine eye for color."

Elizabeth made to follow the trio into the shop but was forestalled.

"I am quite sure you do not need four people to help you choose one length of ribbon, Bertha," Hetherington said. "Miss Rossiter and I will entertain each other by taking a turn down the street. Ma'am?"

He was holding out an arm to her. Blue eyes that she had never seen so steely were boring into hers. The other three members of the group disappeared inside the shop. Elizabeth ignored the proffered arm. She could not bring herself to touch him. But she did turn away from the doorway and begin to move along the street.

They walked in loud silence for a few yards.

"I did not expect to find you so come down in the world,

Miss Rossiter," he said without looking at her. Could that icily polite voice be Robert's?

"Being a governess and companion is respectable employment, my lord," she replied stiffly.

"But you expected more, did you not?" he asked.

Elizabeth looked across at him in astonishment. His words had been sneering. "I do not know how you can say that," she said, trying desperately to hide the slight shake in her voice. "I was never wealthy, and never looked to be."

He looked back at her now, and the sneer was in his face too. "Except once," he said, and looked away from her again.

Elizabeth would not ask him what he meant. She raised her chin and continued to walk beside him. It was he again who broke the silence.

"Time has not been kind to you," he said quietly. "You look a perfect fright, Elizabeth."

Had she not been almost blinded by hurt, Elizabeth might again have been surprised by his lack of manners and by the anger in his voice.

"Thank you," she said, her own voice now shaking with suppressed anger. "I am six and twenty years old, my lord. Alas, women cannot be expected to retain their beauty forever. And the clothes befit my station. I did not have it in mind to please you when I dressed this morning."

They walked on in angry silence.

"We should turn back," Elizabeth said at last. "The purchase of the ribbons must be almost complete."

He turned obediently and they began to walk back in the direction from which they had come.

"And what happens to you when Miss Rowe marries?" Hetherington asked. "The day will come quite soon, you know." The sneer was back in his voice.

"Then I shall find another family in need of a governess," she said, "or I shall go home and be maiden aunt to my nephew. John has a son, you know. But whatever I do, it is no affair of yours, my lord."

"Maiden?" he said softly, looking across at her with one eyebrow raised.

Elizabeth flushed but did not answer. Cecily had emerged into the street, followed by the Prossers. Soon they were all walking back home again, Mr. Prosser with Elizabeth, followed by Hetherington with a lady on each arm. He was oozing charm and good humor again, Elizabeth noticed.

Both Cecily and Mrs. Rowe were ecstatic when the visitors from Ferndale had departed in their phaeton.

"I had hoped that you would make an impression on Mr. Mainwaring, Cecily, my love," Mrs. Rowe said, "but to have taken the attention of the marquess! Why, he had eyes for no one else. Did you not notice, Miss Rossiter? I declare, it was probably his idea in the first place to come this way and invite Cecily to walk with them."

"The marquess is such a pleasant man," Cecily confided to Elizabeth a short while later as they ascended the staircase to their rooms to prepare for dinner. "As soon as we began to walk, I forgot about my shyness and felt quite as if we had been friends for years. His title has not made him a conceited man. He is charming, is he not, Beth? You should know. He was kind enough to walk with you while Mrs. Prosser was choosing ribbons."

"Oh, yes, he is certainly charming," Elizabeth conceded. As she went on her way to her own room, she hoped that Cecily would not fall in love with Hetherington. The girl was too young and inexperienced in the ways of the world to fall prey to a man whose own interests always came first, a man who could hurt another apparently without a qualm.

She went through the motions of changing into the gray silk dress and brushing and reknotting her hair while her mind dwelled deeply on the encounter with Hetherington that afternoon. She had known that he could be cruel, that he was basically heartless, but she had never had face-to-face proof of the fact before. The voice and the facial expression that she had witnessed during that walk along the street in Granby had made him a stranger to her. She had never seen him cold, sneering, sarcastic before. He had behaved as if he hated her. But why? She was the one who had been wronged, hurt almost beyond bearing six years before. Was it conscience that had made him turn upon her with such contempt?

Elizabeth had tried to hate him in that first year when the pain had been intense enough to drive her almost out of her mind. But even then she had not been able to. The best she could do eventually was to dull all feeling, so that a mere empty ache would gnaw at her when her mind strayed to that episode in her life. She had trained herself to think of him, if at all, as he was at the beginning of their relationship.

Their friendship had developed through frequent meetings at *ton* events. Always he would seek her out and spend as much time with her as propriety allowed. But at first it had been pure friendship. They had sparked a note of sympathy in each other. They had found it easy to talk about their deepest feelings and dreams. Elizabeth had told him all about her life at home, her dreams of a home of her own in which family ties would be close, in which love would be the ruling spirit. He had told her about his home life, his sense of alienation from his family. He found his father and his brother too stern and joyless, too much attached to the city, with too little love of the land. They considered him a misfit, a nuisance. Both frowned upon his wish to enlist, yet neither could suggest a useful employment for this younger son. They seemed to expect him to be an idle man-about-town although the family had very little money. Living in a style that he considered appropriate to his rank, the marquess had put too much stress on the income from his estates.

Love had taken her quite unawares. They had both

been attending a ball, but were not together because they had already shared the regulation two dances. Elizabeth had been wearing new slippers, which pinched her toes so badly that she was convinced that she must have at least one blister. The house belonged to the parents of one of her intimate friends. She had hobbled to the library, hoping that her aunt would not miss her presence for a while. She closed the door quietly behind her and sank into the nearest chair with an audible sigh. Moonlight from the full-length windows sent shafts of dim light across the carpet.

"Can it be that the indefatigable Elizabeth Rossiter is actually fatigued?" a teasing and familiar voice had asked.

Elizabeth, startled, had looked across to see a dim form occupying a wing chair beside the fireplace.

"Robert, how you startled me!" she had said. "And what are you doing here, pray?"

"Sulking because I cannot dance with you again," he had replied.

Elizabeth had laughed. "What flummery!" she had said lightly. "Anyway, sir, if you really wish to dance with me, you may do so right here. The orchestra can quite plainly be heard. But you must permit me to remove my slippers and allow my blisters some breathing room."

She had been joking. But he had got up from his chair, come across the room to her, and knelt in front of her chair.

"Poor Elizabeth," he had teased gently, "smiling politely at all your admirers in the ballroom and secretly nursing two feetful of blisters." He had lifted her feet one at a time and removed the shoes. She had sighed with exaggerated contentment, and he had laughed.

"Come," he had said, taking her by the hand, "now you may dance in comfort and I may have the partner of my choice."

But she had stumbled over the abandoned slippers as she rose to her feet and lurched clumsily against his chest. They had both laughed. And then somehow they were not

Mary Balogh

laughing anymore. Their arms went around each other and his lips had found hers in the darkened room.

It had been a long and sweet kiss, her first. She had been surprised by the warmth and softness of his lips, by the feel of his breath against her cheek, his hands roaming her back, and the strength and firmness of his body against hers. But most of all she had been surprised by the strength of her own reaction. The moment had seemed electrically charged. She had felt as if her body temperature had shot up. Eventually they had pulled apart and gazed at each other, wide-eyed.

"I should not be here with you, Robert," she had said shakily. "Aunt Matilda will be looking for me."

"You are right," he had agreed, and then, anxiously, "Elizabeth, have I offended you? I did not intend to take advantage of our being alone together, I swear."

"I am not offended," she had assured him.

He had reached out one hand and run his fingers lightly down one cheek and along her jawline. "I have known for some time that I love you," he had said. And he had bent his head again and lightly touched his lips to hers. "You must go, my love, before you are discovered here with me."

And she had gone, after squeezing her feet painfully into the slippers again. She had been dazed, astounded by the discovery that she, too, had loved for some time without realizing it.

Pushing the last pin into the coil of hair at the nape of her neck, Elizabeth again found it difficult to reconcile that memory of a tender, loving Robert with the afternoon's encounter with the cold, unfeeling Marquess of Hetherington.

3

A few days later Mrs. Rowe and Cecily ordered out the old, ponderous carriage from the coach house and left to pay an afternoon call at Ferndale. The main purpose of the visit was to issue an invitation to Mr. Mainwaring and his house guests to a dinner party the following week. Mrs. Rowe had pondered long on what entertainment she should organize. Should it be a full-scale ball? Would that be too ostentatious? Should it be an afternoon picnic? Was that too informal on so short an acquaintance? On Elizabeth's advice she finally settled for a dinner party, which had, anyway, been her first idea. As Elizabeth pointed out, a dinner party was free to develop in any direction. Music in the drawing room after dinner, or a few tables of cards, or even an informal dance to the music of the pianoforte could all be arranged with the minimum of fuss, depending upon the mood of the party.

Elizabeth did not accompany the ladies to Ferndale. Instead, she sat down to write her weekly letter to her brother. Although they rarely saw each other and although she steadfastly resisted all his urgings to come home, brother and sister remained very close. From his regular letters Elizabeth felt as if she knew exactly what was happening on the estate and in the neighborhood. She felt well-acquainted with her sister-in-law, whom she had met only twice, and with her nephew, Jeremy, whom she had seen only on the occasion of his christening.

The letter writing was interrupted, though, by the arrival of Ferdie Worthing and his sister, Lucy. Elizabeth

was amused to discover that they had come to invite the
Rowes and herself to a ball at the squire's home the
following week, two days before Mrs. Rowe's dinner
party. How chagrined her employer would be! Brother
and sister had issued their invitation to Ferndale that
morning, and had been accepted.

"I suppose Cec is quite excited by the arrival of the two
gentlemen," Ferdie commented gloomily.

Elizabeth smiled. "She seems pleased with all the
visitors," she replied. "She became quite friendly with
Mrs. Prosser when we were out walking a few days ago."

"Those two men are bound to be dangling after her,
though," Ferdie predicted. "They are both top-of-the-
trees, you know. And Cec is the prettiest girl in these
parts."

"You forget your sister and Anne Claridge, to mention
only two," Elizabeth said, amused at the obvious jealousy
of the boy.

"Oh, I know I'm no beauty," Lucy said philosophically.
"If Mama would just admit it too, I should be so much
more comfortable. She is determined I should make a
brilliant match and sees the marquess and Mr. Mainwaring as likely prospects. I shall hate it, Miss Rossiter. I
know she will be forever pushing me at them while they
are here."

"I am sure she will not do anything to embarrass you
unduly," Elizabeth soothed. "She must have your own
happiness at heart, after all."

"Ho, you don't know Mama," Ferdie added.

"I do hope to find a husband during the Season next
year," Lucy added. "But I shall be quite contented with
an ordinary man whom I can respect."

Elizabeth smiled reassuringly and changed the subject.
She felt sorry for Lucy Worthing. She was a thin girl, with
a narrow, pale face and yellow-blond, hair. She would be
quite striking if she aimed for elegance in her appearance
and if her hair were arranged in a smooth, sophisticated
style. Instead, her mother insisted on white or pastel-

shaded clothes, with as many bows, frills, and flounces as could be reasonably added to each garment. Her hair was a mass of ringlets. Obviously the mother assumed that the more she decorated her daughter, the greater the appearance of beauty she would give. The opposite was true.

The pair did not stay long. Once Ferdie realized that there was little chance of Cecily's returning within the hour, he was ready to begin the ride back home again. Elizabeth promised to pass on the invitation to the ball, though she had already decided to refuse herself. The less she saw of the Marquess of Hetherington, the happier she would be.

The following week was one of great excitement among the leading families of Granby and the surrounding countryside. Although entertainments were not unusual, they were normally very predictable events. Very rarely was there any stranger to add interest. And now there were five strangers, and all of them fashionable and apparently wealthy. The austere good looks of Mr. Mainwaring and his connection with the neighborhood, and the title, vitality, and charm of the Marquess of Hetherington everywhere set the hearts of hopeful mothers and their daughters fluttering. The haughty beauty of Miss Norris inspired awe and admiration everywhere.

Elizabeth finally met this lady a few days before the ball, when she rode over with the rest of the Ferndale party to invite Cecily to walk. Elizabeth was in the rose garden cutting some blooms for the house when they arrived. Mrs. Prosser and her sister walked over to talk to her while they all waited for Cecily to run upstairs for a bonnet and parasol. Elizabeth was very glad that the men went inside the house for some refreshment. She had felt a painful stab of the heart at the sight of Hetherington. Like the other gentlemen, he touched his hat in acknowledgment of her presence. Unlike them, he did not smile.

Mrs. Prosser introduced her sister to Elizabeth as Miss Amelia Norris. Elizabeth did not know why she so condescended. The girl was a handsome brunette, though her beauty was marred by a perpetually haughty expression. She succeeded now somehow in looking down her nose.

"Ah, the companion of dear Cecily," she commented, making the word *companion* sound like the lowest of menial occupations, and making Cecily sound anything but dear.

Mrs. Prosser was left to maintain a conversation with Elizabeth. "Mrs. Rowe has told me that you are a sister of John Rossiter," she said kindly. "I knew his wife slightly. She made her come-out in the same year as Amelia. I believe I met him once, too. They made a charming couple."

"Yes, indeed," Elizabeth replied, "and now they have a son of whom we are all proud." She smiled.

"Yes," Miss Norris added languidly, "Louise was, I believe, one of those girls who feel that they must attach some gentleman during their first Season or they are failures in life." The implication was that she had far more wisdom and good taste.

"But it was a love match, I believe," her sister said.

"Sometimes love can be combined with good sense," Miss Norris continued. "When Robert and I marry, there will be no sense of unseemly haste."

"Are you betrothed?" Elizabeth was startled enough to ask.

Haughty eyebrows arched above cold brown eyes. "We have an understanding, Miss Rossiter," she deigned to reply. "I feel almost sorry for all these country girls, who all seem to believe that they can attach the interest of either Robert or William."

She smiled arctically, and Elizabeth understood. Miss Norris had heard, no doubt, that Hetherington had walked all the way to town and back arm in arm with Cecily just a few days before. She was issuing a covert warning to the girl through her companion.

"Come, Bertha," the girl said sharply now, and started for the entrance to the house, where the gentlemen were emerging with Cecily. Elizabeth noticed that she quickly gained possession of Hetherington's arm before it could be decided how the six persons should pair off. He smiled easily down at her and covered her hand with his for a brief moment. Cecily shot Elizabeth a brief, frightened glance as Mr. Mainwaring extended an arm to her. But Elizabeth was not to be drawn. Her presence on this occasion would be decidedly *de trop*. She walked into the house with her armload of roses. Although Mr. Prosser had exchanged a few, brief pleasantries with her, and even Mr. Mainwaring had bid her good afternoon, Hetherington had not so much as glanced in her direction.

Elizabeth ended up attending the Worthing ball after all. She had been determined not to go, and finally Mrs. Rowe had accepted her decision.

"I should find myself in an intolerable position, ma'am," Elizabeth had explained. "It is impossible for me to behave like a regular guest. Yet your appearance there will make my presence as a chaperone superfluous."

"But, Beth," Cecily had pleaded, "a ball is so exciting. You cannot possibly wish to sit at home when you have been invited."

"It is a great shame that you must feel yourself inferior just because you have paid employment," Mrs. Rowe said. "If the truth were known, my dear Miss Rossiter, I am sure you are better born than that Worthing woman. Certainly you never behave with the vulgarity that she displays quite frequently. But as you wish, my dear. I shall not insist you attend if you feel you would be unhappy."

But Elizabeth's relief was short-lived. On the morning of the ball Mrs. Rowe awoke with one of her migraine headaches. Remaining in bed all day and having Elizabeth treat her with vinaigrette and lavender water and compresses failed to bring about a sufficient recovery to enable her to attend the ball. Elizabeth, therefore, was forced to deputize as Cecily's chaperone.

It did not take her long to get ready. She changed into

her best gray silk dress with its high neckline and long, tight sleeves. She did wear a white lace collar as a small concession to the festive occasion. Her hair, though, she knotted at the base of her neck in its usual style.

She waited with Mr. Rowe in the drawing room. But Cecily was not late. She was too eager not to miss a moment of the festivities. She looked remarkably pretty, Elizabeth thought, in her rose-pink ball gown, the new one that Miss Phillips had made for her. Mrs. Rowe was sure the gown was fashionable. The neckline was low-cut, the sleeves short and puffed, the skirt falling in loose folds from a high waistline. The girl's cheeks were flushed with excitement and her eyes shone. Her fair hair hung in soft curls around her face and along her neck. Short ringlets fell from a knot on top of her head.

"I see you are bent on being the belle of the ball, puss," Mr. Rowe said.

"Oh, will I do, Papa?" Cecily asked anxiously, pirouetting inside the doorway.

"Fine as fivepence," he declared.

Elizabeth smiled her agreement.

Cecily looked at her companion. "Oh, Beth," she said, "I do wish Mama had insisted that you have a new evening dress made. I do love you, honestly I do, but must you always wear gray?"

"I shall be sitting among the chaperones," her companion replied lightly. "A fine dress would be totally wasted, now, would it not?"

Cecily made an exasperated sound and turned to her father, who was holding out her wrap to cover her shoulders.

"Shall we go, ladies?" he asked. "And, Miss Rossiter, will you please remember that your coach will turn into a pumpkin promptly at midnight?"

They were not the first to arrive at the ball, but they were before the Ferndale party. Elizabeth was glad. She was able to find herself a chair in the most shadowed corner of the ballroom. Mrs. Claridge soon joined her there.

"I shall sit with you, Miss Rossiter," she said. "At least I can be sure that if you decide to speak at all, it will be good sense. I have heard nothing in the last few weeks but speculation on which girls will be the lucky brides of our two gentlemen visitors. If you ask me, if these gentlemen are still single—and they are neither of them younger than five and twenty—it is unlikely that they will choose any of our local beauties."

Elizabeth murmured her assent.

"I have warned my Anne not to expect anything more than perhaps a country dance with one or other of them," the vicar's wife continued. "I also hear, Miss Rossiter, that the Marquess of Hetherington is all but betrothed to Miss Norris. I do think it rather a shame, don't you? He is such a charming and attractive man. She seems somewhat disagreeable. However, perhaps that is a false impression."

Elizabeth found that she could lend part of her attention to the continuous prattle of Mrs. Claridge while she watched the proceedings in the ballroom. Thus she saw the arrival of the guests of honor. She could hardly have missed it, anyway. A noticeable hush descended on the ballroom as all attention was directed to the entryway.

All five of the guests looked superb, but Elizabeth found to her own annoyance that she had eyes only for Hetherington. He looked quite magnificent, she thought, in cream satin knee breeches and dull gold waistcoat and evening coat. His white linen positively sparkled. He looked full of healthy vitality in contrast to Mr. Mainwaring, who was dressed in black, a fashion that had shocked the *ton* when Mr. Brummell had first introduced it.

Hetherington was smiling his particularly attractive smile at his hosts. Elizabeth shrank further into the shadowed corner and tried to look as if she were en-

grossed in the conversation with Mrs. Claridge, but even
so she felt exposed. She had the strange sensation that
Hetherington had singled her out immediately.

If he had seen her, he gave no sign. He danced first with
Amelia Norris and then with Lucy Worthing, whose hand
had just been relinquished by Mr. Mainwaring. Then he
danced with Cecily, and his whole manner changed,
Elizabeth felt. What had been polite good manners with
his other partners became warm interest with Cecily.
Perhaps the change was not obvious to other onlookers,
but Elizabeth knew him well enough immediately to
assess his feelings. And she worried. Cecily was a giddy
young girl in many ways, but there was a sweetness in her
nature that would develop with maturity if given a chance.
She did not wish the girl to be beguiled by such a practiced
and heartless charmer. She determined that she would
perform her duties as chaperone with extra diligence. Mr.
Rowe had retired to the card room already. It was up to
her to see that Cecily did not spend too much time with
the marquess and that he had no chance to be alone with
her.

Unexpectedly, Mr. Prosser asked Elizabeth for the
supper dance. She had not intended to dance at all, did
not feel it was appropriate to do so, especially dressed as
she was. But as she was about to refuse, she saw out of the
corner of her eye that Hetherington was asking Cecily to
dance again. If she herself danced with Mr. Prosser, she
would have an excuse to go immediately into the supper
room afterward and keep an eye on her charge. She
smiled and placed her hand in his.

It was a country dance. Mr. Prosser led his partner to
join the set of which Hetherington and Cecily were
already part. Cecily waved gaily to her. The girl's partner
looked through her. When the pattern of the dance forced
them to dance together for a few moments, he looked at
her out of cold blue eyes and remarked, "You are looking
remarkably fetching tonight, Miss Rossiter, in your gray
silk."

"Thank you, my lord," she replied in kind. "I thought you would appreciate my efforts."

We are just like a couple of spiteful children, she thought in some dismay as the music forced them to move in opposite directions. The next time they came together, neither said a word.

Mr. Prosser led Elizabeth into the supper room and directly to the table already occupied by Mr. Mainwaring and Lucy Worthing, Ferdie Worthing and Amelia Norris, and Hetherington and Cecily. To her further dismay, her partner pulled out for her the chair next to Hetherington and waited until she had seated herself.

Elizabeth was aware that, had she not felt so conscious of her proximity to the marquess, she might have been highly entertained by the proceedings of the following half-hour. Mr. Mainwaring and Lucy made labored conversation from time to time, but in the main listened to that of others at the table. He was top-lofty, Elizabeth decided severely. He considered himself above his company. Poor Lucy was looking her worst in a lemon-colored evening gown loaded with matching lace. Nervousness made her complexion even paler than usual.

Ferdie and Miss Norris were almost openly tuning in on the conversation across the table, Ferdie glowering moodily at his aristocratic rival to Cecily's affections, Miss Norris showing haughty disapproval.

Hetherington directed his attention to Cecily, talking to her in a bantering manner, almost like father to child, flattering her quite outrageously, and devouring her with his eyes. This last Elizabeth observed in one swift glance. She did not want to be seen watching him. Cecily was glowing happily, apparently quite unaware of the currents of hostility pulsing across the table.

Finally, Mr. Prosser engaged Elizabeth in conversation and she found herself genuinely interested in his accounts of experiences in Portugal. Soon she was engrossed.

Hetherington's voice brought her back to reality. "You

must favor us with your opinion, Miss Rossiter," he was saying, directing the full force of his charming smile at her.

Elizabeth looked up, startled, leaving Mr. Prosser in midsentence. "On what topic, pray, sir?" she asked.

"Miss Rowe and I cannot agree on the location for a picnic on Saturday," he explained. "I favor the riverbank on William's estate. There is a particularly shaded and peaceful area about a mile north of the house. Miss Rowe favors the site of a ruined church on a hill three miles away. What is your opinion, ma'am?"

Flustered as she was by the unexpected attention, Elizabeth could still find time to wonder why he should suddenly decide to speak to her on such a trivial matter.

"A great deal depends on the state of the weather, my lord," she replied. "The river site would be perfect for a very hot day. The church site would be more suited to a cooler day because it is more open. Brilliant sunshine would make it uncomfortable."

"Ah, and do you add weather predictions to your other talents?" he asked, looking so directly into her eyes that Elizabeth was having difficulty breathing regularly.

"I am afraid not, my lord," she replied.

"How absurd you are, Robert," the shrill voice of Amelia Norris said across the table. "I would have thought you had outgrown such childish pursuits as picnics."

He smiled brilliantly back at her. "You may stay at home with your embroidery if you wish, Amelia," he said. "But I am sure that Miss Rowe and I will find others to join us. William, I am sure, will come, and Henry and Bertha. How about you, Worthing, and your sister?"

Ferdie glowered at Cecily, and Lucy blushed a painful red, but both accepted.

"And you, Miss Rossiter?" Hetherington asked.

"If Mrs. Prosser is to be present, I hardly think that my presence as chaperone will be necessary," Elizabeth replied calmly.

"Yes, I do not feel that any servants will be necessary to our party," Amelia Norris commented acidly.

Hetherington smiled again. "Ah, so you have decided to come after all, have you, Amelia?" he said, and turned back to Elizabeth. "But I was not inviting you as a chaperone, Miss Rossiter; I was inviting you as a guest."

Their eyes held for a painful moment. The orchestra could be heard turning up again in the next room. Mr. Mainwaring stood up. "Shall I return you to your mother, Miss Worthing?" he asked. "I believe the dancing is about to start again."

Everyone rose to return to the ballroom. Under cover of the general bustle, Hetherington spoke quietly to Elizabeth. "I wonder if you have the courage to come?" he said, the cold ice back in his eyes and voice. "And to wear a color other than gray."

Elizabeth did not reply. She turned and took Mr. Prosser's arm. Soon she was back in her shadowed corner, listening once more to Mrs. Claridge. She danced only once more that night, with Mr. Rowe, who asked if her glass slippers were pinching her feet yet.

Elizabeth did not sleep much that night. At first she worried about Cecily and about whether she should intervene or not. Someone of Hetherington's charm and experience was dangerous to an innocent like Cecily. And Mr. and Mrs. Rowe might not be able to see behind the facade of charm in time to save their daughter from a broken heart. Only Elizabeth knew that he was capable of subordinating all else to his personal interests. Was it her duty to warn Cecily, or at least Mrs. Rowe?

On the other hand, Elizabeth reasoned, there had been nothing improper in his behavior tonight. He had danced with Cecily only twice; he had danced with Anne Claridge, Amelia Norris, and one other lady as many times. His manner to Cecily at the supper table, although markedly attentive, had not been exactly flirtatious. The man was, after all, supposedly betrothed to Miss Norris, though Elizabeth had seen little evidence of any strong attachment on his part.

And what of Cecily? She had been flushed with pleasure when dancing with Hetherington and at the supper table. But she had looked much the same all evening. She had not looked particularly as if she were languishing after the marquess when she was not dancing with him.

Elizabeth decided that she should wait before saying anything. She was very reluctant to admit to a previous acquaintance with Hetherington. She would observe the two of them at the dinner party two days later and at the picnic on Saturday.

Why had Hetherington so pointedly invited her to that picnic? He had given every sign of loathing and despising her before that invitation. Elizabeth was very inclined not to go, but she really did feel it her responsibility to keep an eye on Cecily. Anyway, the man had dared her to go, had he not?

Why was he so hostile? Elizabeth was completely puzzled. She might have expected him to be embarrassed after the way he had treated her. But hostile?

Their newfound love had developed slowly after that night when, finding themselves unexpectedly alone together, they had kissed. For several weeks they had met as frequently as before, but always in public. Their friendship had grown. Soon Elizabeth had considered him to be her closest friend. She looked forward to meeting him. With him she felt free to pour out her innermost thoughts. It was to him she had confided her worries over her father, who was drinking more and sinking further and further into debt. She had confided her worries over her beloved John, her fear that when the time came, he would have no estate to inherit.

After his one declaration of love, Robert had not broached the matter again for several weeks. Only a new tenderness in his eyes and an occasional squeeze of the hand had convinced her that she had not imagined the episode at the ball. Finally he had spoken. He had invited her to drive with him in the park. He had chosen paths that were somewhat less public than the promenade that all the *ton* frequented on afternoons when it did not rain.

"Elizabeth," he had begun, "you believe that I love you, do you not?"

"Yes," she had replied, looking across at him. He was tight-lipped and frowning, an unusual expression for him.

"You must wonder why I have made no reference to the fact in three whole weeks," he had continued, his voice strained. "After my behavior on that one evening, I owed you an offer of marriage the next morning."

"No," she had said. "I kissed you too, Robert, and I do not believe we did anything so very wrong. I should hate to think that any man felt obliged to offer for me merely because he had kissed me."

"You misunderstand," he had said, distressed. "I want to marry you, Elizabeth. God, how I wish to marry you! But I am afraid I cannot."

Elizabeth had stared at him, wide-eyed.

His eyes had gone hard. "My father is not wealthy," he had said, "and I depend entirely upon him for my living. He opposes my taking any sort of employment and keeps me very much in leading strings. When I am five and twenty, I shall inherit the money left me by my mother. It is not by any means a fortune, but I shall be able to be independent on it."

"You do not need to tell me all this, Robert," Elizabeth had said doubtfully.

"Oh, yes, I do," he had answered viciously. "Do you not see what has happened? For three weeks I have been trying to persuade my father to allow me to make you an offer. It will not do. I must dangle after an heiress. It is useless to argue that I am a mere younger son, that if he were to turn over my mother's money to me now, as he could if he wished, he would be free of responsibility for me. I must marry wealth. I appealed to my uncle, my father's younger brother, to intercede for me. Uncle

Horace was always an indulgent man when I was younger.
But he is worse than Papa. He believes that I should
marry both position and fortune. He is as rich as Croesus,
by the way. I can see no way out, Elizabeth, except to ask
you to wait for three years. I can hardly expect that of
you."

"Three years is a long time, Robert," she had replied.
"Anything can happen in that time to change the situation. For now, it is enough to know that you love me." But
she had been painfully aware that this was probably the
only Season in London that she would be allowed, that
they might have to spend three years without even seeing
each other before they could wed.

Robert had drawn his horses almost to a halt and gazed
across at her. "And you, Elizabeth?" he had asked. "Do
you love me? Will you wait for me?"

"Yes," she had answered with all the ardor of extreme
youth. "I love you, Robert, and I shall wait forever if I
must."

He had glanced hastily around, but there were other
riders in sight. He had had to content himself with lifting
her hand, drawing her glove down to bare her wrist, and
pressing his lips to the pulse there.

"I shall always love you," he had said, and Elizabeth
had believed him.

She laughed harshly now as she stood at the window of
her room in the Rowes' house, made light by approaching
dawn. Forever did not last very long, she reflected.

4

Elizabeth was relaxing in the rose garden the next afternoon when Hetherington and Amelia Norris came to call. She had been into Granby in the morning to accompany Cecily on some shopping errands, and had listened to the girl practicing on the pianoforte after luncheon. Now Cecily was with her mother, and Elizabeth felt free to read at leisure the letter from her brother that had arrived by the morning post.

Although she saw the two visitors arriving on horseback, she did not reveal her presence or make any move to go into the house herself. She was very glad, in fact, to be granted such a fortunate escape.

Baby Jeremy had recently taken his first steps alone, she read with a smile. He had lowered himself down the whole length of the staircase one afternoon, waddled a few steps down the hallway, and toppled a marble bust off a table that he must have clutched for support. The housekeeper did not seem to know whether to scold or to hug the child. Louise was increasing again. John was a little worried, although she laughed away his fears. She was bilious in the mornings as she had not been with Jeremy. But she told him that she was merely looking for excuses to stay abed in the mornings. Elizabeth would be a very welcome visitor. She would be able to offer companionship to Louise, an extra member of the admiring audience to her nephew, and of course, a wonderful source of comfort to her brother.

Elizabeth smoothed the letter on her lap and smiled

down at it. John never gave up trying to lure her home. And the temptation was great, she had to admit that. She could not go back, though, and be dependent on her brother. She could not break in on the family circle there. Although she was really no more than a servant where she was, at least she was supporting herself on her own earnings. She had a measure of independence and self-respect.

She was jolted from her reverie by the sound of approaching voices. She recognized the rather shrill tones of Amelia Norris and the softer, higher-toned voice of Cecily. Perhaps they had left Hetherington in the house. She lowered her head to her letter again, hoping they would pass by without seeing her.

"Hiding, Miss Rossiter?" a deeper voice said from the graveled entryway of the arbor.

"Not at all, my lord," she replied coolly, looking up into his face. "I did not know that my presence was requested."

"What are you doing out here?" Miss Norris asked.

"I have been reading a letter, ma'am," Elizabeth replied, ignoring the impertinence of the question.

"And who is it from, pray?"

Elizabeth's eyebrows rose. "From my brother, ma'am," she said.

"Ah, yes, the one who married Louise," she said. "An unwise marriage for her, I thought. His estate is still as impoverished as it was, I suppose?"

"My brother's affairs are no business of mine, ma'am," Elizabeth replied stiffly.

"He must be doing poorly if you are forced to work for a living," Miss Norris persisted. "And I suppose Louise is breeding whenever she may?"

Elizabeth flushed with anger. Out of the corner of her eye she could see Cecily busily examining the rose blooms, looking embarrassed. She looked directly at Hetherington, who was reclining against a stone wall having the unmitigated gall to look amused.

"Pardon me, ma'am," she said distinctly, goaded as much by that half-grin as by the rudeness of her interrogator, "but I do not choose to discuss my family's affairs with a stranger."

The haughty head tipped back and Elizabeth found herself being viewed along the length of a very aristocratic nose.

"Really, Miss Rossiter," she said shrilly, "I usually do not condescend to show interest in servants. I do so on this occasion only because dear Cecily seems to regard you so highly. In future I shall know how to treat you. You give yourself airs, miss."

Cecily turned away from the flowers looking most distressed.

"Oh, pray," she said, "do not be angry, Miss Norris. You do not understand, you see. Beth is a friend, not really a servant."

Hetherington pushed himself lazily into a standing position. "Amelia, now that you have established the superiority of your breeding, I believe it is time we returned to the house to take our leave of Mrs. Rowe," he said.

Elizabeth was amazed to see that the barb had not found its mark. Miss Norris looked at him with gratitude and turned immediately toward the house. Hetherington offered his arm to Cecily, cocked an ironical eyebrow at Elizabeth, and followed her.

Her own troubled feelings aside, Elizabeth found the evening of the Rowes' dinner party to be an entertaining one. Her employer had insisted that she attend.

"It is quite absurd, my dear," she said, "that you should be obliged to eat belowstairs or above in the schoolroom when you are quite as genteel as the best of our guests. No, you must come, Miss Rossiter. And I don't want any headaches on the night. I know you very rarely get headaches."

Elizabeth gave in. She decided to make the best of a bad

situation and be an observer. And already there were
signs that there might be much to observe: Miss Norris
and Hetherington, Cecily and Hetherington, Ferdie and
Cecily, Mr. Mainwaring and all the hopeful young girls of
the district.

She found herself seated at table between the Reverend
Claridge on her left and Lucy Worthing on her right.
There were sixteen persons at the table, with the result
that conversation was not general. Elizabeth listened to a
health report of all the parishioners on the vicar's visiting
list for part of the meal. Most people avoided the reverend as a bore. He tended to speak in a monotone, with
long pauses between phrases, and about topics that were
dear to his heart but to no one else's. But Elizabeth knew
him as a kindly man, devoted to his parishioners, even the
poorest of them, and an affectionate husband and father
to his large brood. She sat and listened with patience, a
smile of interest on her face.

Eventually Lucy Worthing claimed her attention.

"Miss Rossiter," she almost whispered earnestly, "how
is it that you converse so easily with other people? I think
and think of what I may say to someone and I can never
think of a single thing."

Elizabeth smiled reassuringly at the girl. "I perceive
you have been left to the company of Mr. Dowling too
long," she said, glancing at the gentleman farmer sitting
on Lucy's other side. "He never has two words to rub
together."

"But I am the same with everyone," the girl said
miserably. "You saw at Mama's ball how I could not
converse with Mr. Mainwaring. I felt so uncomfortable.
And all the while you were talking with Mr. Prosser as if
you would never run out of ideas."

"Is it important to you that you be able to converse with
Mr. Mainwaring?" Elizabeth asked, looking into her
companion's face.

Lucy flushed. "Not necessarily," she replied. "But, you

see, I have to meet gentlemen like him when I go to London. And I dread it, Miss Rossiter."

Elizabeth thought for a moment. "Perhaps the problem is that you are always thinking of what you may say," she said finally. "Have you ever asked yourself what your neighbor would like to say? If you know of an interest of his, one well-placed question will probably set him to talking for a long while. If you do not know his interests, a few questions will probably reveal them. You see, the secret of good conversation is perhaps to listen well and to look interested in what you hear."

Lucy stared at her, fascinated. "Oh, do you really believe so?" she asked.

"I wager," said Elizabeth with a smile, "that if you were to turn to Mr. Dowling and ask about his hogs, he will hold your attention for the rest of dinner."

Lucy looked doubtful. "Hogs?" she said.

Elizabeth nodded and turned to the Reverend Claridge, who had directed some comment her way. A few minutes later she noticed that Lucy was at least talking with her neighbor.

The ladies retired to the drawing room a full half-hour before they were joined by the gentlemen. Amelia Norris seated herself at the pianoforte.

"Do come over here, Bertha, and sing," she said shrilly to her sister.

Mrs. Prosser did not move for the moment. "Perhaps Miss Rowe sings or plays," she suggested politely.

"Oh, but, please, you must favor us with a few pieces," Mrs. Rowe begged. "I am quite sure that with London singing masters, your style and repertoire will be superior."

Amelia began to play, a self-satisfied look on her face. She accompanied her sister for a while and then they changed places. Amelia was leaning against the pianoforte singing "Robin Adair," making a thoroughly pretty picture, when the gentlemen entered the room. She was

facing slightly away from the door and pretended to have
been unaware of their arrival, because she completed the
song and affected great surprise at the applause that
succeeded it.

Elizabeth, seated in her favorite window seat, smiled
with great amusement. She watched as Hetherington
stepped forward and kissed the beauty's hand.

"Very nice, Amelia," he said smoothly, smiling charm-
ingly at her. "Shall we move away now so that our hosts
can decide the entertainment for the evening?"

Very well done, Robert, Elizabeth thought ironically.
His charm had worked on Miss Norris as it always had on
her. The girl did not even seem to realize that she had
been given a mild set-down.

It was decided that the carpet would be rolled up and an
informal dance would be held. Mrs. Claridge was re-
cruited to play the pianoforte. Hetherington danced first
with Cecily, Mr. Mainwaring with Lucy. Elizabeth
watched both couples closely. Robert was using all his
charm on the young girl, there was no doubt about it, and
she was glowing with high spirits. Lucy looked as if she
was making an effort to draw her partner into conversation. Was she asking him questions? Elizabeth wondered.
She seemed not to be making much of an impression. His
manner was stiff and solemn. Elizabeth noticed that
Amelia Norris was smiling brightly, her face flushed, as
she danced with Ferdie Worthing.

Mrs. Claridge began to play a waltz next. Elizabeth was
watching Ferdie make a determined effort to reach Cecily
before any other man did.

"May I have the honor, ma'am?" a rich voice asked
close beside her, and she looked up, startled, to find Mr.
Mainwaring looking into her eyes, his hand outstretched.

"Me, sir?" she asked foolishly, a hand at her throat.
"You wish to dance with me?"

"Yes, Miss Rossiter, I wish to dance with you," he said
gravely. "Will you, ma'am?"

Elizabeth got to her feet, feeling self-conscious in her plain gray silk. She had not waltzed for six years.

Mr. Mainwaring was a good dancer. He held her firmly and provided a lead that she could easily follow. But she wondered why he had asked her to dance.

"How do you take to your new home, sir?" she asked, looking up, and found herself gazing into velvet brown eyes.

"Very well, ma'am, I thank you," he said. "My friends and I have certainly been given a warm welcome."

"Ah, that is because you provide novelty and entertainment to a neighborhood that is normally dull, sir," she said, smiling impishly up at him.

His eyebrows rose. "I am devastated, ma'am," he replied. "And I thought they were responding to my own fair self."

Elizabeth laughed outright. "Well, the fact that you are quite personable and, so we hear, rich, certainly helps," she commented.

"Ah," he said, and came very close to smiling, "it is a shame I do not have my friend's title too, is it not? I should take the place by storm."

Elizabeth chuckled again and glanced across the room at that friend, who was dancing with his betrothed, but he was glaring, tight-lipped, straight at Elizabeth! Her eyes dropped in confusion for a moment. Then she glared back defiantly. She was not going to be made ashamed just because he obviously disapproved of a servant—and one dressed drably in gray—dancing with his friend. If he did not like it, let him leave. She turned back to her partner.

"You are a very good dancer, sir," she commented. "I have not waltzed for many years and you have contrived to keep your feet from landing beneath mine."

"A very unwise comment, ma'am," he said gravely. "The music has not finished yet."

Alone in the window seat again a few minutes later, Elizabeth mused on the one major surprise of the evening.

Mr. Mainwaring was certainly not the top-lofty, stern man that she had labeled him. Stiff and quiet as he appeared on the outside, he had a sense of humor. Which was more than could be said of the Marquess of Hetherington.

"Ah, Miss Rossiter," Mr. Rowe said the next morning when he met her outside the breakfast room, "I was beginning to think that Prince Charming was going to ruin our fantasy by refusing to show up. But could he be disguised in the person of William Mainwaring? He seemed quite attentive last evening."

Elizabeth raised her eyebrows. "Indeed not, sir," she said. "The conquest of a mere 'mister' would not be near startling enough. No, no, I wait for someone of more exalted rank."

She would have swept past him with an arch look, but he was not finished. "Ah," he said, "the Marquess of Hetherington, perhaps? He seems quite the Prince Charming. He has the looks, wealth, and rank."

Elizabeth tried to keep her tone light. "He has one missing attribute," she said, pretending to consider. "He refuses to recognize me as Cinderella."

"Foolish man," commented Mr. Rowe. "But I am glad of it. I cannot like the man's attentions to Cecily. He has made her the target of his gallantry, but I cannot fathom why. He treats her much as he would a child. I wonder if he is not trying to make Miss Norris jealous. There seems to be some attachment between the two, though I would guess it is more on her side than on his. Which now makes me wonder, why would he try to make her jealous? My wife always tells me, Miss Rossiter, that one should never try to think before luncheon. I begin to appreciate the wisdom of the lady."

Elizabeth smiled and again would have moved into the breakfast room. He again detained her.

"Miss Rossiter, will you watch Cecily very closely?" he asked. "She is a silly little chit in many ways, but she has a good heart and I should hate to see it hurt."

"Believe me, sir," Elizabeth replied gravely, "I have a deep affection, too, for your daughter, and I take my position seriously. She shall not be taken advantage of if I have anything to say in the matter."

Mr. Rowe nodded vaguely and moved off in the direction of his office.

Mrs. Rowe, meanwhile, was a different story altogether. When she joined Elizabeth at the table, she was bubbling with high spirits.

"Do you not agree that everyone enjoyed last evening excessively, Miss Rossiter?" she began. "Such friendly, informal entertainment, such agreeable company, such stimulating conversation."

"Indeed, ma'am, it appeared to me that your efforts had met with great success," Elizabeth agreed kindly.

"Elva Hendrickson assured me that the evening was a far greater success than the Worthing ball was. Insipid, she called that."

Elizabeth murmured a diplomatic comment.

"I do believe the Marquess of Hetherington is smitten with Cecily, do you not agree, Miss Rossiter?" Mrs. Rowe continued. "He is so particular in his attentions to her. It would be such a splendid match for her. I can hardly wait to see Maria Worthing's face if he should offer for her."

Elizabeth felt that her opinion was being called for. "His lordship is a very charming man," she said carefully, "and of course, he is taken with Cecily's prettiness. I am not sure, though, ma'am, that his behavior amounts to more than gallantry. I believe I have heard that he is something of a rake." Elizabeth had heard no such thing, in fact, but it seemed likely to be true, she assured herself guiltily.

"A rake?" Mrs. Rowe repeated incredulously. "Surely not, my dear. Such a charming man! But I certainly do not like that sharp-tongued Miss Norris, who seems forever to be hanging on his sleeve. She sets her cap at him altogether too openly."

"I believe they may have an understanding," Elizabeth

said hesitantly. "She hinted as much when she was introduced to me."

"Indeed!" the other lady said sharply. "Then perhaps it may be a good idea to keep a close eye on Cecily at tomorrow's picnic, Miss Rossiter. I do not want the girl to be hurt or made to look foolish."

"I shall do all in my power to prevent either, ma'am," Elizabeth replied calmly.

And so, if Elizabeth had not gone to the picnic as a result of Hetherington's dare, she would certainly have gone as a result of the express concern of Cecily's parents.

It had been decided that the old church should be the site of the picnic. Hetherington had taken on the role of host. All the members of the Ferndale party were to be present, and in addition he had invited Cecily and Elizabeth, Ferdie and Lucy Worthing, Anne Claridge, and Mr. Dowling. The party was to assemble at Ferndale at eleven in the morning and travel together by horse or barouche.

After much animated discussion, it was decided that the gentlemen would ride and also Amelia Norris and Lucy Worthing, who was an excellent horsewoman. The remaining four ladies were handed into the barouche by a smiling, high-spirited Hetherington. When it came to Elizabeth's turn, she gathered her skirts together and would have stepped into the conveyance unassisted. But his outstretched hand did not waver. She had to accept his assistance or appear rude in front of an audience.

And so she placed her hand in his and he gripped it firmly. She was touching him again after six long years. For a moment she forgot time and occasion. It could be no one else's hand: warm, broad, capable. She had once thought she could put her whole life in it and be safe. She looked up wide-eyed into his face. His blue eyes looked steadily—and blankly—back into hers.

"Ma'am?" he said politely, and she stepped into the barouche and released his hand.

Once the picnic site had been established, the party broke up into two groups. The picnic blankets were laid at the foot of the small hill, at the only spot that was well sheltered by a clump of trees. And they would need that shelter later on, they all agreed. The sun was already blazing down on them with all its summer heat.

Several of the party decided to stroll beside the stream that meandered around the base of the hill. Hetherington insisted that Cecily show him the old church that she had dragged them all there to see. Amelia Norris, Ferdie, and Elizabeth, for reasons of their own, tagged along too. So did Mr. Mainwaring.

Cecily clung to Hetherington's arm as they climbed the grassy slope. Amelia strode ahead. She was staring scornfully at a half-ruined stone church when the rest of the group came up with her.

"Look at this, Robert," she said shrilly. "It is nothing but a pile of rubble. I told you that we should picnic at the river, as you originally suggested."

"So you did, Amelia," he agreed, "but I consider this an interesting pile of rubble. Tell us about it, Miss Rowe."

Cecily and Ferdie between them told about how the church had deteriorated from lack of use after the town of Granby grew up three miles away.

"The bell was taken to the town church about fifty years ago," Cecily explained, "and that seemed to be really the end. It seems such a shame. This would make a splendid setting for a Christmas evensong or for a wedding, would it not?"

All the while the small group had been tramping around the church through the overgrown grass and weeds.

"Do you remember, Cec, how we used to come up here every chance we could and try to piece together the shattered stained glass from the back window?" Ferdie asked.

"Oh, I say, yes," Cecily replied, her face lighting up with pleasure. "And didn't we have a thundering scold that afternoon of the storm when we sheltered for hours and no one knew where we were?"

"I got more than a thundering scold," he said dryly.

"You also caught cold, did you not, Ferdie?" Cecily asked. "And it was all because you lent me your coat to keep me warm."

"Let's go inside and see if any of the glass is left," Ferdie suggested.

"Oh, yes, do let's," she agreed, and they scampered for the empty doorway like a couple of schoolchildren.

"I am hot and thirsty," Amelia announced. "Escort me back down this hill, Robert."

Hetherington smiled ruefully at the pair disappearing inside the ruins and led away his angry betrothed.

"What is at the other side of the hill?" Mr. Mainwaring asked.

"Oh, merely more grass and trees, sir," Elizabeth replied. "If you wish, we may walk down there and follow the stream around the base of the hill until we reach the picnic site."

"That sounds pleasant," he said. "Shall we go, Miss Rossiter?" He held his arm for her support.

More than half an hour passed before they came in sight of the rest of the party, who were already assembled on the blankets and surrounded by the contents of the picnic hampers. Elizabeth had enjoyed the stroll. Close to the stream and beneath the shelter of the trees that grew on either side of it, they were shaded from the heat of the sun.

And she discovered that she had been right in thinking that Mr. Mainwaring was not as taciturn or as top-lofty as he had at first appeared. He began to tell her about himself. He had been brought up, after the death of his parents when he was an infant, by his maternal grandfather in Scotland. The old gentleman had been stern and something of a hermit. The place had been lonely. The boy had been brought up almost entirely by his grandfather and a crusty old housekeeper. He had been educated at home. It was not until his grandfather died when William Mainwaring was nineteen years old, that the boy fully realized that he had an estate and wealth awaiting him in England. But he had no training for the sort of life he would face. He knew no one in England and, in fact, very few in Scotland.

He explained to Elizabeth that, although he was now thirty years old, he had never quite recovered from the strangeness of his upbringing. He found it difficult to relax and behave with the ease of manner he so admired in other men. He found it difficult to make friends, but found himself firmly attached to those he had made.

Elizabeth could not help allowing curiosity to get the better of her. "How comes it that you are friendly with the Marquess of Hetherington?" she asked. "You and he seem so different from each other."

"Robert?" he said, looking at her solemnly. "Yes, he is the sort of man I should like to be. He has an ease of manner and a charm that come naturally to him. People invariably warm to his personality. However, there is great depth to his character that you may not know on such short acquaintance, Miss Rossiter. Strangely enough, his upbringing was similar to mine in many ways. And I believe he has suffered in his life. He has a sensitivity to the hurts of others that can have come only from personal experience."

Elizabeth hid her skepticism in silence. "Around this next bend we should find ourselves close to the horses and the luncheon," she said.

"Ah," he remarked, "I had forgotten the others. You are an easy person to talk to, Miss Rossiter. Is it part of your profession to set people to talking so much at their ease?"

Elizabeth smiled. "Not at all, sir," she replied cheerfully. "Perhaps it is my plain gray dress that gives you confidence. Maybe you allow a lady's grand appearance to awe you into believing that she is a threat to you."

They had rounded the bend and were now in full view of the others. He looked down at her and laughed. "What a novel idea," he said. "And I only now noticed that you are dressed plainly. Do you always dress so? You must have a powerful personality, ma'am. One tends not to notice."

Elizabeth too laughed, but could not hide a blush at the unexpectedness of his words. "Why, sir, I do believe I have been complimented," she said, looking up into his face, and across into the tight-lipped, glowering face of the Marquess of Hetherington, who had paused in the process of pouring wine for the company. Elizabeth had enjoyed the walk and the conversation with William Mainwaring, and refused to have her mood spoiled. Joining the group, she placed a meat pasty and a buttered bread roll on a plate, and moved over to join Mrs. Prosser and Anne Claridge, who were exchanging views on the latest fashions.

As she ate and listened, Elizabeth let her eyes rove around the company. Lucy Worthing and Mr. Dowling, she was amused to see, were sitting together and conversing—or, at least, Lucy was listening to Mr. Dowling talk. The girl was looking almost pretty today with her sky-blue muslin dress that did not make her hair look too yellow or her complexion too pasty. Ferdie, Cecily, and Amelia Norris formed a group with Hetherington, but Elizabeth noticed that Cecily, flushed and slightly disheveled, was talking animatedly to Ferdie, while Hetherington, looking quite genial again, was entertaining his betrothed. He must have been angry to remember that he had invited her, Elizabeth thought, and that was why he had looked so out of sorts a short while before.

When everyone had eaten his fill and the food was packed away again, Mrs. Prosser got to her feet. "Come, Miss Claridge," she said, "show me this church of yours on top of the hill. Is it worth looking at?"

"Oh, not really," Anne said, standing up and shaking out her skirts, "but there is a splendid view from the top."

"Is there? Come, Henry, I need your arm," his wife called cheerfully.

"May I come too?" Mr. Mainwaring asked, and offered his arm to Anne Claridge.

"Miss Rossiter, I should like to discover the walk you were just showing to William," Hetherington's voice said from close to her shoulder.

Elizabeth turned, startled. She was even more surprised to see that he had put the church group between himself and those who were still sitting on the blankets, so that it was almost a private moment that they shared. He obviously meant that she was to go with him alone, not with a group.

She looked into his face for a clue to his motive. But his expression was polite, impassive. She smoothed her skirt and turned quietly to walk along the bank of the stream again toward the bend that would take them out of sight of the group. They walked in silence until they were unobserved. Then he began.

"What is your game, Elizabeth?" he asked quietly. "Is it Mainwaring you are out to captivate now?"

She looked across at him blankly. "What?" she said.

"Because if it is," he said, his voice now revealing an underlying fury, "I am here to tell you that you will not be allowed to succeed."

"What are you talking about?" Elizabeth stopped and turned to him, a puzzled frown on her face.

"Do you think I have forgotten what you are like?" he sneered. "He is wealthy and he is vulnerable, is he not? And it seems that you need money again. So you have set to work. And your plan is succeeding already, damn you. I have never seen Mainwaring so taken with a lady."

"I believe I have walked into a conversation not meant for me, my lord," Elizabeth said, breathing rather fast. "I have not the faintest idea what you are talking about, except that I realize you are being insulting. I wish you would explain yourself more clearly."

He turned fully to her now, his fury showing in his heightened color and in his flashing eyes. "You wish me to

put the matter plainly to you?" he snapped. "I shall do so.
If your position does not offer you enough in the way of
luxuries, and if you need more money, you may apply to
me for it. I shall give it to you. But you will not ruin a
friend of mine who has had a hard life and deserves some
happiness. You will leave him alone, ma'am."

Elizabeth's eyes had widened. Her body was rigid, fists
clenched at her side. For a moment she could not speak.
"How dare you!" she whispered at last. "By what possible
right could you so insult me?" Her hand rose of its own
volition and cracked across his face.

She watched in fascination as the white marks left by
her fingers darkened almost immediately to an angry red.
Then she met his eyes, which still blazed.

"By God, Elizabeth, you forget yourself," he said
through clenched teeth, and then his hands clamped
painfully on her shoulders and crushed her against his
body. His mouth came down on hers, hard and bruising.

Elizabeth reacted in panic. This could not happen, her
mind screamed. It must not happen. Her only defense
against him was distance. If she did not get away immediately, she would be lost, in the same state of raw pain she
had suffered for months six years before. So she fought.
She clawed at his chest with her fingernails, kicked at his
shins, twisted her head from side to side, and moaned her
protest. His answer was to haul her harder against him so
that hands and breasts were crushed against his coat, and
to open his mouth over hers so that she could not pull
away.

Elizabeth continued to moan, but gradually collapsed
against him and angled her head so that his seeking tongue
could slip past the barrier of her teeth. And he was
Robert, the man she had always loved, the only man who
had ever touched her, the only man she had ever wanted.
And wanted now with a searing passion.

But suddenly she was alone again, cold, back beside the
stream close to her place of employment, only two hands

holding her shoulders in a bruising grip, a pair of cold blue eyes looking at her cynically.

"You could have had it all, could you not, Elizabeth, had you only waited a little while?" he said. "You must have felt that fate had dealt you a treacherous blow. But you have made your choice, ma'am, and you must live by it. You will stay away from William Mainwaring. Do I make myself understood?"

His words had thawed some of the numbness that seemed to grip Elizabeth's heart. "Remove your hands from me, my lord," she said calmly. "I have nothing to say to you, now or ever. I had never thought to hate anyone. But I believe I do hate you."

They stared at each other for a long moment, each cold and unyielding. Finally his hands dropped and she turned to go back the way they had come.

"Let us continue with our walk," he said stiffly. "You are flushed and breathless. I do not doubt that I still have the mark of your hand on my face. It would not do for us to be seen in the near future."

They walked side by side, coming around at the back of the hill, and climbed the slope to join the other group, which was still at the top, sitting on the grass admiring the view.

5

She was listening to her father again, her father without his usual gruff manner, hesitant, troubled, almost apologetic, telling her. After all the agony and uncertainty that had gone before, she finally knew the worst.

"No!" she was saying. "Please, no!"

"I'm sorry, Lizzie," he said. "I can think of no way to soften the blow. Eventually you will realize that you are well out of it, of course, but . . ."

His voice trailed away when he realized that she was not listening. She rocked back and forth on the chair, her hands spread over her face, trying desperately to shut out the truth, to blot out reality, life.

"No!" she moaned over and over. "Please, no. It can't be true. No! Oh, God, no!"

John was there, though she had a feeling suddenly that it was a few days later.

"Elizabeth," he pleaded, kneeling on the floor in front of her and trying to look into her face, "You must pull out of it, love. You have not eaten for days."

"No," she moaned.

"He is a scoundrel, Elizabeth," he said angrily. "You must tell yourself that over and over again. Let me hear you."

"No," she replied, her hands before her weary face again. "No. No. No. *Robert!*"

She screamed the name and clawed at the arms of the chair as she pulled herself upright, gasping for air. John had disappeared. Everything had disappeared. She stared wildly into the darkness, heart thumping loudly, hands gripping bunches of the bedcovers. It took her several seconds to realize that she was in her bedroom at the Rowes'.

Elizabeth slumped back against the pillows and closed her eyes. She put her hands, palm downward, on the bed beside her and concentrated on breathing slowly and evenly. The old nightmare! She had thought she was over them. But, of course, the reappearance of Robert in her life was bound to revive some of the old pain. It would pass again, she told herself soothingly, unconsciously assuming for herself the role that John had played for several weeks six years before.

She would not think about it anymore tonight. She must think of something more pleasant. Elizabeth knew from experience that if she tried to divert her thoughts entirely from that episode in her life, she would fail utterly. She must relive some pleasant memory, before things went bad. She set herself deliberately to recalling the evening when Robert had first told her about his grandmother, his mother's mother.

"She lives in Devonshire most of the time," he had explained. "We used to see her once a year when Papa would send us down there for a duty visit. At least, Tom used to come for the first few years. Then I suppose he felt himself too old, so I used to go alone, with a nurse, of course. I used to be terrified of Gram. A crusty old bird, Papa always called her, and I always felt the description fit."

He had gone on to explain how his grandmother, Lady Bothwell, had never treated him like a child, but always conversed with him as if he were a sensible adult. She had demanded a great deal of him and had occasionally referred to "that young fool, your father." She suffered from rheumatism. Her slow, stiff movements, her constantly tapping cane had frightened the child. It was only as he grew older that he came to appreciate the keen intelligence and blunt good sense of his grandmother. He had learned that the bad feeling between her and his father had been caused by her refusal on more than one occasion to help him out of debt.

Robert had always continued the annual visits to his grandmother, from choice once he was old enough to make the decision himself. He had developed a deep, if undemonstrative affection for her.

And now she was making one of her very infrequent, always unannounced visits to London. She had taken a house for the duration of the Season, refusing as she always did on such occasions to stay with her son-in-law.

"I want you to meet her, Elizabeth," Robert had said, smiling eagerly into her eyes. They were waltzing at Almack's. He always chose waltzes with her, because the dance gave them some time to be together and to talk. It was hard to steal time together otherwise.

"Do you really think I ought?" she had asked doubtfully. "She sounds rather frightening."

He had laughed, his blue eyes crinkling at the corners, white teeth flashing at her. "She will adore you, my love," he had assured her, squeezing her hand tighter. "And do not try to persuade me that you are afraid. You are always easy in other people's presence. You never seem at a loss for topics of conversation."

"But perhaps she will think a visit from me an impertinence?" Elizabeth had suggested.

His eyes had softened as they gazed back into hers. "I love her, Elizabeth," he had said. "I have told her about you and all that you mean to me. She insists on meeting you. I do believe that if you will not call on her, she will call on you."

"But that will never do," she had said, aghast. "How would it look if your grandmother came calling on my aunt when we are not even betrothed?"

He had grinned, looking suddenly like a mischievous boy. "Then you have no choice, do you, my love?" he had said. The music had been drawing to a close. "Tomorrow afternoon?" he had suggested. "I shall call for you at three."

And so they had gone. Elizabeth's Aunt Matilda had raised no objection to her charge's going with Robert Denning to visit his grandmother. Despite Robert's assurances of the night before, Elizabeth had been nervous. Lady Bothwell was the first member of Robert's family to whom she had been formally presented. And she had wondered what he had said about her. Did the old lady really know that they loved each other? Did she know that they had pledged to wait three years until they were free to marry? Would she like Elizabeth, or would she find her ridiculously young and gauche?

That first meeting had certainly been disconcerting. The old lady had risen to her feet when they were announced, and stood with her back to the fireplace, leaning heavily on a cane. She had watched Elizabeth through an old-fashioned lorgnette as Robert led her forward.

"This is Elizabeth Rossiter, Gram," he had said simply.

"I could have guessed that, boy," she had replied gruffly, still surveying Elizabeth. "Well, if her sense matches her looks, it seems you have made a good choice. Come and sit down, girl."

"Thank you," Elizabeth had replied, and she had perched stiff-backed on the edge of a nearby chair.

Robert had laughed, looking endearingly handsome and at ease in this very uncomfortable situation. "Gram, you old rogue," he had said outrageously, "you are deliberately trying to make Elizabeth uncomfortable just to discover if she has character. Now admit it," he had said.

"Hmm," had been her reply as she lowered herself slowly into a wing chair close to the fireplace.

"I told you that she is not a silly, empty-headed chit, now, did I not?" he had said. "She may sit like that, looking ill-at-ease, Gram, but she will not dissolve into tears or the vapors, I do assure you."

"Hmm," the old lady had repeated. "You never did

learn manners living with that young fool, did you, boy? Now, you go upstairs to my room and fetch the paisley shawl I left on the bed. It is chilly here."

And, remarkably, by the time he had arrived back a few minutes later, Lady Bothwell and Elizabeth had been conversing quite comfortably on some topic that Elizabeth had now forgotten. The three of them had taken tea and cakes and talked for an hour or more. For Elizabeth it had been a blissful time. For once she and Robert did not have to steal a little time together in a public place. For once they could talk and laugh and relax together. And for once she felt the delight of being accepted by at least part of his family. There had been better to come. The old lady had finally pulled herself to her feet and grasped her cane.

"I have to go and check on my plants," she had announced. "They almost did not survive the journey from Devon. Old, like me. It takes me ten minutes to water them. No, I do not need any help, boy." She waved aside Robert's outstretched arm and hobbled toward the door. She had shut it firmly behind her.

Robert and Elizabeth had stared at each other incredulously for a moment. Then he had laughed. "Do you doubt now that she likes you?" he had asked, and he had stretched out a hand to pull her to her feet.

They had spent ten shameless minutes in each other's arms, kissing, gazing into each other's eyes, whispering love words, just holding each other. Elizabeth had rested her head against his shoulder at one point. She had closed her eyes and luxuriated in the feel of his warm, masculine body touching hers. How strong his thighs and chest and arms felt! How broad and comforting the shoulder! He was not very much taller than she and she liked him that way. She fit so comfortably against him.

He had nibbled on her earlobe and blown into her ear so that she had raised her head, giggling, to meet his laughing eyes again. They had embarked on another exploration of each other's lips and mouths before they heard the slow but unmistakable approach of the cane again. By the time Lady Bothwell had reentered the room, they had been sitting in their former places, Elizabeth flushed, Robert's fair hair looking less than immaculate.

"Hmm," the old lady had said, "sorry to keep you waiting."

That visit had set the pattern for a series of visits that took place every few days. They would converse with Lady Bothwell for an hour and then she would have to check on her plants. Never for longer than ten minutes. But the visits and the brief times alone had been sufficient for their relationship to grow. Their love had developed out of friendship; friendship helped it deepen.

And what had happened to the friendship and the love? Elizabeth asked herself now. They had seemed strong enough for a lifetime of happiness. But she did not dare let her memories stray any farther forward. Not tonight. She had no idea how late it was, but it felt very late indeed.

How could yesterday afternoon have happened? What was the explanation of his coldness and his anger? Elizabeth had gone over and over his words during the drive back home from the picnic and during the evening, which she had spent in her room, pleading fatigue. But she was no nearer a solution now. He had accused her of setting her cap at Mr. Mainwaring. That was outrageous enough, though at least partly understandable, perhaps, as the man had danced with her a few evenings before and had walked with her that afternoon. But Hetherington had accused her of dangling after Mr. Mainwaring's money. The idea was absurd. When had she ever suggested to Robert that money was important to her? She had been willing to marry him when neither of them had a feather to fly with. He must have known then that she had other admirers, wealthier ones, who might have been brought to the point had she given them the smallest encouragement.

He had seemed almost to hate her when he had charged her not to ruin a sensitive man like his friend. Yes, she had learned for herself that Mr. Mainwaring was a sensitive man, that he could probably be hurt easily. But to suggest that she would lead him on only to hurt him, to suggest that she was somehow heartless and dangerous, was, was . . . absurd! And he had told her to go to him for money. That he would give it to her. The gall of the man! The sheer gall! Elizabeth tapped her palm convulsively on the bed. How she itched to slap him again. She wished she could have hit him harder.

And she wished—how she wished—that she had not responded to his kiss. Perhaps it had not been so obvious, had it? She had certainly struggled hard enough at first. Perhaps he would think she had just grown tired of the struggle, had just gone limp in his arms. Would he? You did not open your mouth to a man when you just went limp, though, did you? And he would not look at you afterward with a contemptuous sneer, would he? Oh, drat the man, he knew, all right.

Elizabeth flushed with mortification and burrowed her head in her pillow, determined to sleep again. Persistence helped her to feel drowsy; she began to drift into welcome unconsciousness.

Suddenly her eyes flew open. Now, what had he meant when he had said that she could have had it all if she had only waited? She sighed and willed sleep to come yet again.

Mrs. Prosser and her sister paid a brief call the following afternoon to invite Cecily to drive into town with them. They also brought an invitation to the whole family and to Miss Rossiter to attend a ball at Ferndale the following week.

Elizabeth went upstairs to help Cecily change into clothes suited for a shopping trip. The girl did not really wish to go.

"I like Mrs. Prosser," she explained, "but I cannot abide that cat, Miss Norris. She forever makes me feel like a foolish country girl, Beth, and she positively glares at me every time the Marquess of Hetherington comes near me. Really, there is no need, Beth. I like him well enough, and he is kind enough to single me out for attention whenever we are together. But really there is nothing between us. The cat is welcome to him, though I do not believe he likes her excessively."

"What makes you say that?" Elizabeth asked casually as she selected a bonnet from a shelf that would match Cecily's primrose walking dress.

"Have you not noticed that he always avoids having to spend too much time with her?" the girl explained. "Why, yesterday he even preferred your company to hers. Mr. Dowling remarked on it and she positively glowered." Cecily giggled. "Would it not be amusing if she became jealous of you, Beth?"

"Yes, indeed," her companion agreed. "Now hurry, Cecily, or the ladies will be tired of waiting."

Elizabeth spent the unexpected free time in the rose arbor writing a letter to her brother. Cecily joined her there on her return from town.

"Well, the cat has thrown down the glove," she said cheerfully.

Elizabeth did not comment on the strange mixture of metaphor. "Oh?" she prompted.

"We stopped for ices," Cecily said, "and she hinted that the ball is to celebrate a special occasion. An interesting announcement is apparently to be made."

"Indeed?" Elizabeth said lightly, not quite understanding the pang of emptiness she felt somewhere in the region of her stomach. "Her betrothal to Hetherington?"

"Oh, I think so," Cecily said, "although Mrs. Prosser looked cross and told Miss Norris not to be premature."

Elizabeth was carefully putting away her writing materials. "Will you be unhappy if it is true, love?" she asked. "Did you mean what you said to me earlier?"

"Oh, it will not bother me," Cecily said airily. "I must admit that at first it seemed glamorous to be noticed by a fashionable man, and a wealthy, titled man at that. But really, Beth, these things do not matter much once you get to know a man, do they?"

"You mean that love and friendship mean more?" Elizabeth asked.

"Well, yes. I mean, yesterday the London people thought the church was rather a joke, did they not? But Ferdie and I have memories attached to it. We could have spent hours there and not got tired."

Elizabeth smiled. "Is Ferdie back in favor again, love?"

"Ferdie?" said Cecily. "Oh, sometimes he can be very annoying and boyish, Beth, and he does like to show off because he has been to London. But, yes, I feel more comfortable with him than all the Mr. Mainwarings or marquesses you could present me with. I do not love him or anything like that," she added hastily.

"No, of course not," Elizabeth smiled, "and you must not be in a hurry to fall in love or to imagine that you should be in love with someone. You are very young, Cecily. Be sure that when you do marry, it is to someone you can trust completely."

"Why, Beth," Cecily said in surprise, "you sound so serious. I am not even thinking of marriage yet, you silly goose. But truthfully, what do you think of the Marquess of Hetherington and Amelia Norris? Will they suit?"

"Yes, admirably," Elizabeth said with more vehemence than she had intended.

Cecily looked doubtful. "I think not," she said. "For all that I do not love him, Beth, I think the marquess is a very pleasant man. She will sour him or make his life a misery."

"I think Hetherington can probably control his own fate," Elizabeth said, gathering her writing materials into her arms and starting off in the direction of the house.

The week was a reasonably peaceful one for Elizabeth. Although she could not ignore the fact that the imminent betrothal between Hetherington and Amelia Norris upset her somewhat, with her rational mind she was glad of it. If they became officially engaged at the ball the following week, they would surely be anxious to get back to town to prepare for the wedding, or if London was too sparsely populated for them at this time of the year, surely there must be any number of family and friends that they would want to visit with their news. Robert had only his uncle left, she believed, but Miss Norris probably had a larger family. Surely they would leave Ferndale soon and then she would be able to begin erecting the wall of quiet serenity around herself that had helped her through her years as governess and lady companion.

Only once during the week was she forced to face the Ferndale party. They all came over one afternoon to take Cecily driving. Elizabeth escaped from the drawing room immediately to fetch a shawl from the girl's bedroom. She handed it to Mr. Mainwaring on her return and would have left. He detained her for a moment.

"I am sorry that we cannot offer to take you up too, Miss Rossiter," he said, smiling down into her eyes from his great height, "but the phaeton will be full by the time we collect Miss Claridge from the rectory."

She smiled briefly. "Indeed, sir, I shall be glad to catch up on a hundred and one little tasks," she assured him.

"We shall see you at the ball?" he asked.

"I—I am not sure yet, sir," she stammered, very aware of Hetherington sitting silent in a chair close by, not participating in the general conversation of the room.

"Ah, but it would be unkind of you to refuse to come," Mr. Mainwaring continued. "I particularly included you in the invitation, ma'am."

"I am much obliged to you, sir," she said, surprised. "I shall attend, then."

He smiled, the expression making his handsome face unexpectedly boyish. "Thank you, ma'am," he said. "Will you save the first waltz for me?"

Elizabeth curtsied and left the room. She had not dared

to glance at Hetherington and yet despised herself for caring that he had overheard. She *would* go to the ball, she decided, and she *would* dance the first waltz with Mr. Mainwaring—if he remembered, that was. But she had the feeling that he would claim the dance.

6

Elizabeth had never actually been inside the house at Ferndale. She had driven past the imposing wrought-iron gates supported by massive stone pillars, of course, and had often gazed at the impressive park that stretched within. During the winter, when the trees were bare, she had even been able to spot the house. But the closest she had ever come to it had been the day of the picnic when she had driven over with Cecily.

She gazed now with interest at the fairly new building. It had been erected a mere fifty years before by Mr. Mainwaring's predecessor when he had been a young man. Elizabeth admired its simple classical lines as she waited with the Rowes for a footman to put down the steps of their carriage and assist them onto the carpet that had been laid out down the marble steps for the occasion.

She felt a sense of anticipation and one of slight dread. On this occasion she was clearly a guest rather than a companion. She had already had her hand solicited for a dance by the host himself. She was wearing a new dress and felt very daring and self-conscious. It was of silk of the palest blue. It was her own creation, very simple as became her station. It was high-waisted with short, tight sleeves and a modest neckline that ended well above the level of her bosom. But it was the first dress she had owned in over five years that was not gray, the first one that did not have long sleeves. She had not quite dared to try a different hairstyle, but she had pulled a few tendrils of rich chestnut hair free of the knot at her neck and allowed them to trail down her neck and her temples.

Cecily was also excited. "Is it not great fun to be going to Ferndale, Beth?" she enthused in the carriage. "I have heard that the ballroom stretches the whole width of the house. Their housekeeper told ours that Mr. Mainwaring had to send all the way to Bath to purchase enough candles to fill all the candelabra. Imagine!"

"He has hired an orchestra from Bath, too," Mrs. Rowe added, nodding until her feather plumes waved back and forth. "Mr. Prosser told Mrs. Claridge so. I do hope Mr. Mainwaring or the Marquess of Hetherington will lead you into the first dance, Cecily. I do declare, one of them ought when we have exceeded everyone else in our civility to them."

"It does not signify, Mama," Cecily said. "Ferdie has asked me for the first dance."

"Fiddle!" said her mother. "You can dance with Ferdie anytime during the twelvemonth, my love."

"And you, Cinderella," said Mr. Rowe, looking across the carriage at Elizabeth, "is tonight the night for Prince Charming?"

"Indeed, I hope so, sir," she replied seriously. "I very much fear that my glass slippers will shatter before I have the opportunity to leave one on the house steps."

"You should not tease her, Mr. Rowe," his wife scolded. "I am quite sure that Miss Rossiter could make a very eligible connection if she but set her mind to it."

"Quite, my love," Mr. Rowe replied indulgently. "I might have suggested Mr. Dowling. He is eligible enough, though a thoroughly dry old stick. But I very much fear his heart may have been conquered already by the Worthing chit. No, Miss Rossiter, I am afraid it will have to be Prince Charming or no one for you."

"My sentiments exactly, sir," she said cheerfully as she gathered together her skirts and took the outstretched hand of the liveried footman who assisted her from the carriage.

Mr. Mainwaring had asked Mrs. Prosser to be his hostess at the ball. The two of them stood at the doorway of the ballroom greeting their guests, who had been invited from miles around. They greeted Elizabeth after the Rowes, Mrs. Prosser with a kind smile and Mr. Mainwaring with a warm smile and a firm shake of the hand.

"I hope you have not forgotten to reserve the first waltz for me," he said for her ears only.

Elizabeth smiled and passed into the ballroom. It was indeed a grand place, stretching the width of the house, its long wall consisting almost entirely of French windows that opened onto a stone balcony. The room was brilliant with candlelight, heavy with the perfume of masses of flowers. A sixth sense drew her eyes across the floor to Hetherington, who was looking particularly dazzling in a midnight-blue satin coat and lighter-blue knee breeches, with gold waistcoat and sparkling white linen. Amelia Norris, in white lace covering lavender satin, held possessively to his arm. But he also was looking across at her, Elizabeth realized with a jolt, his eyes wandering coolly over her from head to foot. She looked sharply away.

Elizabeth felt almost young again during the first half of the ball. She danced almost every dance, with the Reverend Claridge first of all, then with Mr. Rowe and Mr. Prosser. Mr. Mainwaring claimed her for the fourth dance, a waltz.

"Ah, at last," he said, his eyes smiling down at her as he placed a strong hand against her back and moved her into the music. "Now I may relax, ma'am, in your company."

"Oh, beware, sir," she warned, "I am still very likely to tread on your toes during the dance."

"I will not believe it," he protested. "You are by far too charming and too graceful, ma'am."

"Yes," she replied lightly, "but I like to appear modest by pretending that I am not perfect."

He laughed at the exact moment that Hetherington,

staring tight-lipped into Elizabeth's eyes, danced by with Cecily.

Elizabeth tilted her chin upward.

"Miss Rossiter," her partner was saying, "I said a short while ago that I never seemed to notice how you were attired. But I have noticed this evening that you look particularly lovely."

Elizabeth blushed, startled by the sincerity of his tone. "Why, thank you, sir," she said. "I feel very daring, you know, putting aside my gray and venturing into such a startling color as blue."

He smiled. "I do not like to see you in employment," he said. "You grace this ballroom more than any other lady present. It angers me that most of them consider themselves grander than you." His tone had become suddenly serious. He was looking very intently into her face.

Elizabeth did not know how to reply. The conversation, which had begun as light banter, had taken a turn that she found disturbing. "I am honestly employed because I choose to be, sir," she replied carefully. "And, indeed, these people have always treated me with great kindness. I have never felt condescension, not from the local families, anyway."

He danced with her in silence for a while, still gazing down at her averted face. "I have made you uncomfortable, ma'am," he said quietly at last. "I am sorry. I did not mean to do so. I only meant, in my clumsy way, that I wish I might call on you and invite you to drive and ride with me. But I can do so only if I invite others and have you come along as a companion or chaperone. I resent the situation."

Elizabeth looked up at him, startled again. She could think of nothing to say.

"Have you promised the next dance?" he asked. "I should like to walk with you in the garden. It is lighted and there will be others out there. You need not fear that I mean anything improper."

Elizabeth hesitated. "I should be delighted to dance

with you again later in the evening," she said, "but I cannot think it would be quite the thing to leave the ballroom with you, sir. I am but a paid companion, after all."

He sighed as the music drew to an end. "Let it be the supper dance, then?" he said. It was a question.

"It would be my pleasure," she murmured as he led her to a vacant chair close to an open set of French windows. As soon as he had moved away, Elizabeth slipped through the windows and leaned against the rail of the balcony, half-shielded by a large potted plant. The air felt refreshingly cool against her burning cheeks. She forced herself to relax, tried to force her whirling thoughts into some order.

Had Hetherington been right about Mr. Mainwaring? It certainly appeared as if he admired her. And Elizabeth was not quite sure how she felt about that. After several years of living on the fringes of life, so to speak, it was not unpleasant to know that one had attracted the notice of a distinguished gentleman. And Mr. Mainwaring was certainly that. He was undoubtedly handsome, with a very masculine physique. Although reserved to a marked degree, the man had a hidden warmth and intelligence that would surely make him a pleasant companion. Had she met him under any other circumstances, she felt that she might have been tempted to try with him to put the past behind her and make a future for herself that was less bleak than the existence she had been living.

But Hetherington had made that virtually impossible. It was not that Elizabeth was frightened off by his disapproval or his demands. It was simply that, having seen him again, she knew that she would never be free of him. Although she now found his presence oppressive, despised him for his past, was cynical of his false charm, and almost hated him for what he had done to her life, she still felt bound to him as strongly as she had ever been. She could never love him again, but she could never stop loving him, either. She would always know when he was in the same room, and she would always be as physically aware of him across the length of a room as if he were actually touching her. Although she could never be happy in that situation, she could not in all fairness encourage the attentions of another man. Could she? Elizabeth closed her eyes and pictured how pleasant it would be to allow Mr. Mainwaring to call on her, to escort her on various outings. Of course, it was all a wild dream, anyway. She could never enter into high society again. There would always be the few who might have known and would remember. And it would be unfair to drag an innocent man through that old scandal.

Elizabeth's thoughts were finally penetrated by the sound of voices coming from the far side of the potted plant that hid her from view. She recognized the voices immediately as those of Hetherington and Amelia Norris. Their voices were restrained, but they were arguing, she realized. Elizabeth would have withdrawn; she had no wish to eavesdrop. But she could not move away and back into the ballroom without being seen. And she realized that the conversation had been going on for some time, although she had only just become consciously aware of it. If they saw her now, they would naturally assume that she had been listening. She sank even farther into the shadows, against the stone balustrade.

"You know very well that our friends expect an announcement at any moment," she was saying.

"I know no such thing, Amelia," he replied amiably. "If our friends really do so, their expectations can come only from you, my dear."

"How can you say so!" Her voice shook with suppressed fury. "You have been playing with my affections, Robert. You would make me the laughingstock."

"Indeed not," he denied, his tone more serious. "I have never led you to believe that I held you more dear than a friend, Amelia. I am sure that no one has been misled. Your reputation is in no way sullied."

"You are despicable," she spat out. "You must know

that my sister is in daily expectation of hearing that you have offered for me. I am sure that every rustic in this godforsaken corner of England must be expecting an announcement. Have I been dragged here under false pretenses when I could have been enjoying the pleasures of Brighton?"

"Amelia, my dear, please keep your voice low," Hetherington cautioned. "I accepted an invitation here because William is a particular friend of mine. I heard purely by chance that you were also coming as sister of Henry Prosser's wife. I was pleased. I have always found you lovely and pleasant company. But you must not read more significance into our being here together. Indeed, I am distressed to know that you have misunderstood the situation."

"Misunderstood!" she replied. "It is the little Rowe chit, is it not, Robert? How foolish you make yourself, running after a little schoolroom miss that would not hold your interest for a month. Can you contemplate what marriage with her would be like? You would have that dreadfully vulgar Mama forever visiting you and sunning herself in the glory of having a marquess for a son-in-law. And you would probably be saddled with that solemn drab of a governess, or companion, or whatever she calls herself."

"Amelia," he said, his tone colder, harder than it had been, "I am not contemplating matrimony with any woman, and am not likely to in the future. I am sorry, my dear. I am sure that you can make a brilliant match if you will. But it would not be fair to encourage you to dangle after me. I may not marry even if I wished to."

There was no answer to his words, but after a few moments Elizabeth could hear a rustle of skirts and assumed that Miss Norris had swept back into the ball-room in high dudgeon. She dared not move. She had no way of knowing if Hetherington had accompanied his companion. She was relieved a short while later to hear a deep sigh from the other side of the plant and then the

unmistakable sound of his footsteps moving away. Only
then did she feel free herself to return to the welcome
warmth of the ballroom.

The excitement of the evening was still not over. Mr.
Mainwaring claimed the supper dance with Elizabeth, as
he had promised, and led her in to supper. He seated her
at a table with Cecily and Ferdie Worthing. These two
were engaged in a spirited argument about an incident
from their childhood when they had been caught by the
gamekeeper of the previous owner of Ferndale trespassing
and eating apples from the orchard. The argument concerned which one of them had been responsible for getting
them both caught.

Elizabeth and Mr. Mainwaring listened in amusement
to the epithets that flew between the heated pair. Ferdie
was "idiotic, stupid, and clumsy," and Cecily "silly, slow,
and shrill."

Cecily snorted. "It was funny, though, was it not,
Ferdie, when you told him you were the squire's son and
he realized that he could not thrash us?"

"I say, Cec," Ferdie replied with enthusiasm, "you put
on a jolly good show of crying and wailing. The only time
in my life I ever heard you cry."

"It worked, though," she said proudly.

"Yes, I was the only one who was punished," Ferdie
said dryly. "The dratted man sat me down at the foot of a
tree and told me that if I wanted apples, I could have
them. He made me eat one after another until I was sick."

"You ate eight and a half," Cecily remembered.

"And have never eaten one since," he added.

They all laughed. Mr. Mainwaring touched Elizabeth's
hand briefly and smiled directly into her eyes. She had
been glad of the lively conversation provided by the
younger pair. She was thankful now for another interruption. Lady Worthing had touched her on the shoulder.

"May I speak with you a moment, Miss Rossiter?" she
asked.

Surprised, Elizabeth rose to her feet and followed the

older lady into the deserted ballroom. Squire Worthing was there, too.

"Miss Rossiter, will you help us?" the squire's lady asked. She was obviously distraught.

"What is it, ma'am?" Elizabeth asked, helping the lady to seat herself, taking her vinaigrette from her nerveless fingers and waving it in front of her nose.

"Lucy is missing," Squire Worthing said gruffly. "Has been missing for an hour or more. We do not wish anyone else to notice but cannot find her ourselves."

"We know you to be discreet," his wife continued, "and perhaps you would be less conspicuous moving about than we are. The silly girl must be hiding somewhere and does not know how much time has passed."

"Gracious!" said Elizabeth. "Is she alone, ma'am?"

Lady Worthing hesitated. "I believe Mr. Dowling is absent too, Miss Rossiter," she said. "Oh, it is too provoking. I quarreled with Lucy just this afternoon. What does she want with that dull, undistinguished man when her father and I are sacrificing a great deal in order to take her to town next winter?"

Elizabeth bit her lip. "I shall walk into the garden," she said. "Rest assured that I shall keep looking until I find her. There is no chance that she has left altogether, I suppose?"

"Our carriage and Dowling's are both still in the stables," Squire Worthing replied.

"Then there really is nothing to be worried about," Elizabeth said practically. "I am sure it is as you say, ma'am. They have just forgotten the time." She smiled and hurried away.

She stepped out through the French windows onto the balcony and down the steps at one end. Lanterns had been hung in the trees close to the house. Elizabeth wandered over the lawn and peered among the shrubs that surrounded it, but was afraid to go farther as the lighting was not good and she did not know the grounds at all. She decided that Lucy would probably not have wandered

beyond that area for the same reasons. She must return to
the house, it seemed.

The house was difficult to search for all the same
reasons. Most of the rooms were in darkness and Elizabeth had never been inside the house before. She dreaded
being caught apparently snooping. But she felt compelled
to continue with the search. She felt responsible for the
apparent attachment between Lucy Worthing and Mr.
Dowling. It was her advice at a dinner table that had set
Lucy talking to this neighbor, whom she had not noticed
before. And it seemed that the girl was in trouble with her
parents, who looked higher for a husband for their
daughter than to a mere gentleman farmer.

Elizabeth crept down the stairs into the downstairs hall.
There was no one there. Apparently all the servants were
busy either abovestairs with the refreshments or in the
kitchen below. She turned a door handle and peered
cautiously into a darkened salon. It appeared to be empty,
though she whispered Lucy's name and listened a moment
before closing the door again. She repeated the perfor-
mance at a smaller room that appeared to be Mr. Mainwaring's office, and at another, larger room that was
obviously a well-stocked library. From this room she had
an answer.

"Come inside, Elizabeth, if you must," a cool and
familiar voice said from the depths of a large leather chair
close to a window at the far side of the room.

"I shall not disturb you, my lord," she replied hastily.
"I am looking for someone."

"Why would you search for Miss Worthing in a part of
the house obviously not being used for entertainment?"
Hetherington asked.

"Er, I merely thought she might be lost," she replied
weakly.

"No, you thought she might be enjoying a secret tryst
with her country swain," he said with heavy sarcasm.
"And being the good and straitlaced companion that you
are, you must interfere. She could do so much better if she

went to London and hung out for a *suitable* husband, could she not?"

Elizabeth was angry. "You do not know why I am looking for Miss Worthing, my lord," she said, "and you do not know me. I have no desire either to explain or to justify myself to you. Excuse me, please. I must find Miss Worthing."

"Relax," he said, the sneer still in his voice. "She has been found already by the worthy squire and his wife. She and Dowling were in here with me. We were having a pleasant and quite unexceptionable conversation. It was totally improper, of course, for Miss Worthing to be here with two gentlemen, unchaperoned, but sometimes one forgets such niceties. I suppose the young lady will be whisked home early in deep disgrace."

"I am sorry for it," Elizabeth said, "but really her parents' actions are no concern of yours or of mine."

"No, they are not," he agreed. "Come inside and shut the infernal door for goodness' sake, Elizabeth. You look like a bird poised for flight with one hand on the door like that."

Elizabeth did not know why she did as he asked. He just seemed different tonight, sitting there in the darkness. He seemed unthreatening. She crossed the room and sat on the padded window seat.

"You have been drinking," she remarked.

He laughed. "And I believe you have become a puritan," he returned.

"You used not to drink at public entertainments," she said.

"And you used not to moralize, ma'am," he retorted.

"I was not moralizing," she replied, "merely wondering what troubles you."

There was silence for a few moments. Then he laughed softly again. "It seems to me that we have found ourselves in this situation once before," he said.

"Yes," she agreed softly.

They could find nothing to say for a while. They sat

silently, remembering. Elizabeth closed her eyes and wished herself back to that previous occasion when Robert had first kissed her and told her that he loved her. If only they could go back, wipe out the intervening years. If only she could change the way he was, make him become permanently what he had seemed to be then.

"I suppose the young always imagine the good times will last forever," he said quietly, echoing her thoughts. "It is a rude awakening, is it not, to discover that people change, or that they have other facets to their character that we did not suspect?"

Elizabeth could feel tears welling in her eyes and a tickling in the back of her throat. She stared down at the dim outline of her hands, but could not trust her voice for a while. At last she got to her feet.

"I should not be here, Robert," she said, willing her voice to steadiness. "I must go."

"It is a long time since I heard my name spoken like that," he commented. "You always did have a special way of saying it, like a caress."

"Good night," she said, and moved past his chair.

He caught her wrist as she passed and stopped her progress. "You are right," he said, his words slightly slurred. "I have been drinking. And drink makes me sentimental. Tomorrow I shall be able to see you as you really are again and I shall despise myself for having detained you here. But for tonight, Elizabeth, I find you infinitely desirable."

He lifted her hand toward him and pressed his lips to her palm. He held her wrist afterward, closing her fingers over the spot that he had kissed. He got abruptly to his feet, dropped her hand, and faced the window. "Go now," he said harshly, "before I forget that there can never be anything but enmity between you and me."

Elizabeth turned and found her way out of the room more by instinct than by conscious direction. She stood outside, her back against the door, for a whole minute, fighting the bitter tears, deliberately taking deep, slow breaths to calm herself. Finally she forced herself to climb the stairs again and enter the ballroom. She made sure that there was a dance in progress before she did so, and made her way to an obscure alcove of the room, where she escaped attention until the final dance, when Mr. Rowe found her.

"Ah, Cinderella," he said, "I thought you were lost. I was convinced that Prince Charming must have chased you away already."

"Yes, he did, sir," she replied cheerfully, "but I considered it too far to ride home on a pumpkin, so I crept back inside through a rear door."

"Ah," he said. "Wise, if unromantic. Do come and dance, Miss Rossiter."

7

The weather turned rainy the next day and remained gloomy for most of the following week. Cecily was restless. She had become used to the increased activities of the previous few weeks. Mrs. Rowe fretted. She had set such store by the arrival of distinguished visitors in the neighborhood, yet already the round of social activities had slowed down. And neither of the unattached gentlemen seemed likely to attach himself to Cecily. Perhaps just as provoking was the fact that the girl seemed not to mind.

Elizabeth was relieved, though. She wanted to see as little as possible of the Ferndale residents for the time being. She dreaded seeing Hetherington again. That last, strange meeting with him in the library had unnerved her more than she would have expected. She found his coldness and his anger easier to cope with than the melancholy and near tenderness that drink had induced in him that night. It had taken all her willpower in the hours following the ball not to allow the reserve she had built around herself in six years to crumble away. But she had held on and would continue to do so, perhaps, if she could just stay away from him.

And she was pleased, too, to avoid an early meeting with Mr. Mainwaring. She liked him, and her woman's intuition told her that she could attach his affections quite easily if she set her mind to the task. Common sense had already told her that she must not do so. But common sense sometimes seemed a dreary taskmaster. The previous years had been dull and lonely ones. It was pleasing to know that one was admired, especially when the admirer was a handsome and personable man. She felt that he could become a very close friend. And to a lonely person, friendship can seem a likely substitute for love. Elizabeth was tempted, yet she wished to resist temptation. The tedium of being forced to spend the better part of a week indoors was not wholly unwelcome to her, then.

She did have visitors one afternoon. Mrs. Rowe and Cecily had driven over to the vicarage in a desperate attempt to cheer themselves up. Lucy and Ferdie Worthing arrived on a similar errand, Elizabeth decided after one look at the gloomy faces of the pair.

"Went out this morning for a gallop, rain or no rain," Ferdie told her, "and lamed my best horse when he skidded in the mud. Ruined a good coat and pair of breeches, too."

He wandered off to the stables to examine a pair of horses that Mr. Rowe had recently added to his stable.

"I must confess that I had hoped to have private talk with you, Miss Rossiter," Lucy said hesitantly as soon as her brother was out of earshot.

"Indeed?"

"Yes. I am so miserable," the girl continued, "and there seems to be no one else to talk to."

"What is it?" Elizabeth asked encouragingly.

"You must know that I have an affection for Mr. Dowling and he for me," Lucy said. "Mama says I am being absurd, that I merely imagine I love him because he is the first gentleman to take any notice of me."

Elizabeth did not comment. She had to admit to herself that the same thought had passed through her mind.

"It is not true," Lucy continued anxiously. "I know everyone thinks him dull. I know he is not excessively wealthy or very important. But he suits me, you see, Miss Rossiter. You taught me how to converse with people, and it works. Mr. Dowling has much to say to me. And I find him interesting. I like to hear about his farm and his livestock and his plans for the future."

"I am very glad to hear it, Lucy," Elizabeth said gently. "But would you not like to try your newfound skills on other people? Perhaps you will find other gentlemen even more interesting."

"Oh, I think not," Lucy replied. "You see, I have always been shy and awkward. I never feel that other people will like me. But Ira makes me forget that I am not pretty or clever or witty. I feel comfortable with him, Miss Rossiter. And he loves me."

"He has told you so?" Elizabeth asked.

"Oh, yes," the girl said earnestly, "and he has offered for me, you know. But Papa has refused."

"Oh, dear," said Elizabeth lamely.

"Mama will not understand," Lucy went on. "She insists that she has my best interests at heart. I will soon forget Ira, she says, when I get to London and meet other gentlemen. Oh, but I shan't, Miss Rossiter. I know I shan't."

"How old are you, Lucy?" asked Elizabeth.

"Almost eighteen."

"And Mr. Dowling?"

"He is six and twenty."

"Perhaps you should agree to your mother's plans," Elizabeth suggested. "A winter in London can do no harm, you know. It will give you experience and polish and some connections. It will also help you know beyond a shadow of a doubt whether your feelings now are lasting ones. I cannot speak for your parents, but I believe they are not tyrants. Perhaps if they can see next summer that your feelings and Mr. Dowling's feelings have not changed, they will consent to the match. A year is really not that long a time."

"A year is an eternity when you know that nothing will change," Lucy said firmly. "I know our love will never change."

Elizabeth smiled. "Then being separated for a few months cannot really harm you, can it?" she suggested.

Lucy looked doubtful but did not reply for a while. She looked up finally. "You are right, Miss Rossiter," she said. "I believe I must do as you say. But what if he does not wait for me that long?" she added on a wail.

"Then you will be hurt," Elizabeth replied carefully, "but at least you will have discovered before it is too late that he did not really love you. You will have escaped a bad marriage."

Lucy smiled ruefully and got to her feet. "I shall go to London," she said, "and I know that Ira will wait for me and that I shall continue to love him. Papa must consent eventually. Thank you, Miss Rossiter. You always speak such common sense that I wonder afterward why I did not think of the answer myself." She held out a hand to Elizabeth. "I wonder you did not marry. Cecily has told me that you were in society once. You are so beautiful and so wise, I wonder all the men did not love you."

Elizabeth laughed. "There were so many duels over who should have me," she said, "that finally there was no one left alive to claim my hand. I am a very tragic figure, you know."

"And that is something else you do," Lucy said as she drew on her gloves. "You joke a great deal about yourself so that no one can get close to really knowing you."

Elizabeth was startled. Lucy was the last person she would have expected to penetrate so close to the truth.

Finally Elizabeth ventured outdoors. It had rained all morning. She had spent the time in the old schoolroom with Cecily, going through a pile of the girl's clothes, helping her make small alterations to make the garments more fashionable. They had ended up with a lengthy list of small items: buttons, ribbons, lace, and such, needed to complete the transformations. Elizabeth had volunteered to brave the elements and walk into Granby after luncheon to fetch the purchases.

It was a dreary afternoon. The rain had stopped for a while, but the clouds hung heavy and gray and a cold wind emphasized the dampness in the air. The roadway was muddy, the grassy verges wet and cold on the ankles. Despite it all, Elizabeth was glad to be out in the fresh air. She hated to be cooped up indoors for more than a day or two at a stretch. Yet she had hardly set a foot over the doorstep in five days.

It did not take her long to accomplish her errands. She stuffed the packages into the large reticule she had brought with her and started on the return journey. A glance at the sky told her that she must hurry. The rain would not hold off much longer. About half a mile out of town she moved over onto the grassy verge in the hope of saving herself from being splashed with mud by the vehicle coming up behind her. Her head was lowered against the wind.

Elizabeth looked up as a phaeton slowed beside her. She found herself looking into the smiling eyes of Mr. Mainwaring.

"Well met, ma'am," he said, touching the brim of his beaver. "Do let me take you home."

Elizabeth hesitated, but it seemed ill-mannered to refuse. Besides, she felt quite delighted to see him again. Until then, she had not realized just how dreary a week she had just lived through.

She smiled and placed her hand in the one he had stretched down to assist her. "Thank you, sir," she said. "But I am afraid I shall soil your vehicle. My hem and boots are all mud."

He laughed as she seated herself beside him. "How delightful it is to see you again, Miss Rossiter," he said. "How have you been entertaining yourself during this bad weather? By tramping about the countryside regardless?"

"Oh, no," she said, pulling a face, and she proceeded to give him a short account of her week's activities.

"We have fared almost as badly," he admitted. "I could shoot a hole through the next pack of cards I see, Henry declares he will break a cue over the head of the next person who suggests billiards, and Robert has been snapping the head off anyone foolish enough to try to draw him into conversation. He has quite lost his legendary charm. The ladies are no more cheerful. Bertha swears she will scream if she hears another scale on the pianoforte, and Amelia prowls around from morning to night telling us all what delightful entertainment she could be enjoying in Brighton right now. We are all too gallant, I suppose, to remind her that it sometimes rains in Brighton too, despite the presence of the Prince Regent."

"Oh, dear," Elizabeth said, holding out a hand, palm up, and pulling her pelisse closer around her with the other hand, "here it comes again."

And indeed, the rain, having given fair warning that it was about to fall, came sheeting down, blown into their faces and down their necks by the strong wind.

Mr. Mainwaring grasped the ribbons more firmly and watched his horses' footing with care. "Ma'am, we are very close to Ferndale," he said to her, not taking his eyes from the road, which was fast developing into a bath of mud again. "Shall you object if I take you there until the rain has eased again?"

"No, please do," Elizabeth said, bowing her head against the wind again and mindless of everything except the misery of the rain and the cold, which soon seemed to have seeped into her very bones.

It was a very bedraggled pair who alighted a few minutes later at the front steps of Ferndale and who burst unceremoniously into the marble hallway. Mr. Mainwaring threw off his own caped greatcoat and beaver hat and turned quickly to take Elizabeth's dripping bonnet and to help her off with her pelisse.

"Come up to the drawing room immediately and warm yourself by the fire," Mr. Mainwaring said. "Afterward I shall get Bertha or Amelia to lend you some dry clothes. And I shall send a servant to inform Mrs. Rowe that you are safe and sound here."

Elizabeth was still too cold to argue. But she was very conscious of her stockinged feet, the wet and muddy hem of her gray dress, and the heavy strands of hair that had freed themselves from the knot at the back of her neck as she entered the drawing room ahead of her host to find Mr. Prosser taking his ease at one side of a roaring fire and Hetherington sitting reading a book at the other.

"I have brought Miss Rossiter home with me," Mr. Mainwaring announced cheerfully. "I saved her from a certain drowning out there in the storm."

"And it would have been a muddy death," Elizabeth added, gazing ruefully down at her soiled hem.

Both men had risen to their feet. Mr. Prosser came hurrying across the room and grasped Elizabeth by the elbow. "Come to the fire, ma'am," he said, "and warm yourself. You must not risk taking a chill." He led her to the chair he had just vacated and she sank gratefully into it, feeling immediately the welcome warmth of the log fire.

Hetherington had crossed the room without a word and now returned, carrying two glasses of brandy. The one he handed to Mr. Mainwaring, who was also standing before the blaze, his hands stretched toward it. He gave the other glass to Elizabeth, standing before her and looking at her with cold blue eyes as he did so.

"Thank you, my lord, but I should prefer tea," she said hesitantly.

"You shall have your tea, ma'am, but this first," he said, his voice so devoid of expression that Elizabeth shuddered. He stood there until she had taken the first sip and sputtered over it, and then he disappeared from the room. He returned a few minutes later with Mrs. Prosser and Amelia Norris.

"My thanks to you, Robert," Mr. Mainwaring said, "and my apologies to you, Miss Rossiter. I had forgotten that I was placing you in a compromising situation by bringing you into a room where there were no other ladies present."

Elizabeth was beginning to feel human again. She

smiled. "I am afraid that I was so delighted to encounter a fire that I did not notice, sir," she replied.

"My dear Miss Rossiter," Mrs. Prosser said, "you have made yourself dreadfully wet and muddy. Whatever were you doing outside on a day like today?"

"I was in town making some purchases for Cecily," Elizabeth replied. "Indeed, I did not know that the rain would return so soon."

"I do not know what Miss Rossiter was doing walking out in conditions like these," Amelia Norris said petulantly. "Does Mr. Rowe not allow his servants to ride?"

"Don't be foolish, Amelia," her sister said briskly. "Come, Miss Rossiter, we must get you out of these clothes immediately. I am broader than you, but something of Amelia's should fit."

"I do thank you, ma'am," Elizabeth said, leaping to her feet, "but there is no need, I assure you. I must leave for home immediately. Now that I have had a chance to warm myself, it will be no trouble at all. I shall take a shortcut across the fields."

"You shall do no such thing," Mr. Mainwaring said firmly. "It is raining quite as hard as when we came in, ma'am. You would take a chill for certain if you ventured out again. I shall dispatch a servant immediately with a message."

"Oh, but, really, sir," Elizabeth cried, distressed at the awkward predicament in which she found herself, "I could not trespass further on your hospitality. The rain may not ease all night. I would sooner leave now, while there is still daylight."

"I shall have the housekeeper make up a guest chamber for you, ma'am," Mr. Mainwaring said. "I believe you are right. The rain will not let up for a long while. And I am sure that Mrs. Rowe can spare you for one night."

"And you will spare us from the boredom of the same company again this evening," Mr. Prosser added. "Please do stay, ma'am."

"I believe Miss Rossiter should be allowed to do as she

wishes," Amelia Norris said shrilly. "Perhaps she does not feel comfortable in elevated company."

"You speak a pile of nonsense sometimes, Amelia," her sister scolded. "Come, let us find some dry clothes for Miss Rossiter to wear."

Very much against her will, Elizabeth allowed herself to be led from the room by Mrs. Prosser.

"I really do not believe that I have anything suitable," Amelia said as she followed them out of the room.

By the time they had found a gown suitable for Elizabeth to wear, Mrs. Prosser suggested that they all rest prior to getting ready for dinner.

"William keeps country hours here," she explained. "We dine early. I shall send my own dresser in one hour's time to help you get ready."

"I am sure Miss Rossiter is accustomed to do for herself," Amelia said acidly.

"Indeed I am, ma'am," Elizabeth said, smiling at Mrs. Prosser. "I beg you will not inconvenience yourself."

"We shall see," the other woman assured her. "Now, please do rest. I am still worried that you will have caught a chill this afternoon."

Elizabeth did not lie down. She drew a chair to the window and sat looking out. Indeed, it would be madness to venture out, armed as she was only with a heavy pelisse and half-boots. And it would be equal madness to force Mr. Mainwaring to call out a closed carriage when it would get bogged down in the mud in no time at all. Yet even so, she felt wretchedly uncomfortable with her situation. She felt herself to be an intruder, and her ambivalent position as an employed lady did not help her confidence. However polite Mr. Mainwaring's guests might be, they must surely view her as a servant and feel that she did not really belong with them at the dinner table and in the drawing room afterward. To make matters worse, there was the presence of Hetherington. He hated and despised her. She almost knew by the look in his eyes earlier that he believed that she had maneuvered this visit.

She was dreadfully embarrassed. She even considered sending a message at dinnertime to say that indeed she had caught cold and would prefer to stay in her room. But that might be construed as yet another attempt to focus attention on herself.

No, she must go down. She gazed in despair at the gown laid out on the bed. She must wear it. Her own clothes had been whisked away by a maid to be cleaned. Even if they were dry in time, they were not suitable for evening wear. And she could certainly not venture downstairs in the warm but ample dressing gown that she was currently wearing. It had been the plainest gown that Amelia Norris possessed, and she had been noticeably reluctant to lend even that. But its neckline was a great deal lower than anything Elizabeth had worn since she had been a debutante, its sleeves were short and puffed, and its hem was delicately scalloped. And it was of the palest primrose yellow. Mrs. Prosser had lent her a pair of gold slippers. They were a size too large, but Elizabeth was not planning to do much walking.

Finally, when the dresser came to see if she could be of any help, Elizabeth dressed herself. She blushed with mortification when she looked at herself in a mirror. She looked like a girl again, her delicately curved figure accented by the flimsy material of the gown. There was altogether too much bare flesh in evidence for her comfort. The skirt was slightly too long. She would have to hold it up whenever she was on her feet. Her hair still streamed down her back in thick chestnut waves. She hastily gathered together all her hairpins and grabbed a brush. Soon the hair had been tamed into a knot that sat even more severely on her neck than usual.

A tap at the door heralded the return of the dresser. She brought with her a pearl necklace and a warm white shawl from her mistress. Elizabeth was grateful for both. The pearls somehow made her neck and bosom seem less bare. The shawl was something to hide behind.

It took a great deal of courage to leave the room and

descend the staircase to the drawing room. As fortune would have it, only Hetherington and Mr. Mainwaring were yet present, the former looking startlingly handsome in black. They both rose to their feet and stared at her as she timidly entered. Mr. Mainwaring crossed the room in a few long strides and took her hand in his. He smiled dazzlingly.

"I am delighted to see, ma'am, that you are none the worse for your ordeal this afternoon," he said. "And please give me leave to say that you look quite beautiful." He raised her hand to his lips. "Would you not agree, Robert?" he added.

Elizabeth had been aware ever since she entered the room of Hetherington standing with his back to the fire, his face pale, his lips tightly drawn together. He was watching her intently.

He lifted his glass now in a mock salute. "Charming," he said, and raised one eyebrow.

"Do come to the fire, Miss Rossiter, and let me get you a drink," Mr. Mainwaring said, apparently noticing nothing out of the ordinary in his friend's attitude.

He led her to a chair close to where Hetherington was standing, then crossed the room to a sideboard where an array of decanters and glasses had been set out.

"It is the hairstyle that is the real coup de grace," Hetherington murmured, looking into the dark liquid in his glass.

"Thank you, my lord," Elizabeth said sweetly. "I knew I might depend upon you to make me feel at home."

"I thought you might be depended upon to do that for yourself, ma'am," he muttered so that Elizabeth felt herself near to bursting with rage by the time a smiling Mr. Mainwaring put a glass into her hand.

Fortunately, the other two ladies entered the drawing room at that point, soon to be followed by Mr. Prosser. Conversation became general and the party adjourned to the dining room. Elizabeth, viewed kindly by at least three of her table companions, found that the meal was not such an ordeal as she had anticipated. She felt almost cheerful by the time Mrs. Prosser rose to lead the ladies into the drawing room.

Amelia Norris made no secret of the fact that she did not feel it her duty to entertain or socialize with a mere governess.

"Come, Bertha," she said, "play for me while I sing."

Mrs. Prosser groaned. "Must we?" she asked. "It seems we have done little else in a week. I was hoping to have a comfortable coze by the fire with Miss Rossiter."

"There is nothing else to do," Amelia snapped, "and you know that Robert likes to hear me sing."

Mrs. Prosser sighed. "Will you excuse us?" she said to Elizabeth. "Do you sing or play, perhaps?"

"Only very indifferently," Elizabeth replied, shaking her head. "I shall enjoy listening to you."

When the gentlemen entered the drawing room a while later, it was to find Elizabeth sitting a little removed from the fire and the other two ladies at the piano at the other end of the large room.

"Ah, Henry," his wife called, "I need you here to turn the pages of the music for me."

He crossed the room amiably and stood behind his wife's stool. Hetherington too strolled across to the pianoforte and leaned an elbow on it while he watched Amelia singing.

"May I join you, ma'am?" Mr. Mainwaring asked, and seated himself beside her on the sofa.

They conversed about the recent weather, about common acquaintances, about the social activities they had both engaged in since his arrival. He told her about some changes he planned to make in the estate. In particular, he planned to extend the stables and to hire more gardeners to tame the general wildness that surrounded the house.

"Does this mean that you plan to make Ferndale your frequent home, sir?" Elizabeth asked.

"Oh, yes," he replied. "I like it here very much. My estates in Scotland and northern England are rather too remote for frequent visits, and London is rather too busy and too superficial for my tastes. I believe I shall spend a large part of each year in residence here."

Elizabeth smiled. "I am sure your neighbors will be very happy to have Ferndale occupied again," she said.

He looked at her intently. "And you, ma'am?" he asked. "Will you be happy to have me live here?"

"I?" she said. "Why, yes, sir, I value your acquaintance."

Hetherington had moved back across the room and sat now in the chair closest to the fire with his book. He propped one foot against the hearth rail and appeared to become immediately absorbed in its pages. Elizabeth judged that he was out of earshot of their conversation unless he made a deliberate attempt to listen.

"Will I be speaking out of turn, ma'am," Mr. Mainwaring continued, "if I say that you are one of the main reasons why I have decided to make Ferndale my principal home?"

Elizabeth looked at him, troubled. "It is perhaps unwise to allow one person to influence one's decisions," she said. "People can disappoint us, you know."

He was silent for a while, watching her. "May I hope, Elizabeth?" he asked.

She was distressed. She eyed Hetherington uneasily, but he seemed to be engrossed in his book. "For friendship, yes, sir," she replied hesitantly

"But not for anything more?"

"I do not believe so, sir," she said.

He continued to gaze at her. "Does your position as a paid companion make you hesitate?" he asked. "It need not, you know. Your breeding proclaims you every inch a lady, and I find nothing shameful in being forced to work for a living."

"I am not ashamed either," she replied.

"There is someone else, then?" he asked. "Your affections are engaged elsewhere?"

How could she reply? Elizabeth gazed at her hands, which were twisting uncomfortably in her lap.

"Pardon me, ma'am," he said, reaching out and touching her hands briefly. "The question was impertinent. Please do not distress yourself. I believe Bertha and Amelia have tired of their music. Shall we set up a card table?"

He had risen to his feet. The last words were spoken more loudly. Elizabeth gratefully allowed herself to be drawn into the evening's activities. She escaped to her room as soon as she decently could, having avoided any more private conversation with Mr. Mainwaring and without having given Hetherington any further opportunity to cut her with words. She lay down half an hour later, hoping fervently that the weather would have changed by the morning so that there would be no possible obstacle to her going home early.

8

"I must see him for myself," Elizabeth was saying. "I cannot believe it. I will not. He loves me. There is some terrible mistake."

"There is no mistake, love." John's voice was very gentle but equally firm. He was kneeling on the floor in front of her chair. He seemed always to be kneeling before her. "I have talked to Papa and there is no mistake. The man is an out-and-out scoundrel."

"No!" she said, covering her ears with her hands. "No."

The tears were flowing again. She was powerless to resist them. She had lost all pride.

"Love, you must get up from there. You must go outside. You must eat," John coaxed.

"No," she said dully. "No."

"What can I do for you?" he asked, genuine pain in his voice. "I cannot be a substitute for that damned Denning —Hetherington, I should say—but let me comfort you, Elizabeth. Lean on me for a while. You have done enough for me in the last years."

"I must see him," she said dully. "I must see him. I must hear it from him."

"He refuses to have any further contact with you, love. Get angry, Elizabeth. Curse him. Yell. But don't keep on grieving like this. Please, love."

Elizabeth sobbed painfully into her hands again.

He gathered her into his arms and rocked her like a

child. "It will be all right," he crooned. "Everything will be all right."

"No," she wailed.

She was sweating and struggling, fighting for breath. When she opened her eyes against the darkness, she continued to struggle, completely disoriented. It took a while to understand the strangeness of her surroundings. She was in a guest bedroom at Ferndale. She lay still, listening tensely for a while. Had she said anything aloud? Her nightmares had been noisy at first. Many times she had awoken to find John shaking her by the shoulders, telling her over and over that it was just a bad dream and that everything would be all right. No one at Mr. Rowe's house had ever mentioned hearing her call out in her sleep, though several times she had awoken from the nightmare, her face still wet from the tears.

Damn him! Damn Robert Denning, Marquess of Hetherington. How could she be expected to sleep peacefully knowing that he was under the same roof? Was he sleeping dreamlessly? Or was he restless too, troubled perhaps by his conscience? He did not appear to have one, but perhaps it troubled him in his sleep. The thought was somehow comforting.

Elizabeth pushed back the bedcovers impatiently and crossed the room in her bare feet to the window. She pulled back the heavy curtains and stared out into the darkness. It was still raining, though with less force than during the evening. The sky seemed lighter. There seemed even to be some thinner patches in the clouds, though it might have been wishful thinking that made her imagine it.

She shivered. The room felt chilly and damp now that the fire that had been lit earlier in the day had died down. Elizabeth pulled around her shoulders the dressing gown that Mrs. Prosser had lent her, climbed back into the high bed, and sat upright, the bedcovers pulled to her waist, her arms clasped around her knees.

She relived again those few blissful weeks, the best in

their courtship, when they had visited Robert's grandmother frequently and had a chance to get to know each
other and brief minutes to touch and embrace. Even at the
time Elizabeth had wanted those days to go on forever.
Two people had contrived to put a stop to their happiness.

Elizabeth had been surprised one evening at a large ball
to have her hand solicited for a dance by Robert's uncle.
She had seen him before, had even been introduced to
him, but she had never seen him dance, had never seen
him pay any attention whatsoever to young women. He
was a man of enormous wealth and had a great sense of his
own importance. As brother to the Marquess of Hetherington, he felt himself far removed from the common
touch. He was generally disliked, Elizabeth had heard.
She was terrified of him, though Robert felt a deep
respect, even affection, for his uncle. When he asked her
to dance, Elizabeth's amazed reaction was that he must be
putting his public stamp of approval on his nephew's
courtship of her. She could not have been more wrong.

Although he had led her in the direction of the dance
floor, Horace Denning had stopped before they could join
a set, bowed in chilly hauteur to his partner, and suggested that they sit out the dance.

"I have something I wish to say to you, Miss Rossiter,"
he had said.

Elizabeth had been far too young and far too awed to
resist. He had chosen a secluded alcove that had separated
them from the company, though it maintained the proprieties by keeping them in view of the dancers.

"My nephew fancies himself in love with you," he had
begun, coming straight to the point.

Elizabeth had been startled and flustered. "Y-yes, sir,"
she had stammered.

"And I suppose you return the sentiment?" His voice
had been coldly sneering.

"Yes, sir," she had answered more firmly, "but I do not
see what concern it is of yours."

Ice-blue eyes had bored into hers. "You are impertinent, miss," he had said. "It is very much my concern when a member of my family is about to make a fool of himself."

"A fool of himself?" she had echoed faintly.

"He is two and twenty," Denning had continued, "a mere babe. He has obviously succumbed to an admittedly pretty face and figure. How do you think it would appear to the *haut monde*, Miss Rossiter, if the son of the Marquess of Hetherington were to ally himself with the daughter of a drunkard and a spendthrift?"

Elizabeth had felt herself flushing, but she had been too young to dare to let her anger form an answer for her.

"You are a fortune-hunter, of course," the cold voice had gone on, "but my nephew has undoubtedly failed to inform you of the fact that very little of the family money will come his way."

"I am not interested in money, sir," she had found the courage to say.

"Oh, come, come, Miss Rossiter," he had replied, irritated, "we are all interested in money. We are fools if we say we are not. I shall not allow you to have my nephew, you know. When he is older, he will see that it is wise to choose a marriage partner who can increase his consequence. And Robert must marry money and position. It is essential for a younger son to do so."

Elizabeth had stared at him, her chin lifted defiantly.

"How much will it take to make you realize that marriage to my nephew is not a wise course for you?" he had asked.

Elizabeth had not immediately understood. "I beg your pardon?" she had asked blankly.

He had answered impatiently. "I have no time for these missish airs of innocence, Miss Rossiter," he had said. "What is your price?"

She had gaped inelegantly.

"Unlike my brother and his family, I am as rich as

Croesus, as the vulgar saying goes," he had said, "and I believe in investing some of that money in the future welfare of my family."

"Are you offering me money to break my relationship with Robert?" she had asked incredulously.

"How much, Miss Rossiter?"

Elizabeth had risen to her feet, breathing hard. "I have nothing to say to you, sir," she had said. "I notice that the music has stopped. I must return to my aunt."

"I see that I shall have to deal with your father," Horace Denning had said, quite unperturbed. "I shall not find him so scrupulous, I wager."

Elizabeth had felt chilled as she hurried to rejoin her aunt in the ballroom.

Not many days afterward, Mr. Rossiter had appeared in London, claiming that business had brought him there. But Elizabeth had not been surprised when he had taken her to task for her attachment to Robert Denning.

"Did his uncle tell you about this?" she had asked him.

"It need not concern you where I heard about your goings-on, Lizzie," he had said sternly. "It is sufficient for you to know that it will not do and you must see no more of this young man."

"What possible objection can you have, Papa?" she had asked. "He is of excellent birth, as you must know. He has manners and education."

"And not a groat to his name," he had snapped.

"We had not planned to marry until he inherits the money his mother left him," Elizabeth had explained.

"Marriage?" he had said harshly. "And who gave you permission to talk of marriage, miss?"

"We have talked of it, Papa," she had said hesitantly, "though it will be a long while before we can consider even a formal betrothal."

"You can forget the whole idea," he had announced. "Do you think I have raised you and sent you to London, Lizzie, so that you might enter into a lengthy engagement to a penniless puppy? You will do your duty, my girl, and start looking around you for someone whose pockets are well lined. Never mind the handsome faces and the fancy titles. Marry a cit, if you must, but you will marry money."

Elizabeth had said nothing. She knew from experience when it was useless to argue with her father. He had been drinking, as she could tell from his bright eyes and the smell of his breath. If she had tried to reason or argue further, his mood would have become ugly.

But that afternoon had been one of the days scheduled for a visit to Lady Bothwell. Mr. Rossiter had left for his hotel. Elizabeth's Aunt Matilda had raised no objections when Robert came to call on her. So she had gone with him. She had told him during the short journey what had happened with his uncle and with her father, though she had not mentioned the fact that his uncle had offered her money. He had been looking grim by the time she finished.

"Uncle Horace has tackled me with his opinions," he had commented. "I had no idea he would harass you, my love. I am sorry. And your father, is it likely that he will finally give his consent?"

"I fear not," she had replied, "unless you suddenly inherit some grand fortune."

He had gazed at the horses' heads, unamused by her small attempt at humor. "We must go away from here," he had said abruptly.

"Together?"

"Yes, we must. They will never give us any peace if we stay. And in three years they will have driven a wedge between us. It is too long to wait, Elizabeth."

"No," she had said, troubled. "I cannot go away with you like that, Robert. I could not reconcile it with my conscience."

He had looked across at her, startled. "I mean marriage," he had said.

"Marriage?" she had echoed. "You mean Gretna Green?"

"I suppose so," he had agreed. "Oh, you deserve better, my love. Will you mind?"

She had thought as she watched his grandmother's residence approach. "I think being married to you is more important to me than anything else," she had said.

He had flashed her a grateful smile as he tossed the ribbons to a waiting groom and vaulted down from his own seat in order to help her down.

They had not mentioned anything of all this to Lady Bothwell during the visit. But during their ten minutes alone, Robert had held her and kissed her and promised that he would make all the arrangements and inform her of them soon.

"I do not know if what we are doing is best for you, my love," he had said, holding her head against his shoulder and laying his cheek next to hers. "Society will frown on us for marrying over the anvil. Both your family and mine will condemn us and probably disown us. I shall probably have to seek employment so that we may live, but even so, I shall not be able to keep you in the comfort to which you are accustomed. But I cannot think of any alternative. I cannot contemplate the idea of losing you."

"I shall leave the decision to you," Elizabeth had said, lifting her head from his shoulder and putting her arms up around his neck. "I am ready to go with you tomorrow if you wish. But I will not be a burden to you, Robert. If you decide that we must wait, then I shall wait."

He had clasped her to him then and covered her face and neck with hot kisses.

Two days later he had drawn her to one side at a garden party they had both attended. His grandmother had also had an irate visit from his uncle, he had reported. Horace Denning had demanded that she stop receiving Miss Rossiter. But Lady Bothwell was not the sort of person to whom one dictated terms. She had called in her grandson and had a long talk with him. The outcome was that she had offered to use her contacts with a bishop in order to help him procure a special license. She had made an agreement to give her grandson a living allowance, which he was to pay back as soon as he received his mother's inheritance. And Elizabeth was to travel to Devon in her coach in three days' time, while Robert was to accompany them as an outrider. In Devon they were to be married before informing their families of their whereabouts.

"Will you do it?" he had asked anxiously.

"Yes." Elizabeth had regarded him unwaveringly.

"I must not stay with you any longer, my love, or contact you in the next few days. I do not wish to attract the attention of either your father or my family. Can you leave your aunt's house on the morning of Thursday and come to Gram's? I must not come to fetch you."

"It will be easy," she had replied. "I often go shopping in the morning. It should be simple to get away from the maid and the coachman."

"I shall see you then, Elizabeth," he had said. "Three more days and we shall be together for always."

She had smiled brightly for the benefit of an approaching acquaintance. "Yes, sir, it is a perfect afternoon," she had said.

How young they had been. Despite the anxiety of those few days, how easy it had been to believe in a forever-after. Why did young people so readily believe that all problems ended at the altar, that happily-ever-after began right there? Elizabeth, staring through a window at Ferndale at a gradually lightening sky, smiled sadly in memory of her former self, the girl who had believed in fairy-tale endings. No one could have convinced her six years before that the day would come when she and Robert would sleep under the same roof, in separate bedrooms, not only strangers to each other, but bitter strangers.

She raised her eyes to the sky and breathed a prayer of gratitude at the changed weather. She had to get away. She could not stay this close to him and yet this far away from him for much longer. If it would not appear grossly bad-mannered to her host, in fact, she would not wait for morning, but leave now when the sky was light enough to guide her home in safety.

Mr. Mainwaring insisted on taking Elizabeth home himself in the phaeton the next morning. She had had an early breakfast and had tried to insist that she would enjoy the walk across the fields, but he would not hear of her doing so. One thing she was thankful for. She did not see Hetherington. He had gone out riding with Mr. Prosser.

The sun was actually breaking through the clouds when they left the house.

"Ah, I do hope the rainy spell is over," Elizabeth said. "It is so dreary to have to stay indoors for days on end."

"Yes," Mr. Mainwaring agreed. "I have certainly missed meeting my neighbors in the past week. Will you be avoiding me now, Miss Rossiter?"

"Avoiding you?" she asked in surprise. "Why should I do that, sir?"

He smiled wryly. "I made unwelcome advances to you last evening," he said. "I hope you will allow me to remain your friend."

"Indeed, yes," she replied earnestly. "I value your friendship more than I can say, sir. And I am truly sorry about the other. It is just that I—I cannot love. And I could not accept your attentions unless I were free to offer that."

"You do not need to explain," he said quietly. "I shall be here for you, Elizabeth, if you should ever need me. That is all. May I call you by your first name?"

"Yes," she said.

"And I should be honored if you would use mine," he added.

They traveled in silence for the rest of the short distance home. Elizabeth felt strangely comforted. This was how she would want to be loved, with a warmth and an unselfishness that demanded nothing in return. She did not believe that William Mainwaring would abandon her if circumstances changed as Robert Denning had done. If only she could love him! They could have a good life together. And she did not believe he would care even if the old scandalous story were to surface. He cared nothing for London. And town gossip did not reach easily into the countryside to harm one's peace.

She allowed herself to dream as Mr. Mainwaring guided the horses carefully through the mud, of living at Ferndale with him, helping him improve the estate, socializing with him in the neighborhood, bringing up his children. But images of Hetherington intruded. How could she even dream of life with another man when just thinking of him made her heart turn over? She could picture him now as he had looked the night before, sitting relaxed in the chair by the fire, his book resting on his raised leg. It had seemed such a domestic scene and she ached now, as she had ached then, to be a part of it. Instead, she had sat twenty feet away, as far removed from him in spirit as if she had been twenty miles away. Yet she loved him still. Not as she had before, when she had loved him as if he were a prince in a fairy-tale romance. He had been perfection itself. Now she loved him as a woman, with knowledge of all his faults and with full realization that they could never be together again. But she loved him. And for the first time since it had happened, she admitted to herself that she would not have altered any of those events even if she had known of the separation and pain ahead. At least she had known love and at least there was one man in this world who meant everything to her. No, she must never allow her resolve to weaken as far as William Mainwaring was concerned. She could never make him happy. She had nothing of her real self to offer him.

"Here we are," Mr. Mainwaring said cheerfully, "and I did not once upset you into the hedge."

"What a dull and unadventurous life this is sometimes,"

she replied, matching his tone and allowing him to grasp
her by the waist and lift her across to dry ground.

He paid a brief courtesy call in the house before driving
away again. But he left with Mrs. Rowe an invitation to dinner and an evening of charades the following
week.

Mrs. Rowe turned to Elizabeth in some excitement
after he had left. "How splendid for you, my dear Miss
Rossiter," she said. "I was just saying to Mr. Rowe
yesterday that I should not have allowed you to venture
out into that dreadful weather and that you must have got
caught in the rain somewhere and caught your death of
cold when Mr. Mainwaring's messenger came galloping
up to the door. I was never so gratified in my life. Did you
join the company for the evening?"

Elizabeth smiled calmly and gave a brief account of the
card games they had played.

"You have all the good fortune, Beth," Cecily sighed.
"I knew I should have gone to town with you."

"In fact, Cecily, it was an embarrassment," she said
soothingly. "I wore a gown of Miss Norris' that was too
long and too low in the neck, and slippers of her sister's
that I left behind if I did not concentrate on taking them
with me as I shuffled along."

"Oh, bless me," said Mrs. Rowe. "But really, my dear
Miss Rossiter, I do believe that Mr. Mainwaring is developing a *tendre* for you. It was really uncommon civil of
him to escort you home himself when he could easily have
called out his carriage and sent you home."

"Oh, Beth," Cecily chimed in brightly, "do consider me
for a bridesmaid. I have never been one, you see."

Elizabeth blushed, but noticed that the girl's eyes
twinkled. "I believe you should look around for another
bride to befriend," she said. "You may be an old maid
rather than a bridesmaid if you wait for me."

"Well, indeed, I believe it would be a very eligible
connection," Mrs. Rowe declared. "You must have Miss

Phillips make up a new gown for you by next week, Miss Rossiter. And I shall get Rose to come to you and do your hair before we go to Ferndale."

Elizabeth laughed. "And I should be so uncomfortable that I should hide in a corner all night," she said.

9

The neighborhood perked up with the anticipation of new entertainment at Ferndale. It was just what they all needed after the dreadful weather of the previous week, Lady Worthing confided to Mrs. Rowe when she met the latter in Granby one morning when they had both ventured outside to make some purchases and to catch up on local news.

A couple of incidents conspired to prevent the entertainment, though. Mrs. Claridge and Anne arrived to visit Mrs. Rowe and Cecily just two days after the invitations had been issued. The former brought the news that the Prossers and Amelia Norris were planning to leave within the next few days. Mr. Prosser had told the vicar that his sister-in-law was fretting over the fact that she had already missed much of the summer season at Brighton. She wished to be one of the Prince Regent's social set at the Pavilion. She had persuaded her sister and brother-in-law to accompany her.

"I am sure we shall all be better-off here without that young woman," Mrs. Claridge said, "but I shall be very sorry to see the Prossers leave."

"Yes, they are a most genteel couple," Mrs. Rowe agreed.

"Oh, will Mr. Mainwaring cancel the evening of charades?" Cecily wailed. "How provoking that would be."

"I do not see why he would, my love," her mother comforted. "He could hardly withdraw invitations once they are given."

"I wonder why Miss Norris came here in the first place if she so wishes to be in Brighton," Mrs. Claridge said.

"We did hear that she was to be betrothed to the Marquess of Hetherington," Mrs. Rowe replied. "Perhaps they had a falling out."

"I am glad of it," Anne said impulsively. "He is far too handsome and amiable for her, do you not agree, Cecily?"

Elizabeth had been sewing quietly in the window seat. She had not participated at all in this conversation, had not divulged the contents of the argument she had overheard at the ball. She did speak now, though.

"Perhaps we should change the topic," she advised calmly. "The subjects of conversation are presently riding up to the house."

She did not feel as calm as she sounded. In her one glance through the window she had seen that the whole Ferndale party had come. And her heart turned over at sight of Hetherington. It should get easier as time went on to face him calmly, she reasoned as she resumed her sewing. Instead, it was getting worse.

She kept to her seat during the bustle of the new arrivals. Mr. Rowe had met them outside and brought them into the drawing room.

"It seems that we are to lose some of our neighborhood guests," he announced. "Mr. and Mrs. Prosser and Miss Norris are leaving us and have come to say good-bye."

"And very sorry I am to hear it," his wife said, nodding graciously at the three persons indicated. "Do you leave soon?"

"The day after tomorrow," Mrs. Prosser replied, and proceeded to seat herself close to Mrs. Rowe.

Elizabeth had looked up to find Mr. Mainwaring smiling warmly at her. She returned the smile and lowered her head to her work again.

"Miss Rossiter," Mr. Rowe said, walking across to her and putting his hand into a pocket, "I picked up this letter of yours with my bundle this morning and have been meaning to find you out with it ever since." He handed her a letter.

Elizabeth looked at the direction and smiled. "It is from my brother," she said, smiling up at him. "Will you excuse me, sir, while I walk into the garden to read it?"

He nodded his acquiescence and Elizabeth gathered together her work and left the room. She took her sewing and her workbox to her room and wrapped a shawl around her shoulders before going out into the rose arbor with her letter. Even when she was there, she did not immediately break the seal and read it. She savored the moment and drank in the beauty of the scene around her. She felt that she could breathe again now that she no longer shared a roof with Hetherington. She planned to stay exactly where she was until the visitors left, though she felt she owed the courtesy of a farewell to the Prossers.

She finally broke the seal of her letter and opened it on her knee.

A few minutes later, the people gathered in the drawing room were startled by the appearance of a distraught and wild-eyed young woman who flung back the double doors as if she were making a grand entrance on a stage.

"Goodness me, Miss Rossiter, what has happened?" Mrs. Rowe cried, leaping to her feet.

"Pardon me, ma'am," Elizabeth replied, not even having the presence of mind to call her employer out where she could speak to her in private. "I must go."

"Go? Go where, child?" Mrs. Rowe asked.

"Home," said Elizabeth. "My nephew is very sick. He may be d-dying. Please, I must go at once."

Suddenly Mr. Mainwaring was guiding her to the nearest chair and Mr. Rowe was pressing a glass of something into her cold hand.

"Calm yourself," the latter gentleman said evenly. "Tell us what was in your letter, Miss Rossiter, if you will."

"The child toddled off a few days ago in the rain," she said, staring only at Mr. Rowe. "They all searched but could not find him for all of one night. When they did come upon him, he was already in a high fever. And when my brother wrote me several hours later, he was even worse and like to d-die, the physician said. Ma'am"—she turned in frenzy to Mrs. Rowe—"the mail coach leaves town in a little less than two hours time. I must be on it. It is faster than the stage. And my brother and my sister-in-law will need me. Louise is in delicate health again."

"Yes, yes, my dear," Mrs. Rowe agreed, "you must go. But not on the mail. Mr. Rowe will order out the carriage for you. It will be slower, but a great deal more comfortable and suited to your station."

"No, ma'am," she said, agitated. "I would not inconvenience you. And indeed speed is essential."

Mr. Mainwaring bent over her. "I shall take you, Elizabeth," he said, "in my curricle. It is not comfortable for a long journey, but it is as fast as any vehicle."

"It would not answer, William," said Mrs. Prosser. "A curricle will accommodate only two persons. And you could not take Miss Rossiter without a chaperone. It really would not do at all. Even with a curricle you would need to spend a night on the road. Your brother lives in Norfolk, does he not, my dear?"

Elizabeth looked up in an agony of frustration, about to say that she did not care a fig for chaperones or the proprieties, provided only that she reach John as soon as was humanly possible. She met the eyes of Hetherington, who was standing across the room, his face white and drawn.

"I shall drive Elizabeth home," he said distinctly now.

Everyone turned in his direction.

"Nonsense, Robert," Amelia Norris said crossly. "None of this is your concern."

"There would still be the need of a chaperone, Robert," Mrs. Prosser said more practically.

"Not with me," he said, his eyes fixed on Elizabeth's. "A woman does not need a chaperone when she travels with her own husband."

The silent attention that was suddenly focused entirely on his person was worthy of any melodrama.

"The lady is my wife," he said quietly, "and has been for six years."

Pandemonium broke loose. Everyone spoke at once. But the central figures were alone in the room. Elizabeth found that she could scarcely breathe. Even the anxiety over John and Jeremy faded for a moment.

"Was," she said. "Was, Robert. I have been your divorced wife for almost as long."

"Have you?" he said. "That is certainly news to me."

"Beth, this cannot be so, can it?" Cecily was asking, bright spots of color in her cheeks.

"Is this true, Elizabeth?" Mr. Mainwaring was asking.

"Robert, what are you talking about?" Amelia Norris was asking shrilly.

"Well, Cinderella!" Mr. Rowe commented.

"Miss Ross—my wife wishes to leave with all speed," Hetherington said firmly, taking command of the situation and striding across the room toward her. "Go and pack a bag, ma'am. I shall ride to Ferndale and do likewise. I shall be back here with a curricle within the hour. You will get to your brother by noon tomorrow at the latest." He turned, without waiting for her reply, and strode from the room.

There was a stunned silence in the room for a few moments.

"Well, bless my soul," said Mrs. Rowe, "bless my soul."

"Bertha," Amelia Norris said in a brittle voice that sounded close to breaking, "let us leave here at once. I have never been so insulted in my life. Hetherington and a—a governess!" She swept from the room, her back rigid, her head held high, and did not pause to see if her sister was following.

Mrs. Prosser did follow, but she paused beside Elizabeth's chair. "You certainly do not need our presence here to complicate matters, ma'am," she said pleasantly to Mrs. Rowe. She put a hand on Elizabeth's shoulder. "I do hope that you will find all well when you reach home, my dear," she said.

Mr. Prosser bowed to the company and left the room with his wife.

"Come, Anne," Mrs. Claridge said, rising to her feet with obvious reluctance. It was not every day that there was such drama in the neighborhood. "It is time we took our leave, too."

After they had left, Mrs. Rowe turned to Elizabeth.

"Well, bless my soul," she said, "I do not know what to say."

"Then say nothing, my love," her husband suggested. "You can see that Miss Rossiter is in shock. I suggest that you and Cecily take her upstairs and help her pack a bag. Hetherington will be here soon."

"Yes, yes, of course we must," his wife agreed. "But, really, Mr. Rowe, we must call her the Marchioness of Hetherington now. Dear me, and I never even suspected."

"Miss Rossiter has chosen her name," Mr. Rowe answered firmly. "I see no reason why we should call her differently until she asks us to do so."

Elizabeth, on whom her outer surroundings were beginning to penetrate again, shot him a grateful glance and looked up to Mr. Mainwaring, who was standing ashen-faced beside her chair.

"Will you take me, sir?" she asked. "I do not wish to go with *him.*"

He looked deeply into her eyes, and looking back, she could see pain there. "I cannot, ma'am," he said in a strained voice. "I would not interfere between a man and his wife."

She rose and left the room numbly. Mrs. Rowe and Cecily followed her upstairs, though she packed her own bag, mechanically and silently.

"The marquess is here," Cecily said finally. She had been standing looking out the window for several minutes.

She turned away from it, ran impulsively to Elizabeth, and threw her arms around her. "I do not know what happened, Beth," she cried, "but I do know it must have been something dreadful. You are both such dear people, and I know something quite extraordinary must have driven you apart. But I love you, Beth."

"Well, I declare," Mrs. Rowe added, her nose turning pink as the tears started to her eyes, "I am sure this house is much too humble a one for you, my lady, but you are always welcome here."

Elizabeth hugged them both quickly. "I shall write as soon as I have the chance," she said. "I know I owe you some explanation."

Downstairs, the three men stood in the hallway. Hetherington, dressed in a caped greatcoat and holding his beaver hat in one hand, stretched out the other for Elizabeth's bag.

"We should be on our way without further delay," he said briskly.

Mr. Rowe grasped Elizabeth by the shoulders. "Go, Cinderella," he said quietly, "and remember that you have both a home and employment here to come back to." He bent and kissed her on the cheek.

She would not trust her voice but smiled fleetingly and hurried after the striding figure of Hetherington. Mr. Mainwaring came after her and helped her up to the high seat of the curricle while Hetherington was strapping her bag at the back.

"I may not interfere," he said before lifting her up, "but I am your friend, Elizabeth. Always. You may depend on me."

She was swung up into her seat, Hetherington climbed up beside her and took the ribbons from the waiting groom, and they were on their way.

Elizabeth felt all the strangeness and awkwardness of the situation as soon as she turned back from waving to the little group outside the house. The man beside her was silent, concentrating on guiding the horses through the stone gateposts at the end of the driveway and out into the road.

"Why did you do it, Robert?" she asked.

"Do what, ma'am?"

"Why did you tell them about the connection between us? There was a roomful of people to hear. This is the place I had chosen for my new life. Now I do not know if I shall ever be able to return here."

"I beg your pardon," he said stiffly. "I believed that your concern for your nephew and your need to go to your brother were your first consideration. Under the circumstances, I put aside the desire both you and I might have to disown our relationship."

She could feel his anger and it subdued her own. "I am sorry," she said. "Of course, it must have been very painful for you, too, confessing to such a thing in the presence of your friends."

Silence descended on them once more.

"What did you mean," she asked, "when you said that it was news to you?"

"About your being my divorced wife?"

"Yes," she said. "Were you merely trying to make things easier for me, letting those people believe that there is nothing improper in our being together?"

He looked across at her fleetingly. "What made you believe that we are divorced?" he asked.

"But we are," she insisted. "You informed Papa and he broke the news to me. Why do you deny it?"

"Your father was lying to you, if indeed he did tell you that," Hetherington said cynically. "He was probably ashamed of you and wished to ensure that you did not keep coming back to me for more."

"For more?" she asked, puzzled. "What do you mean?"

"Oh, come, Elizabeth," he said impatiently, "let us not reopen that sordid episode in our lives. I do not wish to talk about it. In fact, my dear, I do not particularly wish to talk to you at all. I am taking you to your brother because you need help and because I still owe you the protection of a husband. I do not pretend that there is any sentiment involved. This is no social occasion."

Elizabeth did not feel the set-down because she had heard it with only part of her mind. "Are you telling me that we are still married?" she asked incredulously.

"As tight as parson's mousetrap," he answered. "You are a marchioness, my lady. Are you not highly gratified?"

This time she heard the sneer in his voice. She stiffened, then drew her cloak more tightly around her against the chill of the cloudy summer afternoon and sank lower in the seat. If he wished for silence, she was quite willing to give it to him. And even if he did not want silence, he probably needed it. The curricle was moving along the narrow country road at a spanking pace. She felt safe; even as a very young man, Robert Denning had been a notable whip. She could see now that his ability had not left him. He took hills and corners with a skill that suggested perfect concentration, perfect confidence. And speed was everything. If only she could reach home in time. She dreaded to face the question: in time for what? When the thought that Jeremy might already be dead threatened to intrude, she thrust it resolutely to one side. He could not be dead. By the time she arrived, he would probably be toddling around again and everyone would wonder why she had come. Anyway, brooding would accomplish nothing. She turned her head to one side and tried to concentrate on the scenery.

They were still married. The thought would not dislodge itself from her mind. She was still legally his wife. Why had Papa lied about that? Could there possibly have been a misunderstanding? But no. He had said there was a letter from Hetherington and legal papers of divorcement from his solicitor. He had refused to show her the papers, had not wanted to upset her further, he had said. Why had he done it? The answer seemed obvious enough. He had been unusually concerned about her as she had grieved almost to the point of madness over her broken marriage. He had probably hoped that by telling her Hetherington had divorced her he would force her to face reality more quickly. And he had been right, probably. It was after that news that she had finally taken a hold of herself and started to put her life back together again. Poor Papa. He had done it for the best.

But her marriage still existed. It was as legal and as real as it had been on that day in Devon. It was the day after their arrival from London. They had both been taut with anxiety, fearful that someone would come galloping down from London and prevent the marriage. Lady Bothwell had not raised any objection when they had asked if the wedding could take place in the morning. The elderly vicar from the nearby village had come out to the small stone chapel that was part of the estate, but that was hardly ever used any longer. And in the presence of Robert's grandmother and several of the servants from the house, they had been married. She had worn a garland of fresh flowers in her hair, lovingly fashioned by the countess's ancient gardener, and had carried a small matching posy.

Elizabeth's eyes misted now as she looked back to that day. It was such a cliché to say that it had been the happiest day of her life. But that was the simple truth. There had been a fairy-tale quality about the day. It had not seemed as real as others. She remembered Robert as he had looked when the vicar had pronounced them married. The sun itself had seemed to be behind his smile as he had turned to her and kissed her lightly on the lips. It had seemed that they had conquered fate, that they were now safe forever.

They had walked back to the house and eaten a wedding breakfast with only Lady Bothwell and the old vicar for company, but they had not felt the absence of larger celebrations. They had wanted only each other. Their world had been complete.

When the meal was over and the vicar had taken his

leave, Lady Bothwell had announced that she was going to
visit a few friends for several days.

"They have been inviting me for at least a quarter of a
century, so it is time I went," she had said. "And
newlyweds need to be alone for a while. Mrs. Cummings
and the other servants will take care of all your needs."

By the middle of the afternoon they had been alone.
And they had had two days together, forty-eight hours
into which to cram a lifetime of happiness. No longer.

It was almost beyond belief that the Robert of those two
days was the same person as the man who sat silently
beside her now, the man who had told her only a little
while ago that he had no wish to talk to her at all. He had
talked and talked in those two days, and laughed and
joked and teased. They had walked a great deal along the
cliffs that formed one boundary of the estate and along the
wide, sandy beach that could be reached after a difficult
climb down a winding cliff path. They had cared nothing
for the salt wind that had blown their hair into tangles and
whipped color into their cheeks. They had not worried
about the sand that filled their shoes and found its way
into the rest of their clothing. They had been intent only
on each other, their fingers entwined or their arms encir-
cling each other's waists, since there were no other eyes to
see and to censure them.

And they had made love for two glorious nights—no,
for one glorious night. Robert had not been himself a
virgin, but neither had he had a great deal of experience.
He certainly had not known how to avoid giving her pain.
And she had been hurt at his entry, so much so that she
had cried out. It had not been good. He had finished
hurriedly and then held her, alternately soothing her and
apologizing to her and kissing her face. He had not tried
to take her again that night. Yet even then she had felt a
certain pride in knowing that she was indeed his wife and
that she was now as close to him as any woman could be to
a man.

But the next night had been very different. After a

whole day in each other's company, they had been far more relaxed, far less nervous of what was to come. He had spent a great deal of time kissing her, touching her, and murmuring to her, so that when he had finally come inside her she had let him take her with him until they had been clinging to each other, sated with a shared ecstasy. She had discovered with wonder that that part of marriage was not to be just a necessary ordeal but that it would be at the very heart of her love for her husband. They had turned to each other time and again during that second and last night, one body, man and wife.

Elizabeth clung now to the seat of the curricle as she looked back on that night over the achingly lonely years between. Hetherington just could not be the same man. They could not possibly have grown so far apart after having shared *that*.

"Am I traveling too fast for you?" his cool voice asked now.

"What? Oh, no," she said blankly, startled out of her deep thoughts.

"You are clinging to the seat as if you fear for your life," he said. "I assure you that you are quite safe with me."

"Yes, I know," she said breathlessly. No, it could not be. It could not be the same man. There had been no barriers left between her and that other Robert. They had become one entity.

"You are tired," he said. "We shall stop soon for a change of horses, and you will be able to rest for a while and have some refreshment. But we will press on farther until we are stopped by darkness."

"Oh, yes, please," she agreed fervently.

He said not another word to her until they stopped at a posting house one half-hour later. Although she tried to persuade him then to proceed immediately, he insisted that she step inside the inn. He took a private parlor there and ordered her tea and a meal of beef and vegetables. But he did not join her there. When she questioned him later, he told her that he had eaten in the public taproom.

They traveled on for a few more hours until the growing dusk made the roads hazardous for the horses. Hetherington stopped at the next town only to discover that the inhabitants for miles around had descended on the place in anticipation of a boxing mill that was to take place there the next day. There was not a room to be had in the first two inns he stopped at, and in the third he was successful only because one patron had been invited to stay at a nearby home and had vacated his room only a few minutes before. There was only the one room available, but he dared not take the chance of traveling farther. All the inns of the town were likely to be full, and it was too dark to drive out of town. He took the room in the name of himself and his wife.

10

Elizabeth felt numb again. She knew that there was no use in objecting to the arrangements that had been made. They had been turned away from two other inns already and it was perfectly obvious that the whole town would be the same. She allowed Hetherington to lift her to the ground and take her bag from the back of the curricle.

"You will take my arm and stay close beside me," he commanded. And because the inn yard was bustling with horses and ostlers and guests, she obeyed.

She pressed even closer to his side when they entered the inn and stepped straight into the public taproom. It was crowded and noisy. Men sat and stood and jostled one another in every inch of space, it seemed. Elizabeth lowered her eyes and allowed herself to be guided across the room to the staircase. Hetherington was not a tall or a broad man. But he had a certain presence and a charming smile that did not falter in such situations. A path opened for him as if by magic.

Hetherington led the way up the staircase and into a small, dark room that was wholly dominated by a large bed. A washstand, a table, and a chair filled most of the remaining space. Elizabeth felt herself flush with embarrassment. Although the noise from the taproom sounded almost as loud upstairs, they seemed very much alone together in the room. He set her bag down beside the washstand.

"This is quite intolerable," Elizabeth said in a strangled voice.

He looked at her. "I could not agree more, ma'am," he said coldly. "But if you expect me to play the gentleman and offer to stay downstairs tonight, you will be sadly disappointed. I must have a few hours of sleep if I am to drive you home tomorrow."

Elizabeth walked to the low window opposite the foot of the bed and stared blindly out.

"If you can spare a blanket and a pillow," he continued, "I shall sleep quite comfortably on the floor."

She said nothing.

"I shall go downstairs now," he said. "Lock the door. You must on no account open it to anyone. There are too many revelers around tonight who are in their cups. I shall have the key to let myself in later. Go to bed, Elizabeth, and get some sleep. You have been under much strain today, and tomorrow will not be easy for you. You may rest easy. You have nothing to fear from me."

Elizabeth pressed her forehead against the windowpane and continued to stare out into the darkness. There was silence for a while and then she heard him leave the room and lock the door behind him. She closed her eyes. Robert, Robert, what happened to us? she wondered. But she would not stop to think. She had exhausted herself with memories that afternoon. She must prepare for bed now and climb beneath the covers before he returned. She could not risk being caught in the act of disrobing. In fact, she did not wish to face him in any guise that night.

She wasted several agonized minutes deciding whether to undress or not. Her clothing seemed to offer some measure of defense. Yet her gray cotton dress would be hopelessly creased if she slept in it. And if she removed it to sleep in her chemise, she might as well change into the one nightgown she had brought with her. She undressed hastily, waiting until she was in the relative safety of the nightgown before washing herself at the washbasin.

Then she dithered over another problem. Should she leave her hair as it was, in its tight knot at her neck, or should she brush it out as she usually did at night? There was only one sensible choice, of course. The heavy knot would be uncomfortable to lie on and would look silly too, she supposed. She quickly removed the pins and brushed her thick chestnut hair until it crackled.

Finally she pulled one of the two blankets from the bed and one of the pillows. She tossed them onto the floor and climbed into the bed in panic. He might be back at any moment. But she soon forced herself back onto the floor. The candle was out of reach on the washstand. She did not want that to be burning when Hetherington returned. And if he was to move in the darkness, it would be unkind to leave his bedding in a heap on the floor. He would be dreadfully uncomfortable.

She looked around her and then removed her gray cloak from the hook on the door. She spread it on the floor with his own greatcoat on top of it. She laid the blanket on top and turned down one corner. She plumped up the lumpy pillow as best she could and put it in place. Kneeling back on her heels to view the overall effect, Elizabeth suddenly had a mental picture of Hetherington lying there, and the image sent her scurrying to blow out the candle and climb back into the bed and beneath the covers. She pulled the single blanket up around her ears even though the room was not cold.

Falling asleep was another matter altogether. She found herself constantly listening for footsteps in the passageway outside. There was much traffic to and fro, but the footsteps always passed the door. And the noise from below was incessant. She might as well have taken her bedding into the middle of the taproom and tried to sleep there, Elizabeth thought wryly as she tried to ignore shouts and singing and cups banging over the loud hum of masculine voices.

Then she started to think about Jeremy. She had seen the child only once, at his christening, but she felt as if she knew him very well. John's letters were always full of descriptions of the youngster and bulletins of his progress. She could almost picture the child with his sturdy build

and the blond curls that he had inherited from Louise.
Both parents obviously doted on their son. John would be
devastated if anything happened to him, and goodness
only knew what the shock might do to Louise in her
condition. Elizabeth prayed that the child would recover.
She prayed that whatever happened she would have the
strength to offer both her brother and his wife the help
they needed. Her own problems paled in comparison to
what they might be facing.

She stiffened suddenly. She had hardly heard that set of
footsteps approach and they had stopped outside her
door. As she held her breath, she heard the key turn in the
lock and then she was aware of light through her closed
eyelids.

Hetherington stood there for a while before blowing out
his candle, coming inside the room, and closing the door
softly. Elizabeth lay rigid, almost afraid to breathe, listening to him set down the candlestick and remove some of
his clothing. Then she heard him lie down and move
around until he was comfortable.

There was total silence in the room. Elizabeth found
that every nerve in her body was tense. She was afraid to
move, afraid to breathe even, in case he would know that
she was awake. His own stillness made her wonder if he
too lay awake or if the fatigue of the day had sent him
instantly to sleep. She resigned herself to a sleepless night,
tried to calculate how long it would be before the dawn
would come.

"No," she was saying. "No, it cannot be true. I shan't
believe it."

"I am sorry, Lizzie," her father said, his voice unusually
sympathetic. "It is over. You will have to face the fact.
The man is a scoundrel."

"No," she wailed, rocking herself back and forth in her
chair. "No, please. I must go to him. I have to see him."

"He will not see you," her father said. "He has refused.

You cannot keep on clinging to hope, Lizzie. He does not want you any longer."

"No," she moaned. "I won't believe it. I can't. I have to see him. I have to. Oh, please, please."

John was kneeling in front of her, his hands warmly covering hers over her face.

"Hush, Elizabeth," he was saying, "it will be all right."

"No, it will not," she wailed. "It will never be all right."

"Hush, darling, hush," he whispered. "Oh, don't cry. All will be well. I shall be with you."

"No," she said. "No."

He drew her to him and held her head against his shoulder. His fingers stroked through her hair.

"John, I have to see him," she said against his neck. "I must go immediately."

"Hush, love," he said, "I shall take you to him tomorrow."

And she was tired of the pain, tired of bearing her grief alone. She surrendered to the comfort of her brother's strong arms. She allowed him to rock her in his arms, to lay his cheek against hers, and kiss her temple. She allowed herself to be comforted by the soothing words he murmured the whole time. She felt the whole burden of her agony slipping away.

A needle of light was shining through a chink in the curtains and directly onto Elizabeth's face. She was aware of it and knew instantly where she was. But she did not want to wake up yet. She was too warm and too comfortable. She shifted her position to escape the sunbeam and to burrow more deeply into the warmth.

But sleep was receding. Her mind was reaching back into memory for the source of the smell that now teased her nostrils, a musky cologne that she had not been in contact with for a long time. She could almost smell the salt of the ocean that seemed to be associated with it, could almost hear the sound of sea gulls crying in the early morning. She had a vivid recollection of warm lips on hers and a tongue that teased them apart and probed into her mouth.

She opened her eyes. Her head was resting in the hollow between Hetherington's shoulder and neck. His arm was around her, clasping the arm that was thrown across his naked chest. Although she could not see his face without tipping back her head, she could tell by his even breathing that he was sleeping. She lay paralyzed for a moment, then pushed in panic at his chest and pulled herself into a kneeling position beside him on the bed.

"What are you doing here?" she cried. "What has happened?"

His eyes were open now, though he did not move except to clasp his hands behind his head. "What do you imagine has happened, Elizabeth?" he asked. "Do you believe you have been ravished?"

"You were to sleep on the floor," she accused. "You are not to be trusted, my lord."

"Before you have a fit of the vapors," he said, "may I point out that I am lying on top of your blanket and beneath my own." He turned back the blanket that was covering him to prove the truth of what he said. "And you will also observe, if you have courage enough to look, that I am fully clothed from the waist down. Don't worry, my love, your virtue is quite intact."

She had grown to hate that sneer in his voice. "This is no joking matter," she hissed. "Get out of here immediately."

"Shirtless and bootless?" he asked, not moving. "I fear the landlady would be scandalized."

"Get out!" she shrieked, and she scrambled off the bed, grabbed his shirt, and flung it at him, then proceeded to do the same with his boots, one at a time.

"Stop this, you little wildcat," he commanded, suddenly serious. He too had leapt from the bed; he grabbed her now by the wrists as she was about to pick up his bag. "Do you wish the whole inn to believe that we are having a lovers' spat?''

She struggled against him, but his grip only tightened.

"What was I to do when you were having nightmares?" he asked. Elizabeth went limp suddenly and stared into his eyes. "You were dreaming about your nephew, wanting to go to him at once. You were crying and moaning enough to attract attention. When I came to wake you up, you thought I was your brother. The thought seemed to comfort you."

Elizabeth pulled her wrists from his loosened grip and crossed to the window. She pulled back the curtains and stared down into the yard, where ostlers were already busy grooming horses.

"I shall wash and shave and be out of here in five minutes," Hetherington said. "You can be sure then that I shall not give in to my animal instincts when you strip off that very appealing nightgown. It certainly enhances your maiden-aunt image."

She stood where she was, and not another word was exchanged until he left the room.

"I shall have breakfast sent up to you," he said. "Be ready to leave in half an hour's time."

It was well past the noon hour when the curricle drew to a stop outside her brother's home. Elizabeth was so stiff and sore that she hardly knew how to get down. Hetherington solved her problem by striding around to her side of the vehicle and lifting her to the ground with strong hands. He held to her waist for a moment.

"Are you all right?" he asked. They were the first words he had spoken since they had stopped to change horses several hours before.

"I shall be in a moment," she replied. "You need not concern yourself."

At that moment the front doors opened abruptly and John came out. Brother and sister glanced at each other anxiously and rushed into each other's arms. He held her in a bruising hug.

"You have come," he said. "Thank God! I knew you would."

She drew back and took in his disheveled appearance, bloodshot eyes, and several days' growth of beard.

"Jeremy?" she asked, the name almost sticking in her throat.

"The same," he said abruptly. "The fever has not broken. He is very weak, Elizabeth."

He looked past her to see who had accompanied her. "Good God," he said, "Hetherington!"

"You have the advantage of me," Hetherington answered coolly, extending his right hand. "But I assume you are John Rossiter."

John did not accept the hand. "What are you doing with my sister?" he asked tightly.

"He was staying at Ferndale, which is but three miles from Mr. Rowe's house," Elizabeth explained hastily. "He happened to be visiting yesterday afternoon when I read your letter and kindly offered to bring me home."

John grudgingly shook the hand that was still extended to him. "For that courtesy I thank you, Hetherington," he said.

"I came to offer my wife my protection," Hetherington said, "not to do anyone a courtesy."

"You are several years out of date," John retorted. "Elizabeth is no longer your wife, Hetherington. I shall protect her now."

Hetherington raised his eyebrows but said nothing.

"Papa did not tell you, then, that he had told me an untruth?" Elizabeth asked, and when John looked inquiringly at her, she added, "There was no divorce, John."

Her brother clenched his fists and glared with hostility at his brother-in-law. "Come inside," he said, taking Elizabeth's arm. "Louise is with Jeremy. I will not permit her to sit with him at night because she is not strong. I fear what this will do to her and the unborn child. Come, I shall have some luncheon prepared for you."

"Is there anything I can do?" Elizabeth asked.

"After you have eaten and rested," he said firmly. "You have had a long journey, and by curricle, too." He led them into the house and straight to the dining room. "What are your plans, Hetherington?" he asked. "Are you going to start back today?"

"No," Hetherington answered steadily. "I shall stay to offer Elizabeth my support as long as there is a crisis in the family. And thank you for the invitation, Rossiter."

Elizabeth was indeed thankful to shut the door of her old bedroom behind her, to slip off her dress, and to lie down on top of the bedcovers. After luncheon, which had been a strained occasion, Hetherington had disappeared and John had taken her up to the nursery where Jeremy lay, a flushed and pathetic little bundle lying in his cradle. He had been like this for three days, John explained in a whisper, hot, dry, and delirious. His face had lost some of its baby chubbiness. His blond hair had been clipped very short.

Seeing her sister-in-law, Louise tiptoed out of the room, leaving the nurse to watch her baby.

"Elizabeth, how good of you to come," she said. "You must have come on wings."

"Not quite," Elizabeth replied, "but I left immediately after I read John's letter. I shall help you watch, Louise. You must force yourself to rest. And John, too, looks as if he is sleeping on his feet."

"He has been up for four nights," Louise said, "and will hardly sleep in the daytime."

"Then it is settled that I shall sit with Jeremy tonight," Elizabeth said firmly.

Soon she let Louise go back into the nursery and persuaded John to retire to his room for a rest. Only then did she go to her own room.

But she could not sleep. She kept seeing the baby clinging restlessly and feverishly to life. And she kept seeing the strain and exhaustion on the faces of her brother and sister-in-law. It was bad enough for her to contemplate the death of a nephew whom she had seen only once before today. How must it feel for them, who had given him life and cuddled and watched him daily grow into an energetic toddler? It would be like losing part of one's own life. There had been a span of a few weeks once when she had hoped and hoped that she was with child. She had been so full of pain and emptiness in the loss of her husband. She had wished painfully for his child so that something of their two days together would survive. When she knew for certain that it was not so, she had felt almost as if she had lost a child. But that had been trivial—nonsense, in fact—when compared to the very real experience that John and Louise were going through.

She tried to block out thought and will herself to sleep. She could help John and his family best, not by worrying about them, but by maintaining her own strength so that she could relieve them of some of the burden of watching. But thoughts of the night before intruded, and she could not shake them off. She tried desperately to remember that dream. Usually she woke up in the middle of it and could recall vividly what had happened. But on this occasion she had not woken up. What had she said? She hoped nothing that would be humiliating. But no. He had said this morning that she had been dreaming about Jeremy. Whatever she had said had been ambiguous enough for him to misunderstand.

What had he said to her? She wished that she could remember. He said she thought he was John. What usually happened when John was part of the dream? He always talked to her, held her, soothed her. That was what must have happened. Hetherington had taken her into his arms and she had thought he was John. She must have felt very comforted to have let go of the dream without waking up. She recalled how very comfortable she had been when she woke up that morning. It had felt so good, so right, to be lying relaxed in Hetherington's arms.

She could not recapture her fury of the morning. The experience was one pleasant little memory to cling to. She turned over onto her side, eyes closed, and tried to recapture the feeling she had had that morning. She inhaled, trying to imagine the distinctive scent of his cologne. A tear escaped from her closed eyelids.

His father could not have found a more effective way of breaking up his son's unwelcome romance. After that second night of love, they had had one glorious morning left. Not knowing how soon fate was to separate them, they had eaten a leisurely breakfast, strolled along the beach, and wandered back to the house for luncheon. They had reached their room afterward. Robert was going to make love to her again before they went riding along the cliffs. He had already helped her undo the long row of tiny buttons down the back of her dress. He had removed his neckcloth and was unbuttoning his shirt cuffs, gazing through the window as he did so.

"There is someone riding toward the house," he had said. "In a hurry, too."

She had rushed to his side. They had been expecting someone. Both had written to their fathers after the wedding ceremony to inform them of the fact and to tell where they were. They had guessed that today or tomorrow would bring some message.

Robert had smiled ruefully across at her as he rebuttoned the cuff that he had just undone. "I could have wished him to have better timing, whoever he is," he had said. "Turn around, love, and let me tackle those buttons again."

He had trailed kisses up her spine as he closed the opening of her dress. Then he had turned her to him again and drawn her close. "If it is someone from your father," he had said, "do not be afraid. I am your husband now. He has no power over you."

She had smiled rather tensely and they had descended

the staircase together, hand in hand. The messenger had been directed to a downstairs salon. Robert had recognized him immediately as his uncle's head groom. The man, still disheveled and covered with dust, had handed Robert a letter and regarded him uneasily.

After sending the man to the kitchen for refreshments, Robert had opened the letter and read, while Elizabeth watched him anxiously. He had stopped reading and folded the letter very deliberately.

"What is it?" Elizabeth had asked anxiously.

It took him a while to answer. "My father and my brother have been killed," he had said.

"Oh! How?"

"In some absurd and freak boating accident at a regatta," he had replied.

She had grabbed his arm as his face turned pale.

"I shall have to leave for London immediately," he had said.

"Yes, yes," she had agreed. "I shall pack and order out the traveling carriage."

"No!" he had said sharply. "I must go alone, Elizabeth. It is imperative that I get there as quickly as possible. I must ride."

"I can come with you," she had protested.

"No, love. You know you do not ride well. If you are with me, I shall feel obliged to stop for meals and for sleep. Please believe me, darling, it will break my heart in two to leave you here. But I cannot take you. I must go quickly. Please understand."

Agonized blue eyes searched hers. She felt cold, almost faint. "Yes, you are right," she had whispered.

"I shall write to Gram before I leave," he had said. "She will be back here with you by tonight or tomorrow at the latest. In the meantime, you will be quite safe with Mrs. Cummings. It will be a comfort to me to know that."

He had left the room then, spoken briefly with the butler, and taken the stairs three at a time. She had trailed him numbly and packed a small bag for him while he changed his clothes and wrote to his grandmother. His horse was waiting for him, ready saddled, when they came downstairs together.

He had taken Elizabeth into his arms and held her very close to him. "I love you," he had said against her hair, "and I shall come for you just as soon as I may. Within the week. You must stay here, do you understand me, Elizabeth? Do not try to follow me."

She had nodded and hidden her face against his neck. She had not trusted her voice. She did not want to shame herself by crying.

He had placed a hand beneath her chin, raised her face, and kissed her deeply there in front of the butler and the groom who was holding his horse. Both pretended not to notice.

"Have a safe journey," she had whispered. "I love you."

He had vaulted into the saddle and ridden down the driveway away from the sea and the cliffs, and away from her, without a backward glance. She had watched him, an ache in her heart, until a line of trees finally hid him from view. And that was the last she had seen of Robert Denning, Marquess of Hetherington, until he had walked into Mrs. Rowe's drawing room a few weeks before.

The old marquess had certainly had his revenge. Had he not chosen that moment in which to die, and had he not taken his older son along with him, Robert might never have changed, might never have considered that she was not a worthy wife for him. Or would his underlying snobbery have surfaced at some time anyway, under different circumstances?

Elizabeth gave up trying to sleep and consequently drifted into unconsciousness almost immediately.

11

The family dined together that evening. Both John and Louise had been persuaded to leave Jeremy for an hour with his nurse and to eat in the dining room. Hetherington and Elizabeth were also there. Three at least of the gathering found the mealtime a strain. Hetherington was at his charming best, Elizabeth noted with annoyance. He had obviously set himself to win over Louise, who had been horribly embarrassed to learn of his presence in the house. Good manners dictated that she treat him with courtesy, but loyalty to her sister-in-law made her want to snub him.

His charm had obviously had an effect, though. Louise went with Elizabeth to the drawing room after dinner, though she did not stay long.

"The marquess seems such a pleasant man, Elizabeth," she said hesitantly. "It is hard to believe that he could have treated you so cruelly."

"That was a long time ago," Elizabeth replied. "Since we seem to be stuck with him here for a few days at least, perhaps it would be as well if you forgot about the past and treated him as a new acquaintance."

"But how can I?" Louise protested. "John has told me how he abandoned you so callously after your marriage. It is difficult to like or trust a man when one knows that of him."

Both ladies had retired to the nursery before the men left the dining room. The strain returned to Louise's face as she watched her son toss feverishly in his crib. Elizabeth soon persuaded her to go to bed and try to have a night's sleep. She and John sat up all night watching for the crisis that did not come. Neither could persuade the other to give up the watch.

The doctor came the next day, but beyond shaking his head and advising Louise to force as much liquid inside the child as she could, he was unable to tell them whether to continue hoping or to despair.

Elizabeth slept for much of the day. She had tried to persuade John to do likewise, but feared that he was using his time away from the nursery to accomplish estate business. She looked idly through her window when she awoke in the afternoon and saw that Louise and Hetherington were strolling arm in arm in the flower garden. She had meant it the night before when she had told Louise to forget about the past. But it still annoyed her to see that Hetherington could so easily charm a stranger, even one who knew of his past.

She could not understand why he had decided to stay. He had made no attempt to see her since dinner the evening before, and it must be plain to him that neither she nor John wanted his presence. It merely added to the strain of an already difficult situation. She decided that she would ask for a tray in her room that evening. She wanted to reserve all her energy for the night ahead. John and Louise were almost at breaking point, she felt, and it seemed to her that it was impossible for the baby to continue as he was for much longer. Surely the crisis must be close. She dared not think of what might happen when it did come.

Later that night Elizabeth had accomplished her aim. Louise had gone off to bed at John's bidding. He was a little more difficult to persuade, but Elizabeth, looking at his bloodshot eyes and sunken cheeks, had known that he could not sit up another night without collapsing.

"What good will you be to anyone if you become ill?" she had reasoned with him. "I came here in order to help,

John. Please allow me to do so. I know what to do to care for Jeremy, and you must believe that I will send for you at the least sign of change."

Finally he had given in and retired to his own room. An hour or more had passed since. Elizabeth had just finished sponging the child's burning flesh with a cool, damp cloth and forcing some drops of water between his lips. She sat now quietly watching him and thinking of the man she had seen only briefly today through the window.

Perhaps it had all been partly her fault. At least she might have made it more difficult for him to abandon her if she had obeyed his final request and stayed in Devon.

The hours following his departure had been torture, the night a torment. Lady Bothwell had not returned that day. And during the following morning Elizabeth's father himself had arrived. He had been very angry, threatening to tear Denning apart limb by limb. When his daughter had told him that she was alone, he had turned the full force of his fury against her. His anger was caused not so much by the fact of the elopement, it seemed, as by the poverty of her husband. Had she no sense? Had she no love for the father who had spent years of his life raising her? What did she hope to gain for herself or her family by marrying a penniless pup?

Elizabeth had let his fury blow itself out around her head before telling him about the deaths of Robert's father and brother.

"So you are a marchioness?" he had sneered, and strangely enough, it was the first time Elizabeth had realized the fact. "A fat lot of good such a grand title will do you, my girl, when the father had not a feather to fly with, either."

"We do not care for money," Elizabeth had replied primly.

"You will, my girl, when you find yourself with a position to maintain, and creditors knocking on your door," he had said harshly. "I suppose there is no chance of an annulment?"

"An annulment?" she had asked blankly.

"Has he bedded you, girl?" he had asked impatiently. Elizabeth had blushed painfully, but had not answered.

"Well," he had said, "we shall have to do the best we can. You will come home with me, Lizzie, until the young puppy has finished all his business in London. Perhaps there will be more money than I think."

"I must not leave here, Papa," she had protested. "I have promised Robert that I shall stay, and Lady Bothwell should be here today."

"Nonsense!" he had said. "The old lady may not come at all. Who better to take care of you than your father? And Norfolk is a great deal closer to London than Devon is. He will be thankful not to have to travel so far."

Elizabeth had argued. Even when she gave in, she did so reluctantly. But she had been very young. Obedience to her father had been the habit of a lifetime. She had not yet learned obedience to a husband. Lady Bothwell had not been there to advise her. What her father had said about the remoteness of Devon from London made sense. So she had gone, pausing only to pack her bag and to write a note to Lady Bothwell explaining that her father had come for her and that she was returning with him to Norfolk.

And so she had made it easy for Hetherington. He no longer had her embarrassing presence in his grandmother's home to deal with.

Elizabeth turned as she heard the door of the nursery opening quietly. She opened her mouth to scold John and send him back to bed. But it was her husband who stepped into the room and closed the door softly behind him.

He came across to the crib and stared down at the child for a while. Elizabeth watched him, tight-lipped. He was dressed only in his breeches and a shirt open at the neck.

"Poor little devil!" he said. "Is there no change?"

"None," she answered shortly.

He drew up a chair and sat down beside her. "Can I

persuade you to rest awhile?" he asked. "I do not wish
you to become overtired."

"I slept during the day," she replied. "I do not need rest
now, thank you."

He regarded her in silence for a while. "Why do you
hate me, Elizabeth?" he asked.

She turned to him incredulously. "You ask me that?"
she hissed.

He raised his eyebrows. "Yes, I believe I did," he said.

"I shall not answer," she replied in a loud whisper. "If
you do not know the reason, you must be totally lacking in
conscience and I was the more deceived in you."

"I see that you have convinced yourself that you were
the wronged party," he continued. "I believe that such is
often the case with guilty persons."

"You should know," she shot back.

He leaned back in his chair and linked his fingers behind
his head. He smiled. "You were very young and naïve,
were you not?" he said. "I suppose it did not take you
very long to realize that you had settled for very little.
And you have blamed me ever since. Poor Elizabeth!"

She stared at him stonily. "I settled for very little
indeed, my lord," she said. "I wish you would go to bed
now. Indeed, I do not need your company, and I believe
the room should be kept quiet."

"I shall sit here with you, nevertheless," he replied. He
glanced at the baby, who was becoming restless again.
"Will he live, do you think? Poor little mite! He could be
ours, do you realize that, Elizabeth?"

She made a strangled sound, but clamped her lips
tightly together. And so they sat, side by side, in silence,
watching Jeremy as he clung stubbornly to life.

It was Hetherington who first noticed the change. He
sprang to his feet, startling Elizabeth, who had been deep
in thought.

"There are beads of perspiration on his brow," he said.
"The fever is breaking, love. Stay here. I shall go for your
brother."

He ran from the room and was back in seconds, it seemed, with both John and Louise. The four of them stood and watched tensely as the child broke out in a bath of perspiration, which Louise tried to sponge away with a cool cloth. Eventually the baby lay very still.

"Is he dead?" Louise asked in a voice that sounded shockingly normal.

No one answered for a moment.

"I believe he is sleeping," Hetherington said, and he reached out one slim hand and took the baby's tiny wrist between gentle fingers.

"If he is dead," he said, smiling at Louise, "he has a very steady pulse to take with him to heaven."

"Ohhh!" Louise wailed and collapsed, sobbing, into her husband's arms.

Elizabeth's eyes locked with Hetherington's. He cocked an eyebrow at her as he closed the distance between them.

"I thought you were the stiff-upper-lip type," he said quietly, grinning at her swimming eyes. "But if you must cry, it had better be on my shoulder, ma'am."

She was horrified at her own inability to resist such inappropriate levity. How dare he push his way into such an intimate family scene and proceed to laugh at everyone! She fumed inwardly as she sobbed on his shoulder and leaned into the warm strength of his body. She felt deep resentment against the arms that encircled her and stroked comfortingly over her back. But her anger was all on the surface when she felt him kiss the top of her head. She jerked her head back and glared at him.

Before she could say a word, he had laid a finger to his lips. His eyes were still brimming with laughter. "This is not the time or the place," he said softly.

And she watched him have the great impertinence to turn back to John and Louise and proceed to take charge of the situation. Before any of them could have the presence of mind to realize that he had no right to give orders in that house, Louise had been packed off to bed, John had been sent to rouse the nurse in the next room, the housekeeper had been woken to prepare warm milk to send to her mistress's room and chocolate to send to everyone else's, and John and Elizabeth were also retiring meekly to their rooms.

"You are going to bed too, Hetherington?" John asked in a feeble attempt to have the last word.

"Oh, most certainly," his guest replied. "If I do not have my sleep, I am quite hagged the next day, you know."

Elizabeth hoped that her displeasure showed in her stiff bearing as she walked to her own room. The amusement in Hetherington's eyes as he bade her good night suggested to her that it did.

For the following two days the baby bounced back to health with all the resiliency of childhood. By the afternoon of the second day the nurse was expending all her energy on confining the child to the nursery. Louise and John, too, seemed to recover quickly from the strain of the few days and nights when their son had hovered on the brink of death.

Louise seemed convinced that Hetherington was somehow responsible for the miracle of Jeremy's recovery. She told Elizabeth so as the two of them sat on the terrace on the second morning, soaking up the morning sunshine.

"I really do not know how we should have managed without his cheerfulness and his strength to keep us sane," she said, "and without your devotion during the nights, Elizabeth. John and I were very close to the breaking point when you arrived."

Elizabeth was outraged. "I consider his behavior to have been most inappropriate in the nursery," she said primly. "He was laughing, Louise!"

"Yes, of course, dear, and the rest of us were crying," Louise answered cheerfully. "Neither reaction was suitable to the occasion. But both tears and laughter are ways of letting out emotion when it becomes too powerful to bear."

Elizabeth tutted. "You are very wise," she said, "but I

cannot think the Marquess of Hetherington capable of deep emotion."

"Oh, there you are quite out," her sister-in-law assured her. "Your marquess cares very much, Elizabeth. He stayed here in this house of gloom, did he not, when he could have gone riding back to his friends? And he was sitting up with Jeremy when his fever broke. And he spent an hour with him yesterday. Nurse said he allowed Jeremy to play with his quizzing glass and to pull his hair, and to leave a wet patch on his breeches. No, dear, I do not know exactly what passed between the two of you when you wed, but I must believe that there is some explanation for his behavior."

"How can there possibly be an explanation?" Elizabeth cried. "He would not see me, Louise, would not answer my letters. And then he divorced me."

"But he did not, dear," Louise reminded her. "And if you have been mistaken about the one thing, perhaps you have been mistaken about the whole. Why do you not confront him now that you have the opportunity? Ask him what happened. The worst that can come of it is that you will find that you have been right all along."

"I would not condescend to show him that it matters to me," Elizabeth replied.

Her sister-in-law gave her a despairing glance.

John too was concerned about the relationship between his sister and her husband. He saw her walking past his office later the same morning, called her inside, and closed the door.

"I cannot but feel the awkwardness of your situation," he said. "It goes very much against the grain with me to offer hospitality to the fellow when I have always despised myself for not calling him out all those years ago for the suffering he made you endure. Shall I send him packing, Elizabeth?"

"I am not sure he would go," she said wryly. "He seems to be quite thick-skinned when it comes to insults."

"It is so deuced awkward," he said, exasperated. "The

fellow has been a model guest. He has treated Louise with great courtesy. Jeremy really took to him, I understand. And he has been of great assistance to me, riding for the doctor early yesterday morning and back again to the apothecary later. I would find it hard now to summon the nerve to tell him that he is no longer welcome in this house."

"Then say nothing," Elizabeth said, smiling. "I am sure that he will leave of his own accord within the next day or two. I cannot think that life here has enough of excitement for him."

"And he is your husband still," John added, troubled. "I am not sure that I have the legal right to order him away from you."

In the following two days there was no sign that Elizabeth was right. Hetherington showed no symptoms of boredom or restlessness. It seemed that he was planning to stay. Elizabeth avoided him as much as she could by staying close to Louise. She spent time in the nursery with her sister-in-law and went visiting and shopping with her.

The two of them spent time in Elizabeth's room trying to find clothes suitable for her to wear. She had brought with her only the gray cotton dress that she had been wearing. There were numerous dresses in her wardrobe, but all of them were from six or seven years before, all to a lesser or greater degree out of fashion and some of them quite unsuitable to a woman of six and twenty, Elizabeth believed.

Louise convinced her, however, that several of the dresses would be quite unexceptionable with a few minor alterations. That particular evening saw Elizabeth descending to dinner in a pale-green silk gown whose puffy sleeves had been narrowed, and whose plunging neckline had been disguised with a delicate lace inset. She was self-conscious. As a consequence, her hair had been swept back into its bun with extra severity.

Hetherington and Louise were in the drawing room when she entered. "Oh, you look so lovely, Elizabeth!" Louise exclaimed. "I wish I might throw away that dreadful gray. Perhaps I should instruct one of the maids to burn a hole in it with the iron. An unfortunate accident, of course."

"I have a better idea," Hetherington added, grinning. "Elizabeth should wear it into the nursery when Jeremy is eating bread and jam. It would be ruined beyond repair."

Elizabeth glared.

Louise became flustered. "I am so sorry about your neckcloth, Robert," she said. "But I am sure they will be able to wash the jam out of it belowstairs."

He laughed. "If I had children of my own," he said, "I should probably have learned long since not to snatch an infant into the air when he is in the process of eating his tea. It was my fault entirely, Louise."

If he had children of his own! Elizabeth's fingers itched to slap him. She could recall now the stinging satisfaction she had had from doing so on a previous occasion. And since when had he and her sister-in-law been on first-name terms?

When the butler finally announced dinner a few minutes after John arrived in the drawing room, Hetherington offered Elizabeth his arm with exaggerated politeness.

"I liked it better without the lace," he said quietly to her, his eyes hovering at the level of her breasts.

She shot him a startled look.

"Almack's," he said. "You wore it there one evening. I seethed with indignation while you waltzed with old Ponsonby, because his eyes were definitely not on your face, nor his mind on his dancing, I believe."

"Oh!" Elizabeth said, lost for words.

"Of course," he added, eyeing her hairdo with distaste, "on that occasion you had some curls to cover some of the bare flesh."

"You are insufferable, my lord," she seethed.

He grinned as he held back her chair while she seated herself. "Yes, my lady, I know," he said.

It was the following day that Elizabeth decided that she must confront Hetherington and ask what intentions he had for staying on at her brother's home. She had reached the end of her tether.

Louise had decided on that day that it was time for Jeremy to have an outing. John decided that he would join them and invited Elizabeth. They would not go far. There was a small lake just half a mile distant through the trees. It was shady there and the baby had always enjoyed playing on the grass beside the water. They would take a ball with them to amuse the child, and a picnic tea.

Elizabeth looked forward to the outing. She was enjoying the holiday with her family and felt that she could have relaxed entirely were it not for the disturbing presence of Hetherington. Soon she would have to make plans to return to her position. She had had a letter from Mrs. Rowe just that morning, in fact, telling her that she was missed and that she was very welcome to return if that was the life she had chosen for herself. But she would have one afternoon just to spend with John and his family. Hetherington had ridden off somewhere immediately after luncheon; she had chosen not to ask anyone where.

Elizabeth, dressed in a sprigged muslin dress from which she and Louise had removed the ribbons and flounces, allowed a few loose curls to soften the severity of her hair knot, and tied the ribbons of a large-brimmed straw bonnet beneath her chin. She went along to the nursery, where Louise was struggling to dress her son, who was bursting with energy and mischief.

"Oh, may I carry him for you?" Elizabeth asked, and Louise shot her a grateful smile.

"Indeed, he is getting heavy," she admitted, "and the doctor and John have both forbidden me to carry any loads."

They went downstairs to find John. He was in the

hallway, a small picnic basket at his feet, talking to Hetherington.

"Robert, I am so glad you arrived back in time," Louise called cheerfully from behind Elizabeth. "Our party would not be complete without you."

He bowed his head and smiled in her direction. "I would not have missed your picnic for worlds," he said.

All the sunshine went out of the afternoon for Elizabeth. Now she would have to be prim and self-conscious again. Louise had clearly invited him. She was being quite excessively courteous. And why had he accepted? Of what possible interest could a family outing with a baby be to him?

Hetherington picked up the picnic basket and retained his hold on it even when John protested. "Your wife will have need of your arm, Rossiter," he said. "Mine does not. She already has her hands full."

They set out across the lawn and through the trees. Jeremy was contented for a few minutes, then decided that his new uncle would be a more exciting person with whom to travel. He gurgled, chattered in unintelligible baby talk, and held out his arms to Hetherington so that Elizabeth had to fight to keep her hold of him.

"Put him up on my shoulders," Hetherington said. "He can hold on to my hair."

Elizabeth ignored him until she could no longer control the child's struggles. She glared as Hetherington stepped in front of her and stooped down so that she could seat Jeremy astride his shoulders.

"Let me take the basket," she said.

He turned a laughing face toward her. "Why do you not just relax, Elizabeth?" he advised. "This is a pleasure outing."

"How can it be a pleasure when I can never get away from you?" she cried, and watched the smile fade from his face.

He turned away without another word to her. "Come

on, Jeremy," he said. "Let's make this old horse gallop."
And he trotted away, the child chuckling and then shriek-
ing with delight as he held to his perch with firm fistfuls of
fair hair.

It was at that point that Elizabeth decided that she
would have to have a confrontation with Hetherington.
They stayed carefully apart from each other for the rest of
the afternoon, but she watched bitterly as even John
seemed to warm to Hetherington's high spirits and obvious success with the baby. Tomorrow she would talk to
him.

As it turned out, Elizabeth did not have to put her
resolve into effect. Hetherington joined her and Louise at
the breakfast table the following morning. He helped
himself to food at the sideboard, sat down, and smiled at
Louise.

"I have just been in conversation with your husband,
Louise," he said. "I have been taking my leave of him. I
leave for London today."

Louise's cup clattered back into the saucer. Elizabeth
felt her heart begin to hammer uncomfortably. She laid
down her fork as quickly as possible before her hand could
begin to shake. She did not look up from her plate.

"You are leaving?" Louise said. "Oh, Robert, I had no
idea."

"I have already been here longer than I ought," he
replied. "I had planned to stay only while I felt that
Elizabeth needed my support. With Jeremy in such
bouncing health, I cannot pretend that there is still a crisis
in the house."

"But you do not have to have a reason to be here,"
Louise protested, glancing uneasily at Elizabeth. She
seemed about to say more but changed her mind.

"I really have quite pressing business in town," he said
gently. "But I do thank you for your hospitality. I have
been very happy to make your acquaintance at last,
ma'am."

Louise was speechless for a while. "Jeremy will miss you," she said at last.

He smiled. "And I shall miss him," he replied. He held her eyes and raised his eyebrows, casting a quick glance at Elizabeth's lowered head.

Louise jumped to her feet. "And speaking of Jeremy," she said brightly, "I must see if he had a peaceful night after his outing yesterday. Shall I see you before you leave, Robert?"

"I shall come to the nursery soon," he said.

Left alone, Elizabeth and Hetherington sat in silence for a while. She had not touched any food or drink since he had spoken his first words.

"You finally have your wish, Elizabeth," he said quietly at last.

"Yes."

"You will be free to relax with your family when I am gone."

"Yes."

There was another tense silence.

"What will you do now?" he asked. "Will you stay here? I believe you are needed. And you are certainly loved."

"I shall go back to my position," she replied. "This is merely a holiday."

"You do not belong there," he protested.

She looked up at him for the first time since he had come into the room. "It is not for you to say where I belong," she said firmly. "I shall do with my life as I please, my lord."

He got impatiently to his feet and strode to the French windows that faced out onto the terrace. He stood there with his back to her. "You do not like being dependent on your brother, is that it?" he asked. "You need not be, you know. You are still my wife. I am able and willing to support you in any manner you choose. If you wish to set up your own establishment, Elizabeth, you may send the bills to me. Or I shall make you an allowance so that you do not have constantly to apply to me. Would you prefer that?"

Elizabeth's chair scraped back and she was across the room at his side almost before he had finished speaking, her cheeks flaming, her eyes blazing.

"How dare you insult me so!" she hissed at him. "Have I not suffered enough humiliation at your hands, without this? I would not take a farthing from you, Robert Denning, if I were destitute on the streets and you my only hope of avoiding starvation."

His face had paled and he had flinched when she began to speak as if she had struck him a physical blow. The sneer had returned by the time she finished.

"You have changed, my dear," he said. "There was a time when money meant more to you than all else. Or perhaps you are no different now. William Mainwaring will be in residence alone when you return to your employment. He is clearly besotted with you. And I am sure you are clever enough to spin him a yarn that will overcome his disappointment in finding you a married woman. I would wish you good fortune, ma'am, if I did not feel that the man deserves better of life."

Elizabeth's hands were clenched at her sides. "Do not let me delay you, my lord," she said sweetly. "I am sure you wish to reach London before night falls."

He stared at her blankly, then held out his hand. "I am glad that events turned out well for your family here," he said.

She placed her own hand hesitantly in his. "I thank you for bringing me home," she said. "It was kind of you to cut short your visit to Ferndale."

He looked into her eyes, a half-smile on his lips. "Good-bye, Elizabeth," he said. "I wish things might have been different for you and me."

She willed herself to show no emotion. She steeled herself for the kiss on the hand that she half expected. She came near to crumbling when he kissed her instead, very gently, on the lips. Had he not gone immediately, in fact, without even stopping to look into her face again, he would have seen the tears spring to her eyes; he would have heard the sobs that felt as if they would tear her ribs apart.

But he had gone.

12

Elizabeth stayed home for only one more week. It was blissful, she thought, to be alone with John and Louise and the baby, not to be constantly looking over her shoulder for Hetherington or half-expecting to find him inside every room that she entered. After a few days she could not understand why she was so bored and restless. John was busy for much of each day; Louise was frequently tired and had to rest; Jeremy could not be played with all day long. It was time to go back. At least she was usually kept busy at the Rowes'.

Louise made life uncomfortable for her by refusing to let the topic of Hetherington drop. She had become genuinely fond of him and was convinced that he could not be quite the villain that she had previously thought.

"No one who loves children as he does can be a cruel man," she told Elizabeth on one occasion. "And did you notice how much Jeremy loved him? Depend upon it, children always know who can be trusted. Their instincts never err."

Further, she was convinced that Hetherington still had strong feelings for her sister-in-law. She believed that the marriage could be revived.

"I assure you he is not indifferent to you, Elizabeth," she said. "Why else would he have accompanied you here and stayed for ten whole days? It is not as if we are able to offer much in the way of entertainment. He loves you, you may be sure."

"Nonsense!" Elizabeth protested. "He stayed here merely to provoke me. He did not miss an opportunity to set me down or to sneer. And he has said good-bye, Louise. This is the end of it. I shall not see him again. And I must say, I am greatly relieved to know it. I shall be able to settle to my tranquil life again."

Louise cast her a skeptical look but said no more.

John upset Elizabeth in a different way but on the same topic. He apologized to her for not having taken a firmer stand and ordered Hetherington away from the house at the start.

"It was just so deuced awkward when he had just done you the service of bringing you here so quickly," he told her. "And then afterward he did us so many kindnesses and he really did seem to lift Louise's spirits. I am sorry, Elizabeth."

He proceeded to comfort his sister by abusing Hetherington for the heartlessness that enabled him to behave toward them all as if nothing had happened in the past, and for his hypocrisy. Elizabeth, surprisingly, was not comforted. She found herself suppressing the urge to defend her husband to her brother.

And she could not forget him when she was alone. Try as she would to convince herself that she was happier since he had left, she found herself reliving some of those days when he had been there. He had appeared so lighthearted most of the time. And it was his laughter, his teasing, and his smiling eyes that she had fallen in love with six years before. She remembered his always keeping the conversation alive at the dinner table, his ability to entertain Louise. She often pictured him with the baby, who would bounce with anticipated delight at the mere sight of his uncle.

His uncle! She had caught herself several times when Hetherington was still there wishing that they had a normal marriage. A few times she had had to restrain herself from joining him in a game with the baby. She would have enjoyed sharing some of that relaxed warmth.

She would have liked just one of those radiant smiles to be directed fully at her.

She found that she particularly hugged to herself the memories of the brief physical contacts they had shared. Looking back on that morning at the inn when she had awoken to find herself lying in his arms, she realized with a pang all that she had missed through her broken marriage. Every morning should be like that morning, except that she should have been able to wake him and see him smile at her, turn to her, and pull her into a close embrace. She remembered those moments in the nursery when they had all realized that Jeremy was finally out of danger. He had laughed at her, teased her, but there had been some tenderness surely in the way he had held her and comforted her until her tears had dried. And surely there had been some feeling in his good-bye. He had kissed her on the mouth and said that he wished their marriage had turned out differently.

Elizabeth smiled bitterly. Was he regretting what he had done? Was he wishing that he had stood by his marriage vows even when circumstances changed? It was satisfying in one way to believe so. But it was a hollow victory. She had lost him. It mattered not that she still loved him against all reason, and that perhaps he regretted losing her. The truth was that they could never revive their relationship. There was too much hatred, bitterness, and distrust behind them. They could never forget, and she did not believe that she could ever forgive entirely. Even if she could, she would never be able to trust him again.

It was better this way. He had gone, and to London, not Ferndale. Clearly he did not intend that their paths should cross again. She knew that her only chance of attaining peace of mind was never to see him again. Yet how could she forget him? Dear God, how was she to live without him?

And so that week passed, with Elizabeth alternately relieved and tortured. The only solution was to go back to

her position and begin all over again the task of recon-
structing her serenity and her independence. She ap-
pointed a Monday for her journey, and resisted all the
entreaties of both John and Louise to stay longer or
forever.

At John's insistence, Elizabeth traveled in his coach and
took with her a maid as companion. It was a very different
journey from the one she had made a few weeks before
with Hetherington. The coach was ponderous. Although
they set out in the morning, they were little more than
halfway by nightfall. Elizabeth and the maid stayed together at an inn, where they received deferential treat-
ment because the innkeeper had not much business. They
enjoyed the comfort of a private parlor as well as a roomy
bedchamber that boasted an extra cot for the maid. The
coach finally rolled to a halt in front of the Rowes' house
in the middle of the following afternoon.

Elizabeth received a warm, if confused welcome. Mrs.
Rowe was quite incapable of deciding what she should call
her employee, until Elizabeth laughingly put an end to her
stammerings.

"Ma'am," she said, "circumstances forced the Marquess of Hetherington to reveal what neither of us would
otherwise have told a soul. We were married for a very
brief time. But it was a mistake. It was six years in the
past, and although we are still married in the eyes of the
law, we are in reality strangers whose paths happened to
cross again for a while. But we mean nothing to each
other. I beg that you will treat me just as you did before
you learned the embarrassing truth. Indeed, I am the
same person."

"Well, it is very gracious of you to say so, I am sure,"
Mrs. Rowe replied. "But I always did say that there was
something quite distinguished about you, Miss Rossiter. I
shall respect your wishes, of course. And indeed we are
honored to have you as Cecily's companion. But I do feel
it a sad shame, my dear, that you and the marquess are
estranged. Such a charming gentleman! I did think he was

sweet on Cecily at one time, but I can see now that it was
just his manner to appear courteous to all ladies. Now,
Cecily, my love, you must be sure to do as I do and treat
Miss Rossiter just as if she were not a marchioness."

Cecily's eyes twinkled. "I shall endeavor to remember,
Mama," she said meekly. "Beth, do come upstairs if you
have finished your tea. I shall help you unpack, though I
do believe you have brought back with you almost as little
luggage as you took."

Elizabeth got to her feet, but she turned to Mrs. Rowe
before following Cecily from the room. "May my brother's coachman and maid rest here for tonight, ma'am,
before setting out for home tomorrow?" she asked.

News of Elizabeth's return spread quickly, and most of
her acquaintances paid a visit to the Rowe house within
the next few days. All of them were driven to a certain
extent by curiosity. News of her real identity and exalted
rank had not escaped anyone's ears. All, though, were
brought equally by a genuine affection for Elizabeth, who
had won respect during her years as Cecily's governess
and companion.

Lucy and Ferdie Worthing were the first to call the day
after Elizabeth's return. Ferdie greeted her with courtesy,
but it was clear that the real object of his visit was Cecily.
Elizabeth watched with some amusement as the girl
reacted with impatience and contempt to his account of a
cockfight that he had attended the day before. He answered her just as sharply. Soon they were in the throes of
a full-scale squabble. Elizabeth wondered if they would
ever achieve a more tranquil relationship. It was difficult
to tell if they loved each other well enough to consider
matrimony at some time in the future. But it did not
matter. They were both mere children. They had time.

Lucy was making stilted conversation. They soon exhausted the topics of the weather, Elizabeth's health, and
that of all her family. The girl stammered her way through

an account of the Reverend Claridge's sermon the previous Sunday. Elizabeth finally decided that she must intervene.

"Miss Worthing," she said, "do you not know me? I am Elizabeth Rossiter, with whom you have been most comfortable these several years past. Are you shy with me now because of the story you have heard about me?"

Lucy darted her a glance and blushed. "I am sorry," she said. "I cannot forget, you see, that you are the Marchioness of Hetherington. And I do not even know what I should call you."

"You must call me what you have always called me," Elizabeth said laughingly. "I was a marchioness when you first knew me, Lucy, and I have not changed since then. It is just a word, you know. I have never really acted the part of such a grand lady, and I have no wish to do so."

"Oh, but are you very unhappy?" Lucy asked. "The marquess is such a very dazzling man. I like him. Does it not hurt you to live apart from him?"

Elizabeth smiled. "Not at all," she lied. "Our marriage happened a long time ago, Miss Worthing, and lasted but a very short while. We have both made a new life since. Now we are no more than strangers."

"I do beg your pardon," Lucy said. "I should not have asked you these questions. But, you see, I cannot imagine marrying someone and then leaving him. Was yours an arranged marriage?"

"I am afraid we do not even have that excuse," Elizabeth replied. "No, at the time we supposed it to be a love match."

"I do not understand," Lucy said. "When Ira and I marry, we shall be blissfully happy for the rest of our lives."

"And I hope you are right," Elizabeth replied fervently. "Your attachment to Mr. Dowling still exists, then?"

The girl's face lit up so that she looked almost pretty for a moment. "He has decided that he will spend the winter in London too, Miss Rossiter, so that we may see each other occasionally. It is a great sacrifice for him, because he hates the city, but we cannot bear to be apart for several months, you see." She giggled. "Mama will be furious when she knows."

The quarrel between the other two occupants of the room could no longer be ignored.

"Cruel!" Ferdie scoffed. "What's cruel about matching two cocks to fight each other, Cec? They have an equal chance."

"Indeed it is cruel," Cecily cried, "when you know that one of them must die."

"You're too softhearted," Ferdie said indulgently.

"And you are a hard-hearted brute," she shot back.

"Cut line, Cec," he said, nettled. "All I did is watch, for goodness' sake. Next you will be trying to tell me that fox hunting is cruel."

"And so it is," Cecily replied, her eyes flashing a challenge to battle.

Lucy rose. "Ferdie, we must go," she said hastily. "You know that Mrs. Claridge and Anne are coming to tea and we promised Mama that we would be back."

Ferdie bowed distantly to Cecily. "There is no reasoning with you when you get into one of these silly moods, anyway, Cec," he said. "I shall see you when you have cooled off."

"I do not enjoy conversing with persons who condone the killing of innocent animals," she replied loftily, and proceeded to take a warm farewell of Lucy, to show Ferdie just what he was missing.

Mr. Mainwaring called the following afternoon while Elizabeth was helping Cecily make arrangements of the flowers they had cut from the garden. Both of them quickly removed their large aprons and smoothed their hair into place when summoned to the drawing room by Mrs. Rowe.

He rose to his feet when they entered the room and greeted both warmly. He asked politely about Elizabeth's journey and about the health of her nephew. The conversation became general for a while.

Finally Mr. Mainwaring turned to Elizabeth and asked if she would care to take a short drive with him, provided that Mrs. Rowe could spare her, of course. Mrs. Rowe was all smiling acquiescence.

Elizabeth went to her room for her bonnet. It was a perfect late-summer day, with sunshine and the merest suggestion of a breeze. She did not need a pelisse to wear over her gray cotton dress.

They drove out along the country road away from the town. Elizabeth soon had the impression that he drove without any destination in mind. It was good to be with him again. She felt none of the heightened awareness and self-consciousness that she experienced with Hetherington. She felt relaxed, as with a friend.

After several minutes he smiled down at her. "It is good to have you home again, Elizabeth. I have missed you."

"Indeed," she replied, "I have felt a warmth of welcome from several people. It really feels like a homecoming."

He smiled at her again. "I believe you have avoided the point I was trying to make," he said. "Have you missed me, Elizabeth?"

She considered. "Yes, I have," she said. "I feel relaxed and at home with you, William."

"Nothing more?" he asked ruefully. "I cannot say I feel relaxed with you. I love you, I believe."

Elizabeth said nothing. She kept her eyes on her clenched hands, searching for a suitable reply.

"You do not have to say anything," he said gently. "I really do not have the right to make such a declaration to you. You are the wife of my closest friend. But I have considered carefully those few weeks when he was here. I would never have suspected the relationship between you. Neither of you showed any signs of attachment to the other. It is my hope that you will agree to marry me so that I may go seek out Robert and ask if he will release you. I know that a divorce will cause an enormous scandal for you. But if you are prepared to live here or in Scotland with me, that need not affect us to any great degree."

Elizabeth was agitated. "William, please do not say these things," she said. "We cannot talk of marriage."

"There cannot be any love between the two of you any longer," he probed, "is there?"

"No, of course not," she answered quickly.

He noticed her haste and said nothing for a while. He maneuvered his curricle carefully past a slow-moving farmer's cart and called a greeting to the driver.

"You love him still, then," he said when they had moved out of earshot.

Elizabeth decided not to lie. "Against all reason, yes," she said.

He transferred the ribbons to his left hand and clasped her hand with his right. "I am sorry," he said. "And is there any hope that you will patch up your differences and live together, Elizabeth?"

"Oh, absolutely none," she replied candidly. "I love him, yes, but I could not possibly agree to reconcile our differences even if he wished it."

"Then marry me," he said. "Agree to let me persuade Robert to divorce you. You like me, do you not, Elizabeth? We could have a good friendship, I believe, a good life together. I have enough love for both of us. I should never demand more than you are prepared to give."

Elizabeth was much affected. It was true; she did like him. It seemed unfair that she could not love this man when she agreed that they could have a good life together, while she loved the man she despised.

"It would not be fair to marry you when I do not love you, William," she said. "Such a marriage would not work."

He drew the horses to a stop and faced her eagerly. "And did love work, Elizabeth? How long did your marriage to Robert last? I do not know."

She looked down in embarrassment. "Two days," she replied.

"Two days?" His voice registered shock. "Do you think a marriage based on respect and friendship would so soon come to an end? Marry me, Elizabeth, please."

She looked at him, shaking her head slowly. "I do not know if I could," she said.

He smiled suddenly and visibly relaxed. "I take hope from your words and your manner," he said. "Will you promise that you will consider my proposal, Elizabeth? Indeed, I shall be greatly honored if you consent."

She smiled too. "I shall think about it, William, I promise," she said. "But I cannot at all guarantee that the answer will be yes."

He gave the horses the signal to start again and soon they were traveling lanes and roadways that brought them closer to home.

"There is to be another ball at Squire Worthing's next week," Mr. Mainwaring reminded Elizabeth. "Are you to attend?"

"Oh, yes," she said. "I shall be expected to chaperone Cecily while Mr. and Mrs. Rowe play cards."

"May I expect an answer on that occasion?" he asked.

"Yes," she replied, "by next week I shall have decided."

He reached for her hand while keeping his eyes on the road ahead. "I shall live in suspense until then," he said, squeezing her fingers almost painfully.

The following days were not tranquil ones for Elizabeth. She was unanimously elected to accompany Cecily, Anne Claridge, and Lucy Worthing on a shopping expedition to Granby to buy new accessories for the ball. Since there had already been several entertainments that summer, it was imperative that they wear something different for this, the grandest of all occasions so far. It was Sir Harold and Lady Worthing's five and twentieth wedding anniversary and no expense was to be spared to make it a memorable occasion. As she sat with the three girls sipping lemonade, their purchases all done, before beginning the journey home, Elizabeth listened to their girlish chatter. Cousins and aunts and uncles had been invited from other counties, Lucy announced. That news certainly set Cecily and Anne fluttering, both of them quizzing Lucy about the possibility of any young and handsome male cousins. Lucy's reply that there were several, if only they came, did nothing to dampen their excitement.

Mrs. Rowe had also chosen this particular week in which to make an inventory of all her household effects. Elizabeth helped her count sheets and pillowcases and towels and dozens of other items, classifying them all as good enough for guests, good enough for the family, good enough for servants, in need of mending, or ready for the rubbish heap. When there was no bustling about to be done, she sat and mended and darned, though there seemed to be no bottom to the pile of articles still to be tackled.

But through all this activity, Elizabeth's mind was occupied by the one pervading question: what answer was she to give to William Mainwaring on the night of the anniversary? For the first few days, her inclination had been all for refusing him. She did not love him. And she did love Robert. She was married to Robert. Even if she could extricate herself from that marriage, she did not feel that she had enough to offer Mr. Mainwaring. She liked him well enough and enjoyed his company, but how could she give herself to him when her heart belonged to another man? It would not be fair to accept him, especially as he did love her.

As the days passed, however, she found her feelings changing. It was true that love had never done her much good. It had brought her very little happiness. A few weeks of courtship and two days of marriage did not provide enough happiness for a lifetime. There had been years of pain and emptiness. Perhaps a marriage based on affection and respect would prove more durable. Perhaps there would not be the peak of delirious joy that she had known with Robert. But there would not be the depths of despair, either.

Elizabeth tried, coolly and rationally, to imagine what marriage to William Mainwaring would be like. He would always treat her with kindness and respect, she was sure. She would always feel at ease and cheerful in his company. They would live at Ferndale most of the year, probably. That would certainly suit her, as she felt a deep affection for the people of the neighborhood. They might also spend some time at his estates in the north. She had often thought that she would like to see Scotland.

She pictured life as it would be if she declined the proposal. She would stay with the Rowes until Cecily married, she supposed. That might be for one or two years longer, certainly not more. And then she would seek a position elsewhere as governess or companion. It was the life she had planned for herself and quietly accepted until a few weeks previously. Now the prospect filled her with a nameless terror. Marriage would take away something of the loneliness and uncertainty of the years ahead. She would have a husband's companionship and, probably, children.

It was that final thought around which the whole decision finally hinged. Elizabeth passionately wanted children of her own, and she was six and twenty already. She could have those children if she married William Mainwaring. But it was for Robert Denning's children that her body ached.

Elizabeth prepared carefully for the ball. Whatever her decision was to be, she wanted to feel confident of her attractions on that night. She had Miss Phillips make her a dress of cream silk with an overdress of matching lace. Gold ribbons encircled the high waist, and gold embroidery made the hemline glitter. Most drastic of all, she had her hair cut short around the crown of her head and longer at the neck. Hair that had been wavy when long and thick now clustered in soft curls around her face and down her neck.

"Anyone looking at you and Cecily now," Mr. Rowe remarked at dinner the evening after she had had it done, "would be hard-pressed to decide which is the young girl and which the lady companion."

"Upon my soul," his wife agreed, "it is a vastly becoming hairdo, my dear Miss Rossiter."

"You will cast me quite in the shade, Beth," Cecily added cheerfully, "now that you have got rid of that dreadful old-maidish hair knot. You are so beautiful, I am mortally jealous."

The Rowes were among the last to arrive at the anniversary ball. Cecily was immediately borne away by an excited Anne Claridge. Elizabeth soon saw the reason why. There were two strange young men present, both passably good-looking, as well as three strange young ladies and a few older adults. She assumed that they were the relatives that Lucy had talked about the week before. It did not take long for Lucy to introduce all the young people to her two friends, or for each of them to be led triumphant into the dance by the male cousins.

But Elizabeth did not devote all her attention to these young people. She had immediately looked around for William Mainwaring. He was dancing with Lady Worthing, who had already left the receiving line when the Rowes arrived. He was looking extraordinarily handsome in the black evening clothes that became him so well. He saw her and smiled in her direction, but good manners kept his attention on the conversation of his partner.

Elizabeth watched him covertly. He was indeed a matrimonial prize: handsome, rich, well-mannered. He could not, generally speaking, be called charming. His manner with everyone but her was still somewhat stiff and remote. But she felt that the people of the neighborhood liked him and accepted him as master of Ferndale. She waited cheerfully until he should ask her to dance.

He did not ask her until a half-hour later. But he clearly had not forgotten his purpose. He suggested that, instead of dancing, they step out into the garden. They went out through the French windows and down the steps of the terrace to the flower-bordered lawn below.

"I shall not keep you long," he said to her halfhearted protest. "No harm will come to Miss Rowe in the meanwhile, not with that young sprig of the squire's glowering at her every partner."

"Ferdie?" she said, laughing. "He spends his time quarreling with her when they are together, and giving off sparks of jealousy when she talks to someone else."

"Well, I am not really interested in the course of their love," he said, grinning down at her. "I am interested in you, Miss Elizabeth Rossiter. I always noticed that you were beautiful, but tonight you are dazzling. You cast all the other ladies into the shade. Do I dare to hope that you have made this special effort for my sake?"

"I hate to dash your spirits, sir," she said archly, "but in reality I had to bolster my courage to come here tonight, knowing that I must have been the subject of much gossip in the last few weeks. Hence the new gown and the new hairdo."

"Well, they are most becoming, Elizabeth," he said, "whatever the reason for the change."

They strolled across the lawn in companionable silence until they arrived at a rustic bench beneath an ancient oak tree. By unspoken assent, they both sat down. Mr. Mainwaring took the hand that she had removed from his arm.

"Well, Elizabeth," he began, "have you decided what my fate is to be? Will you marry me?"

"I have told myself repeatedly that I should not," she replied slowly. "I like you very much, William, and believe with all my heart that you would be a good husband. But would I be a good wife? That is the

question. I cannot bring you a whole heart, sir, and I fear
that the future will always be clouded by the experiences
of the past."

"Life is always like that," he said gently. "We are what
we are because of what has happened to us in the past. We
cannot change that and we should not wish to. I love you
as you are, Elizabeth. Perhaps I would not love you as
well if you had not met and loved and lost Hetherington.
Perhaps the experience has given you the air of maturity
and serenity that I so admire in you. Give me your future,
my dear. I do not ask for the past."

"Oh," she said, "I so much want to say yes, William.
But I fear that I am not being fair to you."

"Let me worry about that," he said fiercely, and he rose
to his feet, bringing her with him. Immediately she was in
his arms, her body pulled against his. He sought and
found her mouth in the darkness and kissed her with
growing passion. Elizabeth deliberately arched her body
against his, twined her arms around his neck, and returned the kiss. She deliberately noticed the sensations
created by his hard thighs pressed against hers, her breasts
crushed against his coat, his hands splayed across her back
and finally pressing downward on her hips, his mouth
moving, closed, over her own, his breath on her cheek.

There was nothing at all unpleasant about any of it. She
could even imagine, without distaste, allowing his love-
making to go further. But she was aware that she viewed it
all as a spectator, almost as if she were still sitting on the
bench observing herself in close embrace with Mr. Mainwaring. She felt no spark of passion, could force none into
her reactions. She removed her arms from around his
neck and pushed gently against his shoulders.

"I am sorry," he said, releasing her immediately. "Did
I offend you?"

"No, not at all, William," she replied, "but I would not
wish to be seen."

"Why not?" he asked, and she could see in the moonlight that he was grinning again. "You are soon to be my wife, are you not?"

She stared at him blankly. "William," she said, "you forget that I am married already and that all these people know it. Even if we do marry, it cannot be until after Robert has divorced me, and that may take a long time."

"I think not," he said cheerfully. "I shall leave tomorrow for Hetherington Manor. Robert is there, I believe. I shall tell him frankly that we wish to marry. Someone with his rank and influence can obtain a speedy divorce, I am sure. And surely he cannot have the least objection. He seemed quite indifferent to you when he was here."

Elizabeth winced and turned away. He grasped her by the shoulders.

"I could cut my tongue out, Elizabeth. I am sorry," he said. "I am afraid tact is not my strong point. I swear, my dear, that I shall give you the peace and happiness that you have missed during these years. Only say that you wish to marry me. Please."

Elizabeth leaned back against his tall frame and closed her eyes. "Oh, yes," she said, surrendering to the longing within her, "make me forget, William. Make me love you."

His arms encircled her from behind. "I shall leave in the morning," he said, "and be back in three days at the most, my dear. I shall have you free soon, never fear."

They returned soon to the ballroom, Elizabeth very much aware of the duties she had been shirking.

13

The older generation was somewhat disturbed when they found out that Mr. Mainwaring had left Ferndale.

"He is a quiet sort of a man," Mrs. Rowe told her family and Elizabeth at dinner, "but not bad-natured, I believe. I did think at first that he was conceited, but recently I have been convinced that he is merely shy. What do you think, Mr. Rowe?"

"Indeed, my dear," he replied, "I have not considered the question at all. But now that you press me to do so, I would say I find him a gentlemanly man, a worthy neighbor."

"It seems most extraordinary that he should leave Ferndale without telling anyone," his wife continued. "I wonder where he can have gone and why. And I wonder if he plans to return soon."

"If I had only had an inkling of his going," Mr. Rowe returned, "I should have backed him into the nearest corner, my love, and forced answers from him. As it is, I am afraid I cannot enlighten you."

"Oh, how absurd you are, Mr. Rowe," his wife said crossly. "I am merely showing a neighborly interest in the man."

Elizabeth did not join in the conversation, or tell anyone what she knew of Mr. Mainwaring's journey. She did not want anyone to know of her secret betrothal until Hetherington had sent her the divorce papers. And for all William's optimism, she believed that that could take quite a while.

Cecily too showed no inclination to join in her mother's curious wonderings. She and the other young people of the area were too full of enthusiasm over the presence of the young visitors at Squire Worthing's. While her mother talked, Cecily's head was full of a certain auburn-haired giant who had paid her lavish and quite outrageous compliments the night before. He had also told her that he and his sisters and cousins were staying for a week, perhaps longer.

Elizabeth had expected the following days to drag by as she waited for William to return and tell her how Hetherington had reacted to their request. But she had little time to brood. The young people began a frantic round of activities: riding, walking, shopping, picnicking in the daytime, playing cards, charades, and other games during the evening. Elizabeth accompanied Cecily everywhere and, by popular request, was made the sole chaperone at the daytime activities. This proved to be a dizzying task as the group often showed a tendency to break up into smaller groups that wandered off in different directions. How did one watch a couple visiting a traveling library, while four others had gone for ices, and a few more to a haberdasher's? She finally solved the problem by laying down the rule that no group of fewer than three persons could go off on its own. Once that rule was accepted, she felt that she could relax her vigilance somewhat.

In the evenings, too, Elizabeth was expected to accompany Cecily. The elder Rowes usually went to the same house, glad of the excuse for increased visiting, but they usually settled with the older adults, playing cards or just gossiping. It was again up to Elizabeth to oversee the activities of the younger set and settle the disputes that frequently arose.

One of the most heated arguments arose when Ferdie and the auburn giant, captains of the two teams for charades, were picking their team members. Ferdie took loud exception to the giant's choosing Cecily. But Elizabeth pointed out that Ferdie had had first pick and had chosen Anne Claridge ("because she's the best actress in the whole county," he explained, exasperated) and that the giant was therefore free to choose whomever he would. Ferdie sulked and Cecily flirted for the rest of the evening. Elizabeth was forced to scold her at home later, when they were alone.

"I do not know how you feel about Mr. Harry Worthing," she said, "but you did set your cap at him in a rather vulgar manner tonight, Cecily."

"Pooh," said her charge, "I was merely cross with Ferdie, Beth. Why must he always behave as if I belong to him? I have never even *kissed* him more than two or three times, and he has never made me a declaration. I cannot resist teasing him when he becomes so possessive." She blushed suddenly. "I was not so outrageous, was I, Beth?"

"I am afraid you were, love," her companion replied, "and that young man seems quite taken with you."

"I really did not mean to encourage him so," Cecily said in dismay. "It is exciting to have new company, but I really have not meant to set my cap at anyone."

"I know that, love," Elizabeth said. "But I do not wish anyone to gain the impression that you are fast."

By the fourth day after William's departure, Elizabeth was exhausted. She had a headache by dinnertime and a tickling in the back of her throat that seemed to threaten a cold. She begged to be excused from that evening's gathering at the vicarage.

"Well, of course, my dear Miss Rossiter," Mrs. Rowe said, all solicitous concern. "You must go to your bed immediately. I shall have some warm milk and laudanum sent up to you and a hot brick for your feet. Don't worry about a thing, my dear. I shall watch Cecily tonight. I knew when I saw you outside yesterday without a pelisse that you would catch a chill. I told Mr. Rowe so."

"And so you did, my love," her husband agreed. "But since it was almost too hot yesterday to wear a dress even,

I do not believe the absence of a pelisse caused the cold. I should say that Miss Rossiter is probably hagged from chasing after a pack of young devils for several days."

"Papa!" Cecily complained.

Elizabeth retired to her room, the relief of having a quiet evening to herself already easing the headache. She undressed and sat in her nightgown close to the empty fireplace. She drank the warm milk that Mrs. Rowe had sent up, but set aside the laudanum. She never felt rested after a drug-induced sleep; she would avoid it if she could. She smiled too at the hot brick, wrapped in cloths, that the maid placed between her bedclothes. She would certainly not retire until that had cooled off thoroughly. The night was almost too warm to allow of bedclothes at all.

She took John's latest letter from a drawer beside her bed and sat down to read it again. They missed her. Louise had begged him to tell her that she was very welcome to come home again to stay. Louise was in good health. The tiredness and nausea that had troubled her in the early months had almost disappeared now. The baby was a bundle of mischief. That very morning he had toddled into the flower garden and picked a magnificent bouquet of blooms for his mama. The only trouble was that there was not a stem among the whole bouquet, only heads. John himself had had to leave his office before the gardener was pacified.

Elizabeth smiled. What a lovely family John had. And how envious she was. Would life with William be that cheerful, that full of minor crises? By this time next year would she be married to him, expecting his child, perhaps? Inevitably, her thoughts passed to Robert and the pleasure he had seemed to take in Louise's company and in Jeremy's. She caught herself before she could become too deeply engrossed in the if-onlys. She had decided, on the night of the anniversary ball after accepting William's proposal, that she would no longer allow herself to brood on the past. She had to put Robert finally out of her mind. She would probably never see him again. She must forget

him. She could not be fair to William if she did not. She
got up and put the letter back in the drawer.

There was a tap on the door.

"Come in," Elizabeth called. When she saw the maid,
she smiled and pointed to the empty glass on the hearth.

"You have a visitor, ma'am," the maid said. "The
butler told him you were unwell, but he said it was
important. He is in the drawing room."

"Oh." Elizabeth had been counting the days until
William's return, but she was still taken by surprise. What
would he have to say? What had Robert said? Would he
have sent any message for her? A message of regret,
perhaps, like the very last words he had spoken to her?
Would he perhaps have sent her a letter?

She dressed in feverish haste, selecting the pale-green
silk with the lace inset that she and Louise had altered and
that she had brought back with her. She brushed her hair
so that the short curls bounced into place, and descended
quickly to the drawing room. She smiled brightly as she
opened the double doors.

Hetherington's eyes were a particularly cold shade of
blue this evening, her mind registered as they met hers
from across the room. In fact, his whole face and manner
were stiff and cold. The smile faded from her own lips.

"Oh," she said foolishly.

His eyes traveled slowly and insolently down her body.
"I am sorry to disappoint you," he said. "I see that you
have prepared yourself for your lover. You look extraordinarily beautiful, Elizabeth. It is a shame to waste such a
dazzling appearance on me, is it not?"

"What are you doing here?" she asked, finding the
business of moving her lips and tongue unusually difficult.

His eyebrows rose. "My closest friend paid me a visit
two days ago," he said frostily, "to ask if he might marry
my wife. Is it surprising that I am here?"

"Your wife!" she said contemptuously, crossing the
room toward him. "Why do you persist in this farce,
Robert? I am not your wife. We are strangers."

"Did I imagine that wedding service we attended together in a small church in Devon?" he asked. "Did I imagine that we consummated the marriage in a very thorough manner for two nights?"

Elizabeth blushed hotly. "Such things do not make a marriage," she said. "Soon after that time you wanted me no more. For six years you have not cared if I lived or was dead. Are you now planning to put an obstacle in the way of my marriage to William?"

"The obstacle already exists," he said coldly. "You are my wife, Elizabeth, and my wife you will remain."

"Then you refuse to grant me a divorce?" she asked.

"Of course," he answered. "I do not believe in divorce."

She stared at him in impotent fury. "You are despicable," she spat out. "You have no such scruples. You merely wish to put a rub in the way of my happiness."

He bowed slightly in her direction.

"Then I shall divorce you!" she cried, the idea striking her for the first time. "I do not know how I may go about it, but Mr. Rowe will advise me. I shall ask him tomorrow."

"It will not work," he said quietly. "You have no grounds."

"No grounds?" she repeated. "I shall find grounds and to spare, my lord, you may depend upon it."

He smiled arctically. "Adultery?" he suggested. "It would not be worth your while to try, my love. Unbelievable as it may seem to you, I have been faithful to our marriage. It is quite a joke among my set, you know, that I do not even keep any high-flyers."

She stared at him.

"Desertion?" he continued. "It would not succeed. You left me, remember? It was my express command that you stay at my grandmother's house in Devon until I sent for you. You disobeyed and went home to your father. If questioned, I should make it quite clear that I am willing to return to you anytime you so desire."

"You would be prepared to lie so?" she asked, wide-eyed.

"Oh, I never lie," he said, smiling into her eyes. "I would remind you that there is documentary evidence that you and I spent a night together at a certain inn just a few weeks ago. You are a remarkably attractive woman, Elizabeth, and six years has been a long time. I should not say no to an invitation to your bed."

His hand shot up to grasp her wrist as her hand flashed toward his face. "No, not this time," he said, eyes narrowing. "That last time you had the advantage of surprise, my love, but I learn by experience. Hit me again, Elizabeth, and I may reply in kind. You would not escape with a kiss this time." He released her wrist.

She turned away from him. "Where is William?" she asked.

"He suddenly remembered pressing business that will keep him in London for an indeterminate length of time," he replied.

"And you are staying at Ferndale?"

"Under the circumstances, that would not be good *ton*," he replied. "The inn at Granby seems comfortable enough."

"What does he intend to do about me?" Elizabeth asked, and then despised herself for having spoken out loud.

"What can he do?" Hetherington asked. "I told him that he may not marry my wife, and like the honorable gentleman that he is, he has retreated to lick his wounds."

"You are utterly heartless," she cried, turning on him once more in fury. "You are enjoying this situation, are you not? It gives you pleasure to cause pain for two people."

"You are wrong, madam," he snapped, his face showing anger for the first time. "It is precisely because I care for William Mainwaring that I am behaving as you see. You have ruined my life, Elizabeth, making it quite impossible for me to lead a normal life or to love another woman. Do you think I would stand idly by while you do the same to my friend? He may hate me now, he may be suffering now, but I would prefer to feel his hatred and watch his pain than see him later with all faith in life and love shattered."

Elizabeth had clutched her throat with one hand and sunk down onto a sofa. "What are you saying?" she whispered. "What have I done to make you hate me so?"

He came to stand in front of her and glared down into her eyes. "Money was more important to you than I was," he said, "and you professed to love me. William, by his own account, you claim to hold only in affection. But I'll wager that you love his money, Elizabeth. It will be so much more accessible to you than mine was."

"What are you talking about?" she asked, barely able to get the words past her lips. "This is not the first time you have accused me of being mercenary, Robert. What do you mean? You were poor when I married you."

He smiled unpleasantly. "Ten thousand pounds was so much more attractive to you than a husband who had only love and a title to offer, was it not?" he asked.

"Ten thousand pounds?"

"Had you planned it all along, Elizabeth?" he asked. "Or was it just the momentary temptation to which you succumbed?"

"Oh, Robert," she whispered, feeling the blood draining from her head and fighting waves of faintness, "what are you talking about?"

His expression changed. A kind of wild fear was in his face. He grabbed her by the upper arms. "Are you ill?" he asked harshly, and when she did not reply, he pulled her to her feet and folded her in his arms. She sagged against him, dizzy with faintness.

"Oh, God, Elizabeth," he said against her hair, his voice heavy with pain, "tell me you did not plan it. Tell me that you were merely tempted, that it was a decision you made on the spur of the moment. Tell me you loved me when you married me, that those days and nights in

Devon were not just an empty sham. Please, darling, give me that much consolation at least.''

Elizabeth fought the buzzing in her ears and the coldness in her head. "Tell me what you are talking about," she said.

His hand came beneath her chin and lifted her pale face. "Ah, don't lie to me," he said. "Believe me, I want to understand, I want to forgive. When I see you and when I hold you, I cannot believe that you are capable of the villainy that I have accepted all these years. I want you, Elizabeth."

His mouth was on hers with a passion and an urgency that she could not have denied even had she wished to. As it was, in her semiconscious state, the embrace seemed like one of the many she had dreamed of in the previous years, only more delightful. She pressed herself to the warmth of him and allowed his demanding lips to tilt her head back and part her own. Her mouth relaxed beneath his so that his tongue plunged an easy entrance and set her afire. His one hand had somehow dealt with the row of buttons down the back of her gown and was caressing the naked flesh of her back beneath her chemise. His other hand fondled one breast and then dropped behind her hips and brought her hard against him. She gasped and regained some of the consciousness that had been slipping from her. He was looking at her with passion-heavy eyes and then stooped down and swung her up into his arms.

"Tell me the way to your room," he said, beginning to move around the sofa.

Elizabeth was fully conscious again. "Put me down, Robert," she said distinctly.

"I shall carry you, love," he said, looking down into her eyes. "You always were the merest feather."

"Put me down, Robert," she said again, willing her voice to steadiness.

The passion was gone from his face instantly as he set her feet back on the floor. "You are a tease, ma'am," he said, "and I fell for it again."

"Enough!" she yelled, her control snapping altogether. "I am sick, Robert, sick of hearing your accusations. I am heartless, I am a tease, I am mercenary. I know myself as none of these things. You have accused me of accepting ten thousand pounds for something. I know nothing of ten thousand pounds. I have never even seen so much money. Now, if you care to explain what you have hinted at, please do so. If not, if your purpose here is merely to insult and accuse me, you may leave, my lord. You are not master here, and in the absence of the Rowes, I command. Now, which is it to be?"

She sat down straight-backed on the nearest chair. He too sank onto the sofa that she had occupied earlier. He looked at her narrowly for a long while, and Elizabeth almost lost her nerve. She set her chin and glared back.

"I refer, of course, to the ten thousand pounds that you accepted from my uncle," he said tonelessly.

"From your uncle?" she asked, a frown creasing her brow.

Hetherington got restlessly to his feet and paced the room. "My uncle was opposed to our marriage from the start," he said. "You told me that yourself. What you did not tell me was that he had offered you money even then to break off with me. Two thousand pounds, I believe. You laughed at him and told him it would take a lot more than that paltry sum to buy you off."

Elizabeth had whitened again. "The details are not quite as I remember them," she said, "but yes, he did talk of money."

His penetrating look again almost unnerved her.

"After we were married, he might have let us alone," he continued, "though you probably thought you could push up his price. Circumstances certainly played into your hands, my dear. How you must have cheered when you realized that I was the new marquess. You must have waited in great glee for my uncle to contact you."

Not a muscle moved in Elizabeth's face. "Go on," she said.

"My uncle responded like a puppet on a string, of course," he said. "When he came to offer you eight thousand pounds, you forced him to pay out ten. You were foolish, my dear. He would have paid double the sum to rid the family of such an unsuitable connection."

"Yes, I imagine he would," she commented.

"I was furious with him when I learned what he had done," Hetherington said, his eyes blazing again, "until I had had time to think, of course. Then I realized that it was probably as well to know the truth about you so early. It was a tragic irony for you, was it not, Elizabeth, that my grandmother died just a year later and left me all her wealth? You might have had the title and a great deal more money than ten thousand pounds, my love."

"Have you finished?" she asked. He made her an ironic bow. "I know nothing of ten thousand pounds," she repeated, "and I have not set eyes on your uncle since that night when he asked me to name my price for leaving you alone. All I do know, my lord, is that I waited for a whole week at my father's house after writing to tell you where I was. I excused you in my mind, knowing that you would be contending with shock as well as the business attending on the funerals and their aftermath. But I longed for a letter, just a little note, from you. At the end of that week, I began to write to you, every day, pleading with you to let me come to you, or to write to me at least. For two whole weeks, Robert. Do you have any conception how long a time that seems to a bride who has just been separated from her husband and who cannot understand the reason why?

"And then finally you wrote." Elizabeth glared at him in angry scorn. "But not to me, my lord. Never to me. Could you find the courage to write only to my father? He was never a particularly loving man, but even he felt pity enough not to show me those letters. He tried to soften the blow by telling me himself that you did not want to see me, did not want to be burdened with my letters. I tried to convince myself that you loved me, that you would become yourself again when the shock of your brother's and your father's deaths had worn off. It took John, brought home from Oxford by my worried father, to convince me that you really did wish to be rid of me. Someone of my social standing suited you well enough when you were plain Robert Denning with no expectations. But as the wife of the Marquess of Hetherington I was merely an embarrassment. You must divorce me as speedily and as quietly as possible."

"But I did not," he pointed out quietly.

"No," she agreed, "because I very meekly gave up the struggle. It might have caused some scandal had a whisper of what was happening reached the ears of the *ton*. It was safer to leave matters as they stood, was it not?"

They stared at each other, worlds apart.

"How can I disbelieve my uncle?" Hetherington said finally. "He is my own flesh and blood. He has always devoted himself to my family. He even came to live with me in the months following the accident, to help me adjust. What he did, though wrong, was done for love of me."

"But you will disbelieve your wife?" she cried, leaping to her feet. "You have made your choice, Robert. There is nothing more for you and me to say to each other."

Again they regarded each other across the room. Finally Hetherington withdrew his eyes and, without a word, strode from the room.

14

"But do you know for sure that Mr. Mainwaring is not coming back here?" Mrs. Rowe asked Mrs. Claridge the following afternoon.

"I have it on the firmest authority," Mrs. Claridge replied, nodding confidentially and setting her teacup back in its saucer. "Soames was talking to the vicar this morning. He told him that his master had sent word that his trunks were to be packed and sent to London."

"How provoking!" Mrs. Rowe said. "And just when the life of our neighborhood was becoming more genteel. I do declare, Mrs. Claridge, I shall miss his company, even if it did seem that he was not interested in any of our girls."

The girls did not seem too disappointed over Mr. Mainwaring's lack of interest in them. They were busy commiserating with each other over the fact that the Worthing cousins were to leave for home in two more days.

"But I wonder why he left so abruptly?" Mrs. Claridge said. "The vicar was unable to say. But I distinctly heard Mr. Mainwaring accept an invitation to cards on Tuesday next."

"Perhaps he had bad news from London," Mrs. Rowe suggested. "Poor, dear man. I do hope he comes back here for Christmas, at least. It is most provoking to have the manor close by and no one in residence."

The visitors were gathered as usual in the drawing room with Mrs. Rowe, Cecily, and Elizabeth. Elizabeth was sitting in the window seat, sewing a new ruffle onto Cecily's favorite ball gown. She kept her head down. She was certainly in no mood to join in the speculations about the master of Ferndale. Was he suffering? Had she hurt him badly? She berated herself now for not putting a firm end to his hopes as soon as she realized which way his feelings were inclined. She might have guessed that they would never be allowed to marry. And now she was almost sure that she could not have carried through with her plans, anyway. She was married to Robert and would always be, even if he divorced her a thousand times.

"The vicar heard another extraordinary thing this morning," Mrs. Claridge was saying. "It seems that the Marquess of Hetherington was in Granby yesterday, but he put up at the inn, not at Ferndale. As it turned out, though, he did not even stay the night, but left very late after paying for his night's lodging and a dinner and breakfast that he did not eat."

"That is most peculiar," Mrs. Rowe agreed. "Perhaps he expected Mr. Mainwaring to be here and did not like to stay at the house when he found that he was not there. Though he might have visited us, of course."

Both ladies suddenly became aware of Elizabeth's presence and remembered her connection to the marquess.

"I am so sorry, Miss Rossiter," Mrs. Claridge murmured.

"Did you know his lordship was here, my dear?" asked Mrs. Rowe.

"Oh, yes," Elizabeth answered calmly. "He called here last evening. He brought the news that Mr. Mainwaring visited him a few days ago and has now gone to London. It seems he has unexpected business there and is unlikely to return for some time."

"Well, how provoking!" Mrs. Rowe declared. "Life will seem so dull with the dear man gone, and the Worthings leaving for London after Christmas."

"The reverend has heard that Mr. Dowling is to take in the Season, too," Mrs. Claridge commented.

"Pursuing Lucy, no doubt," Mrs. Rowe said. "Will the squire ever give his consent to that match, do you think?"

The visit continued, with both groups of ladies enjoying a cosy gossip while Elizabeth sewed in the window seat, alone with her own thoughts.

She had hardly slept the night before and even yet was not quite able to think coherently enough to sort out what exactly had happened or how she felt about it. Too much had happened, too many strange and unexpected things.

Had he really held her and kissed her, not in anger, but in real need? Had there been tears in his eyes when he first lifted her against him? Had he called her "darling," as he had done during those days in Devon? And he had been going to take her to bed. She could have made love with Robert last night. Her needle paused above her work as shivers sizzled up her arms and along her spine.

Another memory was trying to surface. He had been talking to her while she was feeling faint. There had been more than the word *darling*. Elizabeth began to sew feverishly as she remembered. He loved her. He must love her. There had been such real pain in his voice as he had begged her to tell him that she had loved him when they married, that their honeymoon had not been a lie. My God, he loved her! Then, why? Why had he done what he did? Why had he abandoned her?

Mrs. Claridge had risen and was taking her leave. Anne was whispering a final confidence to Cecily.

"You will be coming with Cecily this evening, Miss Rossiter?" Mrs. Claridge asked.

"Yes, if I may," Elizabeth replied, quietly folding away her sewing.

"I should be most grateful," Mrs. Claridge said. "This is the evening when the reverend always writes his Sunday sermon and I like to sit with him to mend his pens. But the young people cannot be left alone."

"It would be my pleasure to sit with them," Elizabeth assured her with a smile.

It was not until quite late that night that Elizabeth again had time to herself. She felt deadly tired. A week of busy social activities, yesterday's headache and encounter with Hetherington, today's busy schedule, had all taken their toll on her energy. But she knew she would not sleep until she had somehow sorted through her thoughts about the night before. She pulled a chair to the window, blew out the candle, and sat looking out onto the moonlit lawns and trees.

What had Robert said last night? There was that ten thousand pounds. He had said that his uncle had paid her to leave her husband. He had accused her of accepting such a bribe. Could he be telling the truth? Could he really believe such a thing? It seemed that he must, because his words earlier in the evening had suggested that he really had suffered over the breakup of their marriage, that he really believed she was the one responsible for it. But why, then, had he not responded to all those letters she had written? Why had he not tried to see her? And why had he written those cold and hurtful letters to her father?

One thing at least was beginning to clarify itself in Elizabeth's mind. Their separation had not been brought about by his lack of love or by cruelty. Somehow there had been a massive misunderstanding. For six years each of them had believed the other at fault. Each had carried the pain and the bitterness all that time. She remembered his saying that he had remained faithful to his marriage, that she had spoiled him for all other women. He had suffered as much as she. She closed her eyes and laid her forehead in one shaking hand. What a revolutionary thought! She had accustomed herself for so long to the idea that he was a heartless wretch. Had he just been her own very dear Robert all the time?

Yet they had parted the night before with bitterness, poles apart, unable to communicate. He had left Granby, not even waiting for morning. There was no reason now

for any future meetings. It was likely that there would be
an estrangement between him and William Mainwaring.
Even if they remained friends, it was very unlikely that
they would come together to Ferndale again as long as she
still lived with the Rowes. He had refused to divorce her
or to allow her to divorce him. They had told each other
their stories, yet had failed to understand what had
happened. And they had parted. It was all over.

But why should that be? They had loved each other
passionately six years before, had defied their families in
order to marry, and had grieved for each other ever since.
They loved and wanted each other now. Why should
they be apart forever? Had they not suffered enough?
And all because of the lies and the schemings of one
man.

Robert had said that his uncle always acted out of
devotion to his family. What a twisted devotion it was to
destroy a nephew's marriage and his happiness in order to
protect the great pride of the family name. The man had
lied, of course. He had lied about that meeting she had
had with him before the marriage, and he had completely
fabricated what he said had happened afterward. But
Robert had believed him, had believed all these years that
she had preferred money to him. Although it hurt to know
that he had had so little faith in her, she had to admit that
Robert had known his uncle so much longer and had
always trusted him. And he had been very young at the
time. She too had eventually believed what her father and
John had repeatedly told her, that he was a heartless
scoundrel. And that had been equally untrue, although
they had not deliberately lied to her.

Elizabeth gazed sightlessly through the window again.
Was there any way that she could prove that Robert's
uncle had lied? If she traveled to London and found him
out, would he admit the truth to her? And, more important, would he admit it to Robert? But how could she, a
mere woman, a mere governess, travel alone to London
and seek out a man of Horace Denning's stature? It could

not be done unless she took someone along with her. John? Would he go? Was it just a mad scheme, anyway?

Elizabeth was suddenly overtaken by a gigantic yawn. She realized how difficult it was becoming to keep her eyes open. She would think of it in the morning.

"Beth? Beth, where are you?" Cecily's voice preceded her up the staircase until she burst into the schoolroom, where Elizabeth was kneeling in the middle of the contents of a box of old books.

"Gracious! What are you doing?" Cecily asked.

"Your mama wants me to sort through your old books," Elizabeth replied, "and pick out any that may be of use in the new school that is to open in the autumn."

"Oh," replied Cecily. "Why, I remember this old reader." She bent and picked up a book with a worn brown cover and water-stained yellow pages.

"You sounded excited as you were coming upstairs," Elizabeth commented. "You were certainly yelling my name in most unladylike fashion. Is there another picnic planned?"

"Oh, much, much more than that," Cecily cried, dropping the book and dancing around the room. "Papa has said we are to go to Bath for a few weeks. Think of it, Beth. The Pump Room. The Assemblies. And you are to go with us. Are you not of all things delighted?"

Elizabeth smiled. "Delighted for you, Cecily," she said, "though you should not get your hopes too high, perhaps. Bath is not as fashionable as it used to be, I understand. You are likely to find mainly older people taking the waters, you know. However," she added, seeing the girl's crestfallen face, "I am sure you will enjoy the change of air and scenery. And at least you will see some new faces."

"Yes," Cecily added, "and I shall not have Ferdie glowering at me every time I smile at another gentleman. Oh, Beth, and we shall visit all the modistes and you shall help me choose my winter wardrobe."

"I am afraid not," Elizabeth said quietly. "I plan to ask your mother if I may take a month's holiday. I know I have just come back from a leave of absence, but I have some pressing business that must be attended to. I shall not feel so guilty if I know you are all going to Bath, as I know your mama will delight in accompanying you everywhere."

"Oh, but, Beth, it would not be such fun without you," the girl wailed. "Must you go now? Can you not wait until after we come back?"

"I am afraid not, Cecily," Elizabeth replied, setting aside some of the books in a separate pile and returning the others to the box. In fact, she had made up her mind only when Cecily had mentioned Bath that she must go home and persuade John to go to London with her. In all likelihood nothing could be accomplished even if John agreed to go. Horace Denning would refuse to see them or deny all their accusations. The chances were very good, in fact, that he would not even be in London during these summer months. But she had to try. Her own love for Robert was a strong pain that she would have to bear for the rest of her life if she must. But if there was a chance that he loved her too and that their separation had not been of their own making, then she felt compelled to try to make possible a reconciliation. She had to put every ounce of effort into the attempt.

There was no point in delaying. Elizabeth immediately sought out Mrs. Rowe and explained to her why she could not accompany them to Bath. In the event, though, she did not ask for a holiday. She resigned from her position. Although she had not given herself time to think through the decision carefully, she knew that she was doing the right thing. Her usefulness to Cecily was over; she was not really earning her salary. If she must work for a living for the rest of her life, then it was time that she inquired after a situation as a governess again. And perhaps most important of all, it seemed only fair that she move away rom the vicinity of Ferndale. William Mainwaring would robably not wish to return there as long as he knew that he was close by. Yet, that was his home and he had told er that he loved it and intended making it his principal esidence.

Three days later, therefore, having said her good-byes o all her acquaintances and given promises to write, Elizabeth took a tearful farewell of the employers, whom he now looked upon more as friends.

"Beth, I shall hate not having you to confide in or to cold me," Cecily said, hugging her hard.

"Now, you come back here whenever you wish, my dear Miss Rossiter," Mrs. Rowe said. "I am sure we shall lways find a place for you. I have never met a more genteel young lady, I do declare." She kissed Elizabeth on he cheek and then blew delicately into her lace handker-hief.

Mr. Rowe drove Elizabeth into Granby, where she was o catch the morning stage. She had insisted on that mode of travel despite the objections of her employers. The tagecoach was in the inn yard already, but the coachman vas taking refreshments inside.

Mr. Rowe turned to Elizabeth as she sat beside him in he gig. "Good-bye, Cinderella," he said, patting the gloved hands that lay in her lap. "I am sorry to see you go. believe that Prince Charming has already won the prize ut has not come with the glass slipper to claim it. Am I ight?"

"Sir?" she asked, startled.

"Young Hetherington," he said. "He risked a great deal vhen he admitted that you were his wife, you know. I could not understand why you came back alone again fterward."

She smiled at him. "It is a long story, I'm afraid, sir."

"Yes," he agreed, "they usually are. Come along, my lear. You find an inside seat and I shall see that your portmanteau is tied on securely."

Elizabeth was fortunate enough to secure a window seat. Mr. Rowe came to the door before the coachman closed it. "Good-bye, my dear," he said. "Dorothy and Cecily will wish to hear from you, you know."

She nodded, too choked to speak, and felt unspeakable relief when the coach lurched once and pulled out of the inn yard onto the cobbled street of Granby.

It was a very different journey from the one she had made with Hetherington. It was much slower and more tiresome. They stopped many times to pick up and deposit travelers. They snatched refreshments whenever possible and stopped for the night at an inn where the rooms were less than clean and the service less than courteous. By the time she reached the village two miles distant from John's house, Elizabeth was glad to leave her portmanteau at the local hostelry and walk home in the fresh air, despite her stiffness and tiredness and despite the gathering dusk.

John and Louise were dining when the butler let her into the house. There was great excitement when she was shown into the dining room.

"Elizabeth!" Louise shrieked, rising from the table to display slightly more bulk than when her sister-in-law had seen her last. "We were just talking about you. Oh, how splendid that you have come home again. Are you here to stay this time? And who brought you? Oh, how naughty of you to just come without letting us know. Are you hungry? I shall have an extra place set this instant."

John was laughing, though he too had risen to hug his sister. "Louise is not usually very talkative," he told Elizabeth, "but sometimes she starts and does not know when to stop. Come and sit down, love, and tell us to what happy chance we owe this visit."

Elizabeth sank down into the chair he pulled out from the table for her. "Oh, it is so good to be home," she said. "I have been traveling on the stage for two full days. And yes, Louise, I am home to stay, for a while anyway, though I hope to lure John away for a few days."

"Where?" asked Louise.

"Oh, I am so tired," Elizabeth replied. "Please may I explain everything tomorrow?"

"Of course you may, love," John replied. "Eat now, if you can, then we can show off to you our son, who has two new teeth since last you saw him, and you can go to bed. We will talk in the morning."

"No!" she was saying. "I won't believe it. No, please, no."

"I am sorry, Lizzie," her father said. "I am truly sorry. But he has made himself quite plain. He does not want to see you."

"No!" she protested. "It can't be true. He loves me. Oh, he loves me."

"He is a scoundrel, Lizzie," he replied. He sounded uncomfortable in his role as comforter. "You will have to learn to forget him."

"No! No, there is some misunderstanding, Papa. I can't believe it. I must see him. I must go to him. Please."

"He will not see you," he said again. "He wishes to end the marriage. The likes of us are not good enough for his lordship."

"No," she moaned. "I must talk to him. I must see his letter. Let me see his letter, Papa. There is some misunderstanding."

"I will not allow that," he said, his voice gruff with sympathy. "It would break your heart to read the words in his own handwriting, Lizzie."

"Oh, let me see it, Papa," she begged, "let me see him. Make him come to see me. He loves me. I know he loves me."

"He does not want you anymore, girl," he said.

"No. Oh, no, no. Please, no," she wailed.

John was kneeling in front of her, covering her hands with his, drawing her head down to his shoulder, murmuring soothing words.

"Don't, love," he was saying. "Don't torture yourself like this. Elizabeth, Elizabeth. Elizabeth!"

She woke up with a start to find John sitting on the side of her bed, gently shaking her by the shoulders. Louise was standing behind him, holding a candle in a holder. Both looked deeply concerned. She stared blankly up at them.

"The old nightmare, love?" John asked gently.

She nodded numbly. "But I was right, John," she whispered. "I was right. He did not abandon me. He did love me."

John smoothed back from her face a strand of hair that lay across one eye. His hand was as gentle as a woman's. "Louise will sit and talk to you," he said, "while I go and warm some milk for you. You are at home now, love, and we intend to smother you with so much love that there will be no room for nightmares or bad memories either."

He left the room before she could reply, and Louise took his place at the side of the bed. She talked cheerfully and without pause until he returned with the promised milk. She told Elizabeth all about her pregnancy and her growing contentment as she felt the child move inside her, about her hope that this child would be a girl, though it really did not matter as they intended to have several more babies, "and surely one of them must be a girl, do you not think, Elizabeth? And, of course, girls have to be properly married when they grow up, and they need decent dowries, so maybe it will be just as well if they are mostly boys. Do you think, love?"

Elizabeth was smiling by the time John came back. The smile covered a great surge of gratitude that she felt for these two people, who were so wrapped up in their own love for each other and for their son and unborn child and yet could open their lives to include her too. She drank her milk like an obedient child and allowed Louise to plump her pillows and tuck in the blankets before kissing her on the cheek. John too kissed her before following his wife from the room.

"You are safe now, love," he said. "I shall look after

you now as you looked after me when I was a boy. Go back to sleep. There will be no more dreams."

Elizabeth smiled and felt herself obediently drifting off. In just such a tone of voice John must talk to Jeremy. But it felt so good, so good to let someone else carry her burdens for just a little while.

15

It was after luncheon the next day when Elizabeth finally managed to have a private word with John. She got up late in the morning, having slept surprisingly soundly after her nightmare. She could not remember when she had slept so late before, in fact. Then she sat chatting with Louise over a late breakfast. She was persuaded to go up to the nursery to visit Jeremy, and finally the three of them ended up outside in the morning sunshine, walking across the lawn and through the trees to the lake. Elizabeth had a sharp stab of memory of the last time she had come this way, with John and Robert in addition to the present group. By the time they returned to the house, it was time for luncheon.

Louise was going out afterward to visit a friend. "Do come, Elizabeth," she urged. "You will like Sophia. She has moved here since you left, I believe."

"No," Elizabeth replied. "Some other time, perhaps, but today I must talk to John if he can spare the time."

"I am not that busy that I cannot give a moment to my own sister," he said with a smile. "Besides, I am curious to know what has brought you back home so soon, love."

They went to his office, where they could talk without interruption. John ordered their tea sent there.

"Now, love, what has happened?" he asked, accepting a cup from her and seating himself in the chair behind his desk. "I know you well enough to be sure that something extraordinary has sent you from your employment so soon after you returned with such determination."

"I had a visit from Robert less than a week ago," she said.

His jaw tightened. "Will he not leave you alone?"

"I must confess that he had some reason to come," she added breathlessly. "His friend, Mr. Mainwaring of Ferndale, made me an offer, you see, which I accepted, and he went to see if Robert would divorce me."

Elizabeth gave a brief account of William Mainwaring's courtship and of Hetherington's refusal to set her free.

"Poor love," John said. "Are you quite devastated?"

"No," she assured him. "I am afraid that William might be, for I believe that he truly loved me. But I do not love him, John, and I know now that I did him an injustice by agreeing to marry him. I do not know, but I believe I would not have been able to go through with a wedding even if Robert had not thrown a rub in our way."

"But you still felt obliged to leave the vicinity of Ferndale?"

"Yes," she replied. "But that was not the only reason. Robert said more, John. We finally spoke of what happened six years ago."

"Yes?" John's voice was tense.

Elizabeth told him all that Hetherington had accused her of and all that he had said of his uncle's part in the dealings.

"You see," she concluded, "if Robert's uncle told him these things, he must have been guilty. He deliberately told terrible lies to separate us. I want you to come to London with me, John, to find him. I must get him to admit to what he did. Will you?"

John had turned very white. He was gripping the edge of the desk with both hands. "Are you sure," he said, "are you quite sure, Elizabeth, that Hetherington did not delegate his uncle to act for him? Are you sure he is not guilty?"

"Oh, yes," she said, wide-eyed. "Yes, I am very sure, John. I could tell from his manner that he was as badly hurt by our separation as I was. Besides, there were no ten thousand pounds."

"Oh yes there were," he said in a tight voice.

Elizabeth stared at him.

"When I came home from Oxford," he said, "I tried to learn the business of the estate as quickly as I could. I was somewhat surprised to find that I had no debts to contend with, though I was by no means wealthy. But at the time my mind was occupied with my courtship of Louise and then by our proposed marriage. It was more than four years after your departure when I finally decided to go back through the estate books to examine all the business that had been done before I succeeded. I discovered that my father had been a very poor manager and that, in fact, he had been hopelessly in debt at about the time of your marriage. As you will remember, Papa did not cope easily with adversity."

"No," Elizabeth agreed. "He drank and he gambled."

"Yet soon after your marriage, he paid all his debts," John said. "I could not understand how. I reckoned that somehow he must have got his hands on about ten thousand pounds. It seemed unlikely that he could have won such an enormous sum at cards, but that was the only possibility that presented itself to me for a long while. I made many discreet inquiries in likely quarters, but never with any success."

"Oh, God," Elizabeth said, sinking into a chair and staring, mesmerized, at her brother.

"Finally I could stand the mystery no longer," John said. "I journeyed to London to consult the man of business that Papa patronized whenever he could afford to. The man traced the source of the money. It had been paid to my father in lump sum by Horace Denning six weeks after the date of your marriage."

"Papa!" Elizabeth whispered.

With one hand John was stroking the feather of a quill pen across the palm of his other hand.

Elizabeth rose to her feet. "John," she said, "you knew

this two years ago. Why did you not tell me? I thought you were my true friend. But you made yourself part of the conspiracy against me."

"No!" he cried, flinging down the pen and upsetting his chair in his haste to come to her. "No, love. I did not tell you because I believed Denning had acted for his nephew. I have believed for two years that not only was Hetherington heartless enough to turn you off in order to satisfy his pride but that he had paid our father to keep you away from him. Elizabeth, are you sure he did not? He is a man of considerable charm. Are you sure that he has not decided after all that he wants you and is trying to raise himself in your estimation by making his uncle the scapegoat?"

"Yes, I am sure," she said. "I know that he meant what he said, John. He truly believed that I had abandoned him for money."

He took her by the shoulders and looked down into her eyes. "And does it still matter to you, love, whether he is guilty or not?"

She looked back through the tears that filled her eyes. "Yes," she answered. "Yes. I love him as much as I did on the day I married him."

He pushed her down onto her chair again and sat on the edge of his desk, arms folded, looking down at her.

"John," she asked, her eyes on her hands, "did you ever read the letters that Papa received from Robert?"

"No," he said. "He never showed them to me. When I asked, once, to see them, he said that he had burned them in a fit of anger."

"The letters did not exist, then," she said.

"It would seem not."

"Why?" she asked. "Why would he do such a thing? Did he not love me, John?"

He did not answer for a while. "I believe he was a sick and unhappy man, love. You know that he used to talk incessantly about money and about the necessity of our marrying wealth. The chance of earning ten thousand pounds as a kind of reverse dowry for you must have been irresistible, especially if he really believed that Hetherington would divorce you and you would still have the chance to make an advantageous marriage."

"Did he really believe that I had been divorced, do you think?"

"Probably not," John said, considering. "He did not make any attempt to make a match for you before his death, did he? One would have thought that he might have done so had he really believed that you were free."

"John, I have to go to Robert," she said. "I have to tell him. Will you come with me?"

He thought before answering. "It would not be good form," he said. "Your best course, love, would be to write inviting him here. You could explain perhaps that you wish to share with him some discoveries you have made concerning what happened at that time. If he is interested, if he truly wishes to know exactly what happened, he will come."

"But I cannot bear to wait here doing nothing," she said.

"He will be here within three days, you may be sure," he said firmly. "It is the best way, believe me. It would look most strange for a lady to arrive at Hetherington Manor asking for him. Remember that his household staff probably knows nothing of your existence."

Elizabeth was forced to agree, though reluctantly, that his advice was good. She went immediately to the drawing room and wrote six letters before she was satisfied that she had said enough to whet Robert's appetite, yet not enough to appease his curiosity. She took the finished letter immediately to John, who assured her that it would be on the evening's mail coach, and began the feverish wait.

Although John had said three days, she had convinced herself that it would be four days before she could reasonably expect to see Hetherington, even five if he had any immediate engagements that he felt he could not avoid. She would hope for him on the fourth day, she decided, but expect him on the fifth. It was a very sensible decision, but she found that she started to watch the driveway, at hourly intervals, the same evening as the letter was sent.

Elizabeth was very tired of watching, therefore, when the fifth day came. Louise and John had both done their best to entertain her, and she had tried to cooperate. She had played with the baby; helped Louise go through all his baby clothes and decide what would be needed for the new arrival; helped outfit a new bedroom for Jeremy, as the baby would be needing the nursery within a few months; and played endless games of cards. In the few intervals when she was left to herself, she wrote letters to the Rowes in Bath and to the Worthings and the Claridges in Granby. She sewed herself new gowns for the approaching autumn. But she refused to leave the grounds of her brother's house. When Louise went shopping or visiting, Elizabeth stayed at home. When John and Louise dined out one evening, she stayed at home, although she too had been invited. And always, even against her will, her feet would take her to a window that commanded a view of the driveway.

On the first four days she had consoled herself with the assurance that he would come on the fifth day. But when that day came, she was far from certain. A dread formed somewhere in the pit of her stomach and she knew that the watch was hopeless. He would not come. Why should he? He had been hurt by her once. He had been quite convinced of her guilt. Why should he come now just because she had written to tell him that she had more information concerning that episode in their lives?

Louise had made a point of staying home on that day. After luncheon she and Elizabeth took Jeremy out onto the lawn. She was tactful enough not to suggest that they go anywhere out of sight of the driveway or the main

door. Louise sat down on a bench while Elizabeth rolled a
ball to Jeremy and helped him run after it when it rolled
too far.

"Oh, I wish I might get up and join in the game,"
Louise called to a flushed and breathless Elizabeth. "But
John has made me promise not to undergo any exercise
more strenuous than a walk." She pulled a face. "I am not
that bulky yet, am I?" She patted a thickened waistline.

"No," Elizabeth replied, "but you know you delight in
pleasing John even when he is being just a mother hen.
Besides," she added, puffing and seating herself beside
her sister-in-law, "keeping up with a toddler is a little
much, even for my energy."

They sat watching Jeremy as he toddled across the lawn
and finally sat down with a plop amid a crowd of daisies
and began systematically pulling the heads off them.

"He is not going to come," Elizabeth said tensely.

Louise did not pretend to misunderstand. "Give him
time, love," she said. "You do not know what he was
occupied with when your letter arrived. Perhaps he was
not even at home. He will come, never fear."

"What makes you so sure?" Elizabeth asked.

Her sister-in-law was firm. "I did not know you six years
ago," she said, "and although I heard the story from John,
perhaps I can see things more objectively than either you
or he can. When I met the Marquess of Hetherington
when Jeremy was so ill, I was fully prepared to dislike,
even hate him. But I could not, Elizabeth. He has a charm
that is not all of the surface. He was genuinely concerned
about the baby and about my health. And you may not
believe this, love, but I could see that he was very
concerned about you. I know he disliked your working for
a living and dressing like a governess. But it was more
than that. I suspected that he loved you. I told John so,
but of course he would not have it, either. But I have
hoped ever since that somehow you would resolve your
differences. I have even schemed for ways of bringing the

two of you together again. He will come, Elizabeth, I know it. Even if it is not today or tomorrow," she added.

Jeremy had tired of the daisies and was headed for the trees that led to the lake. Elizabeth was forced to chase him and then to devise a game that would head him back toward his mother. The topic of conversation was changed, by tacit agreement, when they did rejoin Louise. The three of them went inside for tea.

The following two nights and the day in between were torture for Elizabeth. She wanted to take comfort from what Louise had said. She wanted to believe what her own senses had told her at her last meeting with Robert. In her heart she was convinced that he would want to hear what she had to say. But her head told her that she could watch that driveway until she was old and gray, but that Hetherington would never ride along it toward her.

She sat at her window on that second night, unable to sleep, unwilling to wait like this any longer. Notwithstanding John's advice, she was going to have to go to Hetherington Manor herself. Surely he would not refuse to see her if she came. Even if he rejected her story, even if he refused to believe that she had known nothing of the agreement between her father and his uncle, she would have the satisfaction of knowing that she had done all she could. And at least then she would be certain. If rejection was to be her fate again, she could at least then begin the dreary task of piecing together a meaningless life. Anything was better than this endless waiting. Perhaps even, as Louise had suggested, Robert was away from home. Although she would still then have to await his return home, she would be able to do so with some renewal of hope. Tomorrow, after breakfast, she would talk to John. She was sure that he would not refuse to accompany her.

Elizabeth slept for the rest of the night, somewhat comforted by her decision to do something.

Her plans were disrupted the following morning, however, by the arrival of a letter from Hetherington Manor.

Elizabeth knew as soon as John came into the breakfast room and handed it to her, that it was not from Robert. But she broke the seal feverishly and spread the letter out on the table. It was a short, terse note from his secretary, telling her that his lordship wished to inform Miss Rossiter that he was extremely busy at present and was unable either to answer her letter or to pay the requested visit, but that he would do the former when he found himself at more leisure.

Elizabeth sat, stunned, reading the note over three or four times without realizing that she did so. John came up quietly behind her and read it over her shoulder. He reached down and took it, folded it, and put it away in his pocket.

"Perhaps you were right," he said wearily, seating himself beside her at the table. "Perhaps I should have taken you to Hetherington. Maybe the message in your letter was not clear enough. What do you wish to do, love? I am entirely at your disposal."

When Elizabeth looked up at him, her face was flushed and her eyes flashing. "What do I wish to do?" she repeated. "Nothing! Nothing more, John. I would not speak to the Marquess of Hetherington now if he came through those doors at this moment on his knees. I must give him audience whenever it is his gracious pleasure. I was forced to allow him to bring me here when Jeremy was sick; I had no choice in the fact that he stayed here for days disturbing my peace; I was forced to speak with him and suffer his insults and his unwelcome advances after William had gone to him. I must suffer all these things because I am merely a wife. Yet when I request a meeting with him on a very important matter, I do not even merit a reply in his own hand. He gives me a set-down by way of a secretary. No more, John. I have done with that man."

"Steady, love," he said soothingly, laying a hand on her arm. "Let us be very sure this time. I shall go to see him. He will hear my explanation, I warrant you."

"If you take one step in his direction, I will never speak

to you again," his sister cried, pushing back her chair and getting to her feet. "I would be most obliged, John, if I never hear his name in this house again."

She swept out of the room, leaving her brother scratching his head in perplexity. A visit to his wife's bedroom, where he shared her breakfast and a lengthy consultation, did nothing to solve the problem. After six years of misunderstanding and bitter hard feelings, it seemed that this marriage was not going to be easily resurrected.

Elizabeth, meanwhile, had gone to the drawing room, taken paper, ink, and pens from the desk there, and returned to her own room, where she was soon busy drafting a notice to several London newspapers offering her services as a governess. She would personally see that the notices went out with that day's mail, she decided, so that they would appear in print in two days' time. She resolved to take the first post offered, especially if it was far away from London.

Five days later Louise was still watching the driveway for Hetherington and looking through the day's mail for a letter from him. She was convinced that the other letter had been a mistake, that somehow he would come and allow Elizabeth to tell her story. She was convinced that love would triumph in the end.

For his part, John was still in a quandary. He felt he owed it to his sister this time to help her, to find out Hetherington and explain to him what her letter must have only hinted at. Surely the man would want to come himself to see her if he knew the truth. On the other hand, Elizabeth had very specifically begged him not to have any contact at all with her husband.

Elizabeth was the only one who was not troubled. Since the morning when the letter had arrived, she had blocked Hetherington from her mind and her heart. With a cheerfulness that alarmed her brother and sister-in-law, she helped Louise with household duties, played with Jeremy, and prepared for her own return to service. She had bought several yards of gray wool material and was making herself some serviceable gowns. Although it would be several months before her hair would be long enough to be forced into its old, severe style, she found that she was able to coil the curls at the back so that her appearance became somewhat less frivolous.

Five days after she had sent her advertisement to the newspapers, Elizabeth began to look for a reply. She had none by the morning post, but a messenger in the early afternoon brought word that a Mr. Chatsworth was at the local inn and would be pleased to interview Miss Rossiter that same afternoon for a position as governess.

"Pray do not go, Elizabeth," Louise begged when she was shown the letter, "or send word that your services are no longer available. Indeed, we need you here and we love you."

John was white-faced. "Indeed, love," he said, "Louise is right. We know you are wretchedly unhappy and we cannot do much to ease the pain. But at least here you know that you are with loved ones."

"I am not at all unhappy," Elizabeth replied brightly. "On the contrary, I look on this as a new adventure. Unknown people, an unknown place. It is what I need. I thank you both for your concern, but it really is unnecessary. This is your home, but it is mine no longer. I have to find my own place."

They were forced to let her go. She declined even to let John accompany her to the inn, but drove herself in the gig. She wore her best governess clothes, the gray silk covered with a gray cloak to ward off the chill breeze, and a matching bonnet.

Mr. Chatsworth was lodged in the only private parlor the inn boasted, a tiny, smoke-blackened room, usually used by the landlord's more-favored patrons for their gambling card games. Elizabeth knocked on the door and closed it behind her when she was called inside.

Her prospective employer was a tall man, portly, fashionably dressed, his hair curled high at the front. He leaned with studied casualness against the mantel and studied her minutely from head to foot through a quizzing glass.

"Mr. Chatsworth?" she asked.

He inclined his head. "Miss Rossiter?"

She dropped him a curtsy.

He waved her to a chair beside the table and began the interview. His home was in Yorkshire, Elizabeth learned, where his invalid wife and two young sons lived. He was a mill owner and wished to give his sons all the advantages that he had not had as a child: a governess for a few years, public school after that.

It would not be an easy job, Elizabeth knew. She judged the man to be conceited, with a grudge against the noble class who had birth and breeding even if they did not have his wealth. He would be the sort of man who would treat his servants as inferiors in order to convince himself of his own superiority. She had also been uncomfortably aware all the time they talked of his eyes roving over her body. She judged that at some time in the not-too-distant future she would have to repulse his lecherous advances.

Yet when Mr. Chatsworth made her a firm offer of employment at the end of a half-hour, Elizabeth accepted. What was the point of waiting for a more pleasant post? There was no such thing as pleasure in life for her anymore.

"I wish to leave here before ten o' clock tomorrow morning," Mr. Chatsworth announced. "May I expect you to be ready, Miss Rossiter?"

"I shall be here by then, sir," she assured him.

"I shall look forward to furthering our acquaintance on our journey," he said, taking her hand in his plump and moist one and squeezing it rather hard.

Elizabeth refused to think during the drive home. Yorkshire would suit her fine. She would be far away from all the places and people she had ever known. She knew that she should be uneasy about making a journey of a few days alone with a stranger. John and Louise would probably try to insist on sending a maid with her. Perhaps she would even allow herself to be persuaded if it would make them feel better. She really did not care. Not anymore. It was safer not to care. Already she felt better than she had felt for several months.

The butler was in the hall when Elizabeth let herself into the house.

"Are Mr. and Mrs. Rossiter indoors?" she asked him, removing her bonnet and throwing it down on a table.

"In the drawing room, ma'am, taking tea," he said. "And, er. . . ."

"That is all right," she said. "I shall join them there."

Elizabeth donned the mask of cheerfulness that she had worn at home now for five days and opened the double doors of the drawing room.

John and Louise, one at either side of the unlit fireplace, Louise looking bright-eyed, John acutely embarrassed, were indeed taking tea. But the Marquess of Hetherington was not. He was standing very much as Mr. Chatsworth had stood when she had walked in on him earlier, except that his stance looked genuinely relaxed. He had one elbow propped on the mantel and one booted leg crossed over the other.

His blue eyes met Elizabeth's across the room and he smiled.

16

Elizabeth did not relinquish her hold on the handles of the doors. "What are you doing here?" she asked.

"It seems that you ask me that every time we meet," he said, "and I always have the same answer. I wish to talk to you."

"I have no interest in anything you may have to say to me, my lord," she said coldly, "and I have nothing whatsoever to say to you. Good day."

She stepped backward and began to close the doors in front of her.

"Elizabeth," Hetherington said, and he was still smiling, "how rag-mannered you have become. I have traveled so far just to see you, and you refuse to grant me even a few moments of your time."

Elizabeth deliberately stepped inside the room and quietly closed the doors behind her. She crossed the room until her own blazing eyes looked directly into his intense blue ones.

"I understood that you were busy, my lord," she said. "Pardon me, it was *extremely* busy, was it not, John? I understood that you were to write to me when you had more leisure. Have you found yourself with a great deal of leisure, my lord, so much so that you have found the time to pay me a personal visit? Pardon me for not being quite overwhelmed by your generosity. You are at least five days too late. I do not believe, Robert, there is anything you could say to which I would deem it worthwhile to listen."

He tipped his head to one side and regarded her closely. The smile was gone from his lips, though it was still in his eyes. "What are you talking about?" he asked.

Elizabeth clamped her teeth together and glared back at him.

"I believe she is referring to that letter you had your secretary write," Louise said timidly.

"Carson?" he said, frowning and turning his gaze on Louise.

She nodded.

"You have had a letter from Carson?" he asked Elizabeth, looking at her closely once more.

She continued to stare stonily at him.

"Why did he write to you, love?" he asked gently. "I was unaware that he even knew of your existence." He turned to Louise when it became obvious that Elizabeth was not going to answer him. "Do you know what this is all about, Louise?" he asked.

She looked hesitantly, first at her sister-in-law and then at her husband. "After Elizabeth had written to ask you to come here," she said, "she had a letter from your secretary to say that you were too busy either to write or to visit, but that you would write as soon as you were able."

"You asked me to come?" he said, turning back to Elizabeth in wonder.

When she still did not answer, the rest of what Louise had said seemed to penetrate his mind. Unexpectedly, he chuckled. "Carson was my father's secretary," he explained. "He was more like a parent to me when I grew up than my own father was. Now he seems to feel that every female has designs on my title and my fortune, not to mention my person. He has taken it upon himself to protect me. This is not the first time I have had evidence that he has discouraged bold females in my name."

"You mean you knew nothing of Elizabeth's letter?" John asked stiffly.

Hetherington looked at Elizabeth as if it were she who

had asked the question. "Do you not know me well enough," he asked, "to know that I would have come to you as fast as horse could gallop at any time I had received such a letter from you in the last six years?"

Elizabeth looked blankly back into his now entirely sober face.

"After I saw you at Mr. Rowe's house," he said, "I returned home for one night. I have been traveling ever since. I have not been home at all. Please believe me, Elizabeth."

John rose to his feet. "Come, Louise," he said, "our presence is not needed here."

Elizabeth whirled on him. "I do not wish to be left alone," she said. "I have nothing to say to the Marquess of Hetherington. And I have a great deal to do. I leave for Yorkshire tomorrow morning with Mr. Chatsworth. He has hired me."

"Elizabeth," John said, and his voice was unusually stern, "if I have to lock you in this room, I shall force you to speak with Hetherington this time. It seems to me that the two of you have had your marriage blighted by misunderstandings and suspicions and missed opportunities. This time, talk! At least then, if you continue with this idiotic notion of moving to the wilds in order to teach other people's children, it will be a decision made out of sanity and common sense."

Elizabeth, stunned, looked to Louise for help. But her sister-in-law merely gave her a nervous little half-smile and reached for her husband's arm so that she could be escorted from the room.

Neither of them broke the silence for a while. Elizabeth stood, still facing the door. Hetherington stood a few feet behind her. He spoke first.

"Why did you wish me to come, Elizabeth?" he asked.

She did not turn. "It was nothing," she said. "It does not matter."

"It does matter," he insisted. "Whatever it is, it was important enough to you a week ago that you sent for me.

And I know you well enough to realize that, to do that, you would have to go against all the pride you have built up in the last years. Do you not believe me when I say that I know nothing of your letter? Is that it?"

"I am weary, Robert," she said, turning to face him, "so weary of the misunderstandings, the waitings, the confrontations. I have trained myself since losing you to avoid strong feelings and unpredictable circumstances. I have learned to value tranquillity."

"And have you been happy?" he asked gently.

"Happy?" she repeated, eyes flashing. "Happy! Happiness is a much-overrated emotion, my lord. I was very happy once and I ended up more miserable than I knew it was possible to be. I am not interested in happiness. I wish to be left in peace."

"With your Mr. Chatsworth?"

"Yes, with Mr. Chatsworth and his wife and sons. I can start a new life there and forget again. Oh, God, I want to forget."

"Elizabeth!" he said with such quiet tenderness that her eyes flew to his face and her senses reeled for one unguarded moment. He pushed himself away from the mantel and walked past her.

"We were so young, were we not?" he said, walking to the window and gazing through it. "I cannot now believe that we allowed all those things to happen to us without blazing a trail back to each other. I cannot quite understand why I did not fight my way through hell, though God knows I believed I had done all I could. I was so damned young."

Elizabeth had moved only enough that she could watch him where he stood by the window. She did not say anything.

He turned to look at her. "If you will not tell me why you summoned me, may I tell you why I came?" he asked.

"It seems I have no choice but to listen," she said, but there was no hostility in her voice. She moved to the wing chair beside the hearth and sat quietly on the edge of the seat.

"I knew when I spoke with you last," he said, "before I left you, that you had spoken the truth. I knew what must have happened. All I could think of doing was reaching my uncle and forcing the truth out of him. That proved a most difficult and most frustrating task."

He walked across the room and took the chair opposite Elizabeth. He watched her downcast eyes as he spoke.

"I went home for one night and then went to London. The man he had left there to care for his house told me that he had gone fishing in Scotland with friends, though he did not know the exact location. It took me almost two days to discover who the friends were and where exactly they had gone. I was weary enough when I arrived there, but when I found the place, the friends informed me that my uncle had returned home just two days before. Somehow I had missed him on the road. To cut a long story short, I finally ran him to ground in Paris less than a week ago."

Hetherington paused and looked expectantly at Elizabeth, but she did not say anything or raise her eyes.

"I discovered the truth," he said.

"That my father took the money," she said very quietly, "that the two of them conspired against us, my father for money, your uncle for family pride."

"You know, then?" he said.

"Yes."

"And that is why you called me?"

She did not answer.

"Did you know," he asked, getting restlessly to his feet, "that my uncle intercepted your first few letters to me and that your father intercepted mine to you? Afterward, they had an agreement to stop our letters at their source. Most of your letters never left this house and most of mine did not leave London."

Elizabeth had her hands over her face.

Hetherington went down on his knees in front of her. "Did you know," he asked, "that I came here, that I ranted and raved to your father, begging and demanding to see you, threatening him even? He gave in in the end and went to find you, but he came back to repeat what he had said all along, that you would not see me." He covered her hands gently with his own, cupping her face.

It was her dream again. It was the dream, except that usually it was John there on the carpet before her, touching her hands and her face.

"No," she moaned. "No." And she began to rock herself protectively.

"Hush, love," he said. "Don't grieve so. Everything will be fine now, I promise you."

"No," she wailed, her eyes tightly closed.

He rose to his feet and brought her to hers, one hand grasping each arm. He took her hands and removed them firmly from in front of her face.

"Open your eyes, Elizabeth," he said.

"No," she moaned.

He pulled her roughly into his arms, cradling her head against his shoulder with one hand.

"Elizabeth," he murmured, "this is Robert, your husband, love. I am the man who eloped with you and married you in Gram's chapel, the man who wandered cliffs and beaches with you and made love to you to the sound of gulls and the smell of the sea. This is the man who loves you, darling, who has loved you for six long and lonely years. Open your eyes and look at me, love."

He was rocking her in his arms, kissing gently her forehead, her closed eyelids, her cheeks, her lips. And it was there finally that he felt a stirring of response. He continued to kiss her, undemandingly, until, opening his own eyes, he found her looking up at him.

"It is all over now, love," he said, a smile lifting one corner of his mouth. "We do not have to part ever again. I can take you home with me."

She pushed away from him. "No, it is too late, Robert,"

she said tonelessly. "There has been too much of pain for you and me. I cannot face making myself vulnerable again."

"Elizabeth—" he began.

She interrupted, talking quickly. "I am glad that we discovered the truth. We do not need to hate each other anymore. We can think kindly of each other and be friends if we ever meet again. But I think it best if we live separate lives. I have a new life to start tomorrow and I have a great deal to do before morning." Her voice had gained brightness and confidence.

"What are you saying?" he asked incredulously.

"I mean that I must go now," she replied. "I am sure John will be in his office if you wish to take your leave of him. Good-bye, Robert. And I thank you very much for coming." She smiled brightly and extended her hand.

Hetherington ignored the hand. "I wonder if I shall understand you even at the end of a lifetime," he mused, folding his arms across his chest. "Are you a coward, love?"

The smile still stretched her face. "I must go, Robert," she said.

"I wish you to tell me something first," he said, head to one side, regarding her closely. "Do you love me?"

"Love?" she said scornfully. "I have never found love to be a desirable emotion, my lord. It is a fable told to the romantics, I believe."

He bowed over her hand, which was still extended, and kissed it formally. "Thank you, ma'am," he said. "That is all I wished to know." And before she could take her leave, he brushed past her and left the room.

Really, the whole situation had ended most satisfactorily, Elizabeth told herself several minutes later as she cheerfully packed her bags ready for the next day's journey. The years had been painful because of her terrible disillusionment over Robert's behavior. Now that she knew that he had been in no way to blame, and now that he knew that she had been innocent, the past could be allowed to fall into memory. And she would be happy to remember those weeks of courtship in London, those few days of marriage in Devon. She was free now to remember Robert as he had been, graceful and yet very masculine, handsome, sunny-natured, affectionate, passionate. She would be able to remember their encounters in the last few months with some pleasure, certainly without bitterness.

But she could not revive her feelings for him, of course. She had finally killed those five days before when she had realized her extreme stupidity in opening her heart to rejection and pain yet again. She had learned her lesson well this time. But she was very pleased that he had come. It was good to know that that unkind letter from his secretary had not been dictated by Robert himself.

Yes, Elizabeth concluded with a smile as she folded the skirt of her best gray silk very carefully into the portmanteau, it was all over now, and a very satisfactory ending it was, too. She had been a little surprised when Robert had left so quietly. She had expected more trouble with him. But that was good, too. It showed that he understood the good sense of her decision.

Elizabeth repeated all these thoughts to Louise, who came into her room and sat quietly on the bed to watch her pack, and at the dinner table to John, who smiled and told her that she knew what was best for herself, that he would not try to interfere in her life anymore.

Elizabeth was pleased to avoid the emotional confrontations she had expected. Both John and Louise conversed on general topics during the evening. Neither tried to dissuade her from accepting her new employment; neither even mentioned the necessity of taking a ladies' maid on the journey with her. They had finally accepted her adult right to make her own decisions and to order her own life.

Louise cried a few tears as she kissed her sister-in-law good-bye the next morning on the stone steps outside the house. John hugged her rather too hard and too long. But

Elizabeth felt a sense of relief as she set her face for the village, seated beside her brother's groom in the gig. It had been surprisingly easy to begin a new life.

When she asked at the inn for Mr. Chatsworth, Elizabeth was directed to a traveling coach in the yard outside. The Yorkshireman had requested that she await him there. A footman standing by the open door helped her inside, assured her that her bags would be taken care of, and closed the door.

She found herself in an interior of opulent luxury. Well-cushioned seats of gold velvet were complemented by a paler-gold rug and brocade wall and ceiling coverings. Brown velvet curtains were looped back from the windows, but could give total privacy and darkness to the travelers whenever the master wished, Elizabeth judged. When she sat down rather uncertainly on one of the seats, she sank into warm softness and felt the coach sway slightly. It was very well sprung.

Mr. Chatsworth was a very wealthy man, then. The long journey to his home would be a reasonably comfortable one, despite the deplorable condition of most British roads. But Elizabeth began to feel uneasy. It had been fine yesterday to imagine that she would be quite safe traveling alone with a strange man. She was wearing her plainest wool dress and pelisse, her most no-nonsense bonnet. Together with a chilly, distant manner, her appearance would serve to dampen any ardor that the man might be capable of, she had thought. But now she was not so sure. She remembered the speculative way in which Mr. Chatsworth had looked her over the day before. And she looked again at those velvet curtains.

She felt the coach sway again and heard voices outside. The coachman was apparently climbing into his seat. The door opened again and the footman's face appeared momentarily. Elizabeth leaned a shoulder against the side of the coach and set her face into what she hoped was a polite but chilly smile.

"Good morning, my lady," the Marquess of Hetherington said with his wide white grin as he vaulted into the coach and took a seat next to her. The door closed quietly.

"What are you doing here?" Elizabeth demanded, sitting bolt-upright. She staggered forward at the same moment as the coach was set into motion.

Hetherington put out a steadying arm, but she shook it off.

"What is happening?" she asked. "Where is Mr. Chatsworth? And what are you doing in his coach?"

"To answer your questions in order, love," he said, beginning to check them off on his fingers, "the coach has begun to move; on his way to London, I would imagine, to find himself a new governess; and this is my coach, not his." He smiled at her.

She stared back, wide-eyed. "I have a position with him," she said frostily. "I demand you let me down, my lord."

He crossed his arms on his chest and placed one booted foot against the seat opposite. "My apologies," he said, still grinning hugely. "I told the man that he could not have my wife as a governess for his children. I enjoyed doing so. I disliked the man on sight. You would not have been safe with him, Elizabeth."

"Not safe with him!" she sputtered. "You are the one abducting me! Stop immediately, or I shall, I shall . . ."

"Shall what?" he asked, chuckling. "Throw yourself out of the coach? The doors are locked, love. Scream? The horses may be alarmed, but my men are more than capable of handling them."

Elizabeth sank back into her seat again and glowered at her tormentor. "What do you want?" she asked.

He grinned again. "You," he answered.

"I am here against my will," she said, "and yesterday I said no. How can you expect to achieve anything from such a situation?"

He settled his shoulders against his corner of the coach and looked at her. The grin had faded, though he still smiled. "I have excellent hopes," he said. "I have ached for you for six years, and you have suffered too, I know. I love you now as I have from the beginning, and you love me. I believe we have a chance for a good marriage."

"What makes you believe that I love you?" she asked frostily.

"I have it on excellent authority," he replied. "William Mainwaring, Mr. Rowe, your brother and sister-in-law."

She looked sharply across at him. "Mr. Rowe?" she asked, frowning.

"He told me so at Bath a few days ago," he replied.

"At Bath?"

"How do you think I knew you were here?" he asked with a sigh. "When I found my uncle in Paris, I thought that my wanderings were over. But when I arrived in Granby to claim you, I was told the Rowes were in Bath. I found them there, but not you, love."

Elizabeth turned to stare out the window. "Robert, take me back," she said, "or let me down here. Please."

"No, I cannot do that, love," he said very quietly.

She sat stiffly in her place, staring sightlessly at the passing scenery. Several minutes passed in silence.

"Robert," she said at last, "you cannot take me to your home like this, with no warning, with no one knowing who I am. Your staff will all think me some kind of doxy."

He chuckled. "A very strange kind of doxy dressed like that," he said. "You do look a perfect fright, you know, Elizabeth. Did you hope to hold Chatsworth off with such a costume? You would not have succeeded. Your charms show through quite shockingly." He reached out a hand and flicked a chestnut curl on her neck.

Elizabeth turned to him with pleading eyes. "I cannot go to Hetherington Manor with you, Robert," she said, "indeed I cannot. I am not ready. Please take me back."

He smiled into her eyes, and the hand that had touched her hair moved to cup her chin. "We are not going home yet, love," he said. "We are going to Devon."

"To Devon?" she echoed.

"My grandmother's house passed to me on her death," he said, "though I have not been there since then. But now is the right time. We have a honeymoon to complete."

"No," she said breathlessly. "No, don't take me there, Robert."

He still held her chin. "Do you remember the salt smell of the air, love?" he asked, holding her eyes with his. "Do you remember that wide golden beach, the sand, the waves, the cliff path, the gulls, the view from our window? We were standing there when our honeymoon was interrupted, although at the time we did not know how long that interruption would be. I had just finished unbuttoning your dress, I believe?"

As he spoke, Hetherington had untied the ribbons of her bonnet and tossed it onto the seat opposite. Her pelisse had been unbuttoned and thrown back from her shoulders. His hands held her shoulders now. He gazed tenderly into the white face that looked back at him.

"I can't," she whispered. "I am so afraid, Robert. I am afraid to love again."

"I know," he said, "but I am afraid not to. Look ahead, Elizabeth. Ten years. Twenty years. Thirty. Can you bear to think of the emptiness? I cannot. I need you and I believe you need me just as much. Come back to me, love. Please."

Elizabeth felt the tears springing to her eyes. She moved forward to hide her face against his coat, and his arms came around her to hold her to him.

"Will it be the same?" she asked. "Will the magic be gone, Robert? I am afraid to go back."

He laughed. "Have you grown so fearful, love?" he asked. "I remember the time when you defied the world to run away with me, although I was a penniless nobody at the time. Do you remember the ocean, love? Have you ever seen it before or since? And did you notice any difference? Some things always remain the same. We are not the same people we were six years ago. We will have to get to know each other again. But our love has survived, has it not? Can we not give it a chance again, Elizabeth? You do love me, do you not?"

"Yes," she admitted hesitantly against his coat, "I always have."

"Well," he said, chuckling against her hair, "you have sealed your doom now, love. You cannot expect me ever to let you go after you have admitted that, you know."

"Would you have let me go had I not said so?" she asked, her voice muffled by his coat.

"No," he admitted.

"You see?" she said, raising her head, her eyes flashing, her cheeks flushed. "You do not play fair, Robert Denning."

"No," he said, "I don't, do I? And are you not glad of it?"

She glared at him, until her face dimpled suddenly. "I promise you, you will not win all our arguments so easily, my lord," she assured him severely.

"Have I won this one?" he asked meekly.

"Oh, Robert, please kiss me," she begged suddenly. "Make me forget all my fears. John and Louise are very much in love with each other and they are perfectly happy. There is not any reason why we should not be, is there? If we really try. . . ."

"Elizabeth," he said, pulling her close against his chest again, "you asked me to do something. Now would you have the kindness to allow me to do it?"

"Oh," she said, "is it advisable to kiss on an open highway, Robert?"

He clucked his tongue in mock annoyance and turned to pull the cord that held the curtains back from the window. He leaned across Elizabeth to do the same at her window. The interior of the carriage immediately became intimately dark.

"The answer to your question is yes," he said, grinning

down into her upturned face, "but I am having the forethought to realize that I may want to do a great deal more than kiss you once we get started."

"Oh," she said. "Should we not wait, Robert? The servants mmmm—"

"Thank goodness I have a wife who knows when to stop prattling," the Marquess of Hetherington said with a self-satisfied smile several minutes later. "Now, if I could just train you not to wear these gowns that have a few score of buttons down the back, love!"

"Robert!" she protested, horrified, as she felt his fingers working the buttons free of the loops. "We are on a public mmmm—"

About the Author

Raised and educated in Wales, **Mary Balogh** now lives in Saskatchewan, Canada, with husband, Robert, and children, Jacqueline, Christopher, and Sian. She is a school principal and an English teacher.

More Regency Romances from SIGNET

**Buy them at your local
bookstore or use coupon
on next page for ordering.**

SIGNET Regency Romances You'll Want to Read

Other Regency Romances from SIGNET

on next page for ordering.
bookstore or use coupon
on next page for ordering.

SIGNET Regency Romances You'll Enjoy

27 million Americans can't read a bedtime story to a child.

It's because 27 million adults in this country simply can't read.

Functional illiteracy has reached one out of five Americans. It robs them of even the simplest of human pleasures, like reading a fairy tale to a child.

You can change all this by joining the fight against illiteracy.

Call the Coalition for Literacy at toll-free **1-800-228-8813** and volunteer.

Volunteer Against Illiteracy. The only degree you need is a degree of caring.